THUNDER, AZ

THUNDER, AZ

❖

ARI LOEB

For My Father,
HAROLD LOEB

*Though is it ever too late
to destroy the World?*

—Mark Z. Danielewski

PROLOGUE

THEY SAID IT was a hurricane that did it. That was part of it, sure. A convenient way to cover up what had really happened. But no, it was not a hurricane. It was far more sinister than that, and its deadly claws reached much farther than Navajo territory.

Conspiracies were never pursued. Though the terrifying mystery never became a blockbuster movie, it would've made for a great one.

The hurricane began two thousand miles from the Eastern Seaboard. *That* was the mystery. "Desert Typhoons" became the new hot topic—a scientific horror that hooked the world.

It only took three days: cold and cloudless February days. And despite all the running, screaming, and praying, the whole town vanished with smooth efficiency, more like a scheduled event than a natural disaster.

Scientists sought answers in all the wrong directions. They should have been looking underground.

They might have even seen it coming.

PART
ONE

1

"S HIT, WE CAN'T do this." Charlotte took a deep breath and held it, eyes shut against the world. She was trembling, although from fright or from the cold it was hard to tell. She wore a miniskirt and leggings, which was about as warm as it looked on a February night.

"We can't!" she cried. "Change of plans! Let's put watermelon kombucha in her locker. All her fucking books will stick together! We can sip it up out of the bottle, then spit it through the little vents there. That would be funny as *fuck*!"

Despite the nature of the moment, there was no humor in Charlotte's voice. She felt as if she were swimming against some horrible riptide, the practical joke pulling her in.

She and Bobbi were walking along Eighth Avenue in Manhattan, beside a row of stopped New York City buses.

The bus at the front of the line was an old one, Charlotte noticed. To her it resembled a beached, dying whale. The hiss-and-fart sound of the air brake reminded her of a whale spitting mist out its blowhole, willing itself to roll over toward the water before it would dry up into a dead bus-like structure in the sand. An effortless smile spread across her face.

She glanced over to her friend, Bobbi, for whom she had waited and rehearsed her lines ("change of plans," and, "we'll sip it out of the bottle, then spit it through the little vents there"). They'd planned to do something to Gwenn, Bobbi's little sister.

Little did they know their plan would go right out the window.

The two girls walked among an enormous crowd of New Yorkers. To Bobbi, they all looked similarly fickle. No hard-walk-hard-cock New Yorkers here. *New York is just a big contradiction*, she thought. *In the city that never sleeps, everyone walks around like insomniacs. They don't show that in the movies. Well, maybe Taxi Driver.*

They're all so fragile, she mused. She conjured the image of thin shells with gas inside of them, ready at any moment to flake or crack and spill an unholy reek of madness and tragedy. Insomniacs with poisoned inspiration. Bobbi imagined driving a car through the crowd, half of them popping like balloons, and the other half failing to budge. They'd just keep on walking. Yeah, the tourists would pop like balloons. The locals would keep on walking.

Bobbi spat. "That's fucking gross. Watermelon kombucha?"

"Gwenn hates watermelons!" Charlotte was ready with the retort.

"It's just not classy, Char. Also that stuff rots your teeth. Why can't we just go to Starbucks? It's right here."

Charlotte was ready for that, too. "Because Starbucks is owned by Walmart. It's literally Walmart coffee."

Before Bobbi could argue her facts, Charlotte halted right in front of an old-looking bus and yelled, "God damn! These tights are always bunching in my heels!"

As she bent down to adjust her tights, miniskirt opening its coy eye to the public, the bus began to move.

2

THE DRIVER OF the old bus was John Walter.

Born in the Bronx sixty years back, Walter had attended Brooklyn College, and at one point in his life, he'd aspired to be a writer.

While working on his college thesis, Walter had gone to live on the street to study the homeless.

He drank whiskey and discarded half-drunk cokes. He gave himself three weeks, as an experiment. At first it was easy (only spring when he'd started, and still warm outside), but eventually Walter had submerged himself so deep into the Meisner Technique that he forgot what he was doing. So he sought truth at the bottom of a bottle. He wanted to find a truth so brilliant that it burned his mind and branded his writing. He wanted to put a patent on the mythic nature of modern man. He wanted his novels to be famous for it. He said he would either find this great treasure in prison or in the frozen parking lot of some church on 65th Street, drunk.

John Walter, like Bobbi and Charlotte, had spent his high school years denying his lessons, mocking his mentors, and laughing at the word "wisdom." They'd all gone to college like bong-toting babies, Christmas lights and hair extensions flapping in the breeze.

Walter went crazy on whiskey and his desperate quest for the knowledge that most men already know in their hearts. Charlotte and Bobbi went crazy on social media and reality television.

7

Walter was mostly bald now and looked much older than sixty. He'd spent twenty-six years on the street, homeless, smelling like corpse feet, drinking whatever he could find.

Eventually, to clean up New York City, Mayor Rudolph Giuliani took as many homeless New Yorkers as he could find and turned them into MTA workers. Better buses and subways and cleaner church parking lots. Win, win!

Walter checked the side-view mirror and started the classic heroin lean off the curb into traffic. He had no vantage on Charlotte, who had crouched, adjusting her tights, just inches from the bus's looming face.

Bobbi was dimly aware of the bus moving and automatically took a step back. But Char, from that shoelace-tying position, still concentrating on finding a detour for Bobbi's insane and totally unimportant plan, didn't see it.

The bus lurched forward in first gear, and nudged Charlotte, who swiveled and fell to the ground, like a little Charlie Chaplin in a miniskirt.

Walter the bus driver didn't notice. Nobody noticed, at first.

Charlotte noticed only dimly, and it took her a moment to convert the observation into belief. *Maybe,* she thought, she'd just lost her balance because the bus was so close and large that the proximity gave her vertigo. Yeah, that, and *maybe* she got a head rush from being crouched for so long. In any event, the bus would stop.

The bus did not stop. The front-left tire, four feet in diameter, caught her right hand and crushed it up to her elbow. She brayed quietly, like a trumpet with a mute. She was too focused on her survival to just let loose and scream. It was a distant yet audible shrill, and the New Yorkers in the vicinity noticed her at once.

Not a moment later, the bus crushed Charlotte's right shoulder, collar, and finally her head. Blood burst from her deflating body and sprayed into the traffic, slashing cars and onto the sidewalk. It misted the entryway of the Starbucks Coffee that Charlotte had been boycotting. The bus looked like a huge, grotesque street-cleaning vehicle.

On the street, steam billowed, and a faint hissing sound whispered to onlookers, unsure whether it had come from the bus's front tire or Charlotte's decimated throat.

3

Jimmy was laughing like a drunk hyena, half propped against the wall, half sliding under the table, stunned by the world's most perfectly timed joke. His grin felt etched in cement. For the moment he was brainless, seized and spiraling his way under the table.

Chester was laughing too—partly empathizing with Jimmy's elation but mostly pleased by his own comic timing. *Another slam dunk,* he thought. If he had been Shaquille O'Neal, fifty thousand dollars would've been direct deposited into his checking account at once.

"If you could only get her to grade you while you—" he gasped, but he was laughing too hard to finish. Jimmy would need a new beer to wash this one down. Apparently, sleeping with your teacher is the funniest thing you could ever do at Columbia University.

Jimmy and Chester had another round of beers, and the talk remained bubbly. They were the classic image of best friends. They'd known each other since they were kids, growing up in Thunder, Arizona.

Chester Gall was originally from Texas, and his southern accent was unreasonably thick. He'd moved to Thunder, Arizona when he was eight. He was thin, and he wore old, gaunt cowboy boots that matched his narrow, all-angles face. A New York counterpoint, he looked about as native here as he would in China. He was half gunslinger, half unsung comedian.

Jimmy Johannsen had been born in Thunder, and his round, duck-feather face was caught in perpetual enjoyment of the view. His bright green eyes seemed to understand almost everything at once, and what they did not understand would brighten them up more, widening them to take in more pleasure.

The two boys were at The Dockside Tavern in Harlem, their usual spot. They had a good drunk going on. All their knowledge of the world was safely locked away for later, along with their nerves and their judgement, password protected.

The Dockside had an original maritime decor overlapped with a *Star Wars* theme. Hanging on the wall to Jimmy's right was a painting made by someone who had to have been in college. It was an image of Luke Skywalker, passed out face-down in a swampy bog. Yoda sat next to him, holding a bottle of wine. The words, "Twisted by The Dockside, young Skywalker has become," were painted in a lumpy word bubble.

Chester really scored, man—shit! Jimmy thought.

"Chess," he said. "How come drinking makes me feel so *me*, man?" His blazing green eyes shone pink around the edges. They looked like chameleon eyes, pleading with Chester for some fun science facts—or better even, another knee-slapper.

"I don't know, Rubber. You are what you eat!" A shadow of self-consciousness flashed across his face before evaporating in the bar's warm light.

"Does that mean you're my Chem teacher?" Jimmy asked.

Another laughing spell ensued, but they were losing power now, their laughter weakening as their lungs grew sluggish. Their stamina was about to forfeit.

The drunk was still mostly good, but the alcohol had begun to turn in their blood, sneaking sickeningly toward the surface. Soon they would be nothing but fuming bags of nausea and regret. They both knew IPA hangovers were the worst kind, but they'd binged on them anyways. They called it "the inverse function of alcohol and judgement." They had been at The Dockside for five hours, give or take a little. They had accomplished the task of getting drunk and were beginning to think about how class would feel in the morning.

Chess never composed himself before leaving the bars. He simply moved himself in whatever condition right out the front door and into the real world, head embalmed and fuming freely. His legs never faltered. Jimmy thought Chess's legs didn't get drunk.

His tongue got *very* drunk, though. Sometimes Chess lost all control over his tongue, Southern accent and all, as if he had gargled Novocain. His friends could barely understand him when he spoke, "Ain-ways ye don't look like you. You look like a 'rangatang shaved off its hair n' jumped out an errplane. Why d' you wear that stupid Ghoss-busters T-shirt?"

"Dude this is like the oldest shirt I have!" Jimmy said, as he slowly began to pull himself to standing. Then he halted, swaying over the table. Unlike Chess, Jimmy needed a second to compose himself before leaving the bar. *Legs? Check. Wallet? Double check. Phone?*

"Shots!" The call rang out through the tavern, and Chess and Jimmy knew they'd have to claim them. It may as well have been a death rattle, and they both recoiled, as if in defeat.

It was Jackie Wells. Gorgeous, young, and their favorite waitress in the whole universe. There was no saying no to shots—not in college and not to Jackie Wells.

Jimmy sat back down. He assumed Jackie liked Chester and him because they weren't as loud and abrasive as the other college guys. Around Columbia, the bars were practically reserved for the students, even though technically they sat right in the middle of Harlem, and anyone could stroll in and ask for a Manhattan and a side of olives. Jimmy thought that only college kids came in here because they were the only people who could handle hanging out with other college kids. He was probably right.

Shots. He knew Chester would oblige. Chester was as optimistic as they come. Like a kitchen knife, he cut through the world as if it were butter. Never doubtful, never dull. That was his motto. He was a little naive but intuitive and lucky. Jimmy, on the other hand, had to think about it. He wondered how his actions today would look in playback tomorrow. He had class at eight the next morning.

But then there was Jackie, and she set his mind at ease. Jimmy willed himself to look sober as Jackie approached the two of them, carrying all the necessary gear.

The shots were never traditional at the Dockside Tavern.

"Fireballs for the road!" she bellowed, as she tossed a small sharing plate on the table between Jimmy and Chester. These were Jackie's idea, a gift she'd brought to the Dockside after a semester abroad in Italy. She placed some sugar cubes on the plate, then took an absinthe bottle and poured it over the cubes, creating a tiny green pool of fuming pastis. She set the bottle on the table, then lifted her chin and shook her head to sweep her blonde hair safely behind her shoulders. She pulled out a lighter, lit the small absinthe pool on fire, and everyone reached into the flame, grabbing a cube and tossing it into their mouths. Slushy warm treats. "Fireballs," she called them. Nothing said Wednesday morning like a head full of cracked cement and a burned upper lip.

They each did a round, caught a glimpse of each other with a half-blind eye and a smile, then set up for round two.

"Here's to the weirdest night ever," Jackie said, as she fumbled with a few more sugar cubes. Something was on her mind, Jimmy could tell. She hardly paid attention as she poured a hearty splash of absinthe over the whole shababble.

Her black apron pressed against the edge of the table, creating a fourth wall, drawing a safe little home in which Jimmy could comfortably spiral somewhere under the table.

"Death the Hammer, Hammer a Thor!" Chester boasted, for

no apparent reason. Jimmy and Jackie were quiet as Jackie struggled to get her BIC to light. The three of them swayed stiffly like cacti in a desert wind. From across the tavern, one might have mistaken this for a moment of profound reflection.

"I gaa thought," said Chester. "Why are blowtorches illegal in New York, and fireballs ain't?"

Great question, thought Jimmy. Blowtorches, commonly used to caramelize the surface of a crème brûlée, were illegal in New York restaurants. But it was perfectly A-OK to hurl streaking fireballs at one another from across the bar. Charming, even. A contradiction served daily, New York-style.

Jackie replied, "Because fireballs get you drunk! Also because no one ever burned down a bar in New York with a fireball. And because you're an idiot." Jackie could flick lighters and rib Chess simultaneously.

"Wow, Jackie, how articulate!" Jimmy said.

Jackie smiled, finally lighting the saucer. It looked like a strange alien soup, green broth with white geometric shapes in it. It flared up, the blue light curling around the dish into an awesome cone. The table now had a beautiful electric centerpiece. Like a sacred glowing heart or something out of an *Indiana Jones* movie.

Jackie put the remaining unused sugar cubes back in her apron. Jimmy enjoyed watching her hand dip and reappear in her apron pocket, like a tiny strip tease of the hand against a black backdrop. Jackie seemed to notice Jimmy's trance and slowed her movements, savoring the appreciation.

The sugar cubes gave a soothing, oily hiss.

Chester persisted, "well then how come prossitution's illegal, but pornography ain't? Ain' one just like proof of the other? It's like prossitution's a crime, unless you have good hard evidence that you committed it! What the fuck? Ann' ideas, Rubber?"

"Please don't call me Rubber in front of the ladies." At first Jimmy was defensive but then pleased to show how nice and easy going he was. He got to parry and be light-hearted at the same time—an artful dodger.

"Whole damn country's run by lawyers," Chester said. "How come nuclear power plants er legal, but nuclear-powered *pants* are still up in front of the board?"

Jimmy didn't reply. He pretended that he didn't have any idea what was to come. Chester didn't know it yet, but he was about to work himself into a small frenzy. When Chester started to talk about the law, he was mildly annoying, but when he started talking about nuclear power plants, he was beside himself. *Power plants,* according to Chester were enormous time bombs just waiting to obliterate everything. As ridiculous and brazenly foolish as the world's tallest, blind guard dogs. It would be only a matter of time before the dogs forgot their allegiance and killed their masters, and everything else living. One day, he believed, a couple of rods would crack, and everyone would get microwaved for a few years, and then the world would revert to the Old West. Jimmy had heard it a thousand times. If they were lucky, they'd take some recipes for medicine. Maybe the elephants would become ever larger, the cheetahs faster, the squirrels cuter.

"That's a good question," Jimmy finally managed.

"Yerr 'n good question," Chester piped.

"Whoa, *totally* uncalled for." Jimmy was now using Chess's momentum, the best defense against an impending diatribe. Give him some slack, and he'd forget what the other end was attached to. Maybe he had already forgotten about the power plants. *That's great,* Jimmy thought. *His lizard brain walked right up to his favorite rant subject, probably automatically, and then wandered off like he didn't even see it!*

Meanwhile, the fireballs were heating up. The liquor seeped fruitfully towards their centers, combining, changing, a string quartet of liquid, solid, gas, and flame.

Jimmy knew that absinthe burned at a low temperature. That

was why blowtorches could burn down restaurants, but fireballs couldn't, unless they soaked for too long, bonding the alcohol to the sugar, and then burned for too long, linking the innocent loft flame to the real core flame. That flame burned at a higher temperature. A more contagious temperature.

All at once, in a burst of consciousness, Jimmy straightened up and looked at Jackie, who looked to him like an edible Michelangelo. He wanted to paint her and eat her simultaneously. Maybe that was why Cézanne had stuck with fruit.

"Ready?" he asked, letting loose a whisper of a grin. But his smile was thwarted by a sudden stomach pain, as subtle and ominous as the lights dimming, *threatening.* "I think your bar is haunted," he mumbled.

Chester's head lolled. Yes, he was drunk. *His feet could probably dance the Firebird Suite right now,* Jimmy thought. *He could spin like a bird, while his head lolled and flapped on top like a balloon on a stick.*

Jackie glanced around at the other tabletops. She had been here too long already. There were thirsty people everywhere, and these guys were charming, good looking, but they were utterly useless, even as customers.

"HERE'S T'ALL THE MICE IN THE WORLD!" Chester bellowed. He always toasted a different species of animal. It was something everybody loved. It was very un-Texan. Very Arizonian.

They all grabbed at the flame. Then they screamed, surging backwards, as if recoiling from a rat or a hairy spider. They screamed again, and Jimmy and Chester stood up, knocking the table over, glowing heart, green bottle and all, sending it crashing onto Jackie's feet. All three of them looked down in horror at their hands on fire, immediately strumming and snapping them in spasms, whipping from right to left, looking frantically for something water glass-like to douse them with.

Jackie sprinted for the bar, waving the flame over her head like an Olympic baton. She was heading for the ice basin behind the bar. The flaming liquid had caught on her apron when the table capsized, and it dripped as she ran, leaving a stippled line of light on the floor.

There were thirty people in the bar, roughly. They straightened up stupidly and began to chortle and laugh. But their laughs were half-hearted, without any conviction. They sounded more like embarrassed laughs, self-conscious reactions to their sudden confusion.

Then the bar fell quiet, as if waiting for some kind of underscoring to start up and complete the dramatic effect. The jukebox lulled between songs. Well technically, the jukebox had just finished its last song—unbeknownst to the bar.

Jimmy and Chester both climbed up on their booths and tried to scramble over the toppled table, but they misjudged their ability to move quickly, and Chester fell on top of Jimmy.

On the other side of the table, on the floor, a puddle of fire burned where the absinthe bottle had shattered. The puddle crawled backwards towards the table. It was a big table—a heavy, masculine six-top. Fire lapped up the top of it like a tongue until it consumed the whole thing. People started to scream.

Jimmy and Chester untangled themselves and dove out from either side of the fallen table, landing drunkenly on the floor and rolling through the glass over their burning wrists, putting *that* fire out before it could finish melting their hands. They knocked the table onto its top edge, spewing liquid fire all over. The tavern grew lighter, an eerie natural brightness, as the reality of what was happening became clear.

Christian, the bartender, lunged for the extinguisher behind the bar.

Jackie reached the ice basin, screaming, partly in fear but mostly in terrible pain. She failed at extinguishing the fire, partly because her flesh had caught, and partly because a basin of ice wouldn't put out a fire right away, not if it was fresh ice that hadn't yet begun to melt. She looked down at the flames catching on her apron.

Without thinking, she went for the bow on the back of the apron. She wouldn't be able to get the damn thing off without releasing the bow! But her hand was dissolving in pain, and her apron refused to untie. To make matters worse, her flickering hand was now directly under her fall of blonde hair.

Christian, the bartender, saw this and dove at her in a classic football tackle. Now everyone in the bar was screaming. Seeing a man tackle a woman was a bewildering, terrible sight.

Jimmy pulled himself off the ground as others rushed for the door.

Jackie and Christian were on the floor by the entrance to the bar back, on the porous rubber mat, under the wooden flap. They both caught fire.

The extinguisher was behind the bar, discarded on the floor. The only way for a customer to access it would be to climb over the end of the bar, grab it, and then climb back over the bar again. But no one seemed interested in nitrogen. Only the door.

Jackie and Christian scrambled quickly to their feet, knocking bottles off the bar back. Jimmy was blinded by one thought: *The extinguisher! If they don't get that extinguisher to somebody they're going to die!* He watched as Christian's flannel shirt caught fire, and the flames lapped at his face, reaching for his eyes. A large, framed photograph crashed down behind the bar—a close-up of Darth Vader, with a caption at the top: "You underestimate the power of The Dockside."

The tavern filled up with black smoke. Disoriented, Christian put his arm out for purchase. He tried to feel his way to the extinguisher, but his flaming arm blew up another absinthe bottle on the spot—followed by a third and then the last absinthe bottle. Next the infusions went, then the strong gins and whiskeys. A horrible cherry and gin stench blew through the bar, joining the smoke and the less perceptible stink of burning hair and skin.

Jackie and Christian looked ridiculous, like flaming bartenders, frantically preparing the world's most important cocktail. The Pope's gimlet. Then they both flew out from behind the bar, across the tavern, screaming. They looked like orange angels, with their arms outstretched in a black heaven.

Almost everyone made it out of the bar.

Jimmy and Chester made it out; although, they both would be left-handed for a long while.

A girl named Carol Lee (from Jimmy's mythology class) was shoved in the commotion, missing the door and falling into an umbrella stand. She hit her head and flipped onto her back just as the infusions exploded, and liquor fire rained all over her.

A boy named Chris Gibbons practically flew out of the tavern. He ran past Jimmy and right into a speeding yellow cab. His right femur snapped in half like a stick, but he lived. Drivers in New York, if they saw smoke coming out of a building, they'd speed up—they wouldn't slow down.

Jackie and Christian were still inside. So was Carol Lee.

The tiny crowd watched from the street, backing up as the ash fell harder. Their silhouettes wavered in the glow of what used to be The Dockside Tavern, and the apartments that stacked on top of it. The building was a cyclone of flame, hurling cinders into the street. Jimmy didn't find himself to be enjoying the view. Not this time.

4

THE FIRE DEPARTMENT still hadn't come.

It was 2:12 in the morning, February 24, 2021. Jimmy's hand was a bright Belgian waffle of agony. He swooned as the drunk threatened to come back.

Chester was breathing hard. He looked more concentrated than Jimmy, as if he were trying to swallow his pain. His shoulders were pressed down, bearing the weight of the horrific events. Just three minutes ago his neck had been wet tissue, barely able to support his head, but now the cords in his neck were taught and thrumming like bass guitar strings.

Each of their right hands were now marbled claws. They looked like dead fetuses at the end of their arms, and they smelled like rotten cream and burnt oranges.

The tenants of the building were standing in the street, barechested or in bathrobes and pajamas. They huddled close to the building, using the warmth of their roasting homes to survive the frigid night. At this distance, large chunks of burning ash hit the street all around them, scattering embers everywhere, undoubtedly destroying every car's paint job. One car had caught fire alongside the building. The flames were so thick, cascading up towards the night sky, that onlookers could not see the building or the car beneath them.

Finally, the fire department came.

A woman was shrieking at everyone, at no one. "Juana! Has anyone seen Juana?"

A chill scuttled up Jimmy's back. Juana was an elderly woman who lived in apartment 2A. Jimmy had met her once. There was no way she'd be out at two in the morning. Juana was in the building.

"Has anyone seen Marc from 3B?" another man asked around. He had on one shoe, a pair of sweats, and nothing else. The combination of his hair sticking out like a tumbleweed and black ash smeared on his face made him look like a chemist who'd just failed comically at an experiment. Chester chuckled self-consciously, then suddenly remembered what he was going to say about nuclear power plants.

The Fire Department fired up their routine, hoses on full blast, knocking off corners of the building in all directions, tossing blankets and jackets into the crowd. Everyone backed up farther.

"Ok, I think it's time to go," Chester said. "I feel awful."

Their stomachs and lungs were full of soot. The alcohol in their blood sent waves of nausea through their bodies. The relentless, throbbing burn in their hands was constant. They felt as if they were standing with their hands in a deep fryer.

The cops arrived along with the paramedics. Then vans with "Homicide" painted on the sides showed up, apparently from out of nowhere, even before the news vans arrived.

Jimmy's green eyes were set, staring at the building. "Chess," he said. "Maybe we can see the paramedics."

"You're stoned," Chester said. "Let's just go. There's no point anyways. What are they gonna do, Jimmy? Tell you that you burned your hand? Give you some Vaseline and a lollipop? Come on. Let's just bail."

"They won't let us leave, man. People are dead. That means possible homicide. That's why CSI is here. We all need to offer a statement to the cops. They'll chase us if we bail."

Chester stood still a moment then nodded. Jimmy was right.

They would have to stay here in the cold for at least an hour, filling out police forms with their left hands until God only knows when.

5

Jimmy hadn't brought his phone out of his pocket for hours.

He'd just learned about Jackie's death. And the others. At least four people were dead, so far.

He reached for his phone in search of comfort. He wanted to see a missed call or a text from anybody, a hello, a warm hand on his shoulder, a familiar face.

The pain in his hand seemed to be getting worse, mocking him. *Yeah, motherfucker! You ain't shit, motherfucker! Your ass is mine!*

Jimmy raised the bright phone up to his coal-smudged face. At first, he couldn't read the screen.

"Thirty-one missed calls?" He staggered.

His mother.

There was no way the news could have gotten to her so quickly. Not in Thunder, Arizona. No way in hell. Not in time for her to call him thirty-one times. That would have taken over ten minutes, if she called three times a minute. And the fire only started five minutes ago. Plus, why would she be calling him? *He* wouldn't be in the news, anyways. Only Jackie, Christian, and Carol Lee. And whoever the fourth was.

Jimmy didn't think about it too much. It wasn't unusual to panic when you got thirty-one missed calls from your mother. He called her back with one flick of the thumb. No use spiraling over it.

His mother answered before he even heard a ring.

"Jamie!" she sobbed into the phone. "Jamie, I need you!"

Jimmy's heart sprang. She hadn't called him Jamie since before he started high school. He waited, trying not to imagine what was happening to his mother. Her breathing was loud in his ear, even with the fire department and everyone yelling around him.

"Jamie... Charlotte... she's gone. Your sister... she's *dead!*" Silence overtook the line, and Jimmy imagined his mother trying to ditch the phone, dropping it like a stone, throwing up her hands and saying, "Done! What's my time?" But he knew she couldn't. Now she had to give comfort to her son. She had to hold onto the phone and stand there, drawing the moment out for as long as it took to—well, what? What would come next?

Jimmy's twin sister was dead.

6

Bobbi was screaming. The loungers in the Westin Hotel bar heard her in the street, and they gathered at the windows overhead.

It only took twenty-six minutes. Just under half an hour for all the cleanup, gathering of police details, and news crews rounding up their stories with passive efficiency. They put Charlotte in a bag, and the rest was history. New York was on to the next. 43rd & Eighth went back to normal.

Bobbi Baker hung around 43rd and Eighth for a while, stunned, not exactly confused but rather oblivious. She felt as if she'd just gotten off work, and her feet didn't prefer any direction in which to walk.

Almost every subway line in New York intersects in Times Square Station, and Bobbi couldn't decide which one to take. Walking had completely lost its glam. Moving was doable but going somewhere was not possible—it seemed somehow wrong.

A tourist in a bright, terrible outfit approached Bobbi. "Excuse me, miss. I'm turned around. How do I get to Broadway?"

Bobbi looked at her slowly, as if coming out of a dream. "A lot of fucking practice," she spat, then walked away because now she had something to walk away from.

After 9/11, New York had become a very pleasant place to live. People on the street had become friendly and supportive, like a fraternity. New Yorkers turned to safety and alliance, not fear. But over the following ten years or so, with some guidance from the nightly news and other television programs, society degenerated into a suspicious and fearful thing once again.

Nowadays, it was hard to come by directions on the street—not because folks assumed you were a terrorist, but because you were a *stranger*. Bobbi fucking hated strangers more than anything.

Charlotte was never like that. She'd trusted people, and she rarely complained. Her and Jimmy. A pair of positive thinkers.

Bobbi pulled out her phone to call Jimmy. She would be the first to tell him (if she could put to words) what had happened to Charlotte. She liked Jimmy the way crappy people were sometimes drawn to nice ones.

Bobbi held her phone up to ear and stared at the spot where Charlotte had died. It was just off the curb, in its place a big wet spot where sanitation had sprayed the blood away. The phone rang, and after five seconds or so, Bobbi forgot who she was calling. She had begun to forget that she was calling anyone when Jimmy's voice startled her out of her trance.

"Hey, HEY! It's Jimmy Jay! Tell me what you called to say and have yourself an awesome day!"

Bobbi hung up. What had just happened wasn't voicemail material. She thought about Jimmy for a moment—sloppy, no style, no backbone. Now he had no sister. He wouldn't react well to this. He'd be reduced to something even less suited for this world than he already was. She didn't want to be the one that might level him. She slipped the phone back into her pocket.

Eventually she left, descending into the nearest subway station and warping home.

7

Jimmy and Chester were back in their dorm room. They had spoken to the cops about their situation. They had lied about their melted hands, saying they'd been trying to put out some spilled flames and got ensnared in some kind of liquid fire trap—it was hard to explain. Their hands were now blistering fast. The pain surged up their wrists like venom.

Jimmy was crying. He used his left hand to rummage through his desk drawer in search of some Advil.

"I gotta... get a... plane ticket right away..." He said no more, feeling too many things at once. Charlotte, his twin sister, his other half, was gone. She'd died. She'd gone through the process of dying. How much agony and humiliation had she suffered before she could go into the next world? What kind of horrible gang-like initiation? What had she done? Had she died with her skirt up, humping the air while her soul had already departed? Had she felt the worst pain of her life? Had she suffered her worst fear? The most desperate humiliation?

And then there was the hole—the hole where his other half had been. Jimmy was speedy, hysterical at the thought of Charlotte experiencing death, but also he was afraid and confused, because now she *was* dead, and he would be keeping his life a secret from her for as long as he lived. Never again would he tell her anything, and he would watch her only from his memories, young and pretty, begging him to let her in, to tell her what's up. How that broke his heart. He screwed up his duck feather face again, his expression looking almost as melted as his hand—his cauterized severance point from his former twin.

"I'd like to go with you," Chester said, as if respectfully asking Jimmy's permission. Of course he was coming with him. They were practically family. The Galls and The Johannsens, from Thunder, Ay-Zee.

Jimmy's hand hissed up in his mind once more, mocking him, testing him, *Look at you, fuck! You're fucked!*

"Blows my *weekend!*" Jimmy cried before bursting into a fit of sobs, grey snot and duck feathers flying everywhere.

8

THUNDER, ARIZONA HAD been hardly more than a four-road crossing and a church.

9

Jimmy and Chester stepped off the plane onto the sunbaked tarmac, and both could tell—they could *feel*—that something was upon them. The air, which Jimmy recognized as home air, was pristine compared to that of New York. Even though the island of Manhattan was windy and flanked by rivers, it smelled like piss everywhere. Every doorway in the entire city had a different urine smell looming all year round. But somehow this air was *too* clean. The sun seemed too bright, and the sky was a new profound shade of blue, one he'd never seen before. Even though he couldn't explain it, Jimmy felt as if he had gone back in time, that his small Boeing aircraft had actually been a time machine, and he was now descending the vessel's staircase into a world of dinosaurs—a land that had existed long before humans.

Chester seemed caught in a similar thought. He had an odd look in his eyes. With his face pushed forward, Jimmy could imagine whiskers twitching, as he barometrically adjusted to this new atmosphere. Chester was gaunt and gangly, like Heinlein's *Stranger in a Strange Land*. But this wasn't his first trip from New York through Phoenix International to this landing strip in the middle of nowhere. Not his millionth, but not his first. Chester didn't speak, as he balanced the sorrow of Charlotte's death with the new strangeness of his hometown.

They walked slowly towards the terminal, a couple of young cowboys in their homeland, nervous at noon, seeing their world for the first time.

Half of the airport was shut down. Jimmy and Chess had to walk all the way around the terminal to baggage Carousel 2, which was rarely used.

Carousel 1, where they would normally claim their bags, was closed, and as they walked along the edge of the tarmac, with the building close by on their right, they could see inside. Nothing was there—no security, no people at all, and no remnants of construction, which might have explained the closure. And it wasn't as if it had been under any construction; it was as bleak and old looking as it always had been, an antique landing strip from the fifties. It hadn't been modified since '62, when the state had decided that northeast Arizona would be the new frontier for nuclear testing, only to "change its mind" a year later.

In 1963, President Kennedy signed the Nuclear Test Ban Treaty, an agreement between the United States, the United Kingdom, and the Soviet Union. The NTB Treaty banned nuclear testing in the atmosphere, underwater, and in outer space. But *underground* testing was as legal as lollipops, and the US had desperately needed tech advancement, what with the Soviet Union starting to spread like a grin, eyes locked tightly on their competitors to the west. Jimmy thought that the US needed to advance its nuclear technology like it needed an ass full of electrified pufferfish. Chester likely thought the same thing but with flaming piranhas.

There was no known documentation of underground test sites in Thunder, but Jimmy and Chester found those old mines pretty suspicious. Some of them had open doors—dark portals that would stare at you like lidless eyes in the mountain. Sentient eye sockets of enormous half-buried skulls.

This half of the airport was dim. No light but the weird sun bled in. Carousel 1 looked like an Italian post office during siesta on a Sunday.

Carousel 2 was not much different. There'd been only twelve

people on the flight from Phoenix to Lang Field, and they'd all been quiet, subdued passengers. There were a group of four people who looked like a family, another three who looked like another family, and an old, defeated-looking man who appeared to have been crying.

They'd had one flight attendant, one pilot who hadn't spoken throughout the whole flight, and then there was Jimmy and Chess. The flight attendant might have been pretty, but Jimmy couldn't see her face. She'd worn a blue surgical facemask. He'd wondered if he'd known her from the Thunder area. Why the mask? He thought that was only for Asian people in New York.

The passengers all slumped around carousel 2, the silence broken only when the conveyer belt started up. They looked like they were claiming coffins, not Samsonites. Jimmy saw one woman—the mother of one of the families—wipe her eyes with a tissue, then use the same hand to cross herself.

Jimmy looked for the flight attendant in the baggage claim area. He wanted to see her face. It only took a moment to notice that she wasn't there. *Where is she?* He thought. *Cleaning the air-craft? No, that would have taken all of thirty seconds. Seriously, where is she?* The old 1960s tape on the wall that announced the following departures was blank. No more flights today. The pilot was here with the rest of them; he must have cut the generator and locked up the aircraft. So where was the flight attendant?

Jimmy let it go. Surely his mind was trying to distract him from his pain, to make him forget Charlotte, at least for a moment, and to forget his bulbous right claw.

It had been fourteen hours since the fire at The Dockside, and his hand screamed and screamed. It was as if every hour on the hour he dipped his hand in a vat of fresh acid. And now it was one o'clock on the dot, fresh acid-dipping time.

Think about something else, man, anything else. Say, "Doesn't stuff 'round here look different these days?"

They grabbed their suitcases, then went back out into the sun to greet their families.

The Galls were sitting there in a brand new Subaru, parked.

Alice Johannsen sat in her rusty white Tacoma. She looked dazed and eerily exhausted, as if she had killed her own young herself. Well, *half* of them. Neither the Galls nor Alice seemed particularly excited to see their sons. All the enthusiasm had been sucked out of the world, and it wasn't because of Charlotte. Something huge was happening. Jimmy didn't need to have big, inquisitive eyes to see that.

As they drove away, the terminal at Lang Field seemed to disappear behind them. It went dim, then popped out of existence.

.

10

ALICE DROVE MOST of the way home without speaking. Her vacant expression somehow seemed to intensify as they got closer to Thunder, making her appear ghostly, less there. The road was completely straight, and at times, she didn't move at all, her eyes trained on the expanse ahead. Alice had always been thin, but Jimmy noticed that within the last few months she had become much thinner. Her hands reminded him of long, white spiders. Charlotte's death might actually kill her, Jimmy thought. Blow her over the edge like a leaf.

"Ma... what's going on around here?" Jimmy asked, cautiously.

But she didn't answer. Was she in shock? Could people drive while in shock?

Jimmy thought for a moment that this might be a dream. Was he still on the plane? He knew that he had vivid dreams when he slept on airplanes. Sometimes he would believe that he was on the plane, in his seat, and then something unusual would happen like it would start to snow inside the plane, or the Captain's PA would start announcing eerie, droning babble that got under his skin, and it would go on and on, getting spookier and spookier. One time he dreamed that he was sitting there in his window seat with a fresh ginger ale, cold condensation on his fingertips, and the plane just crashed, bursting at the middle, sending the nose upward, like a roller coaster, the tail end dropping where the middle was, spilling passengers out into the sky like rain. Then he popped out of it, back in his window seat in the world of the conscious.

Yes, airplane dreams could be vivid, but here he was in his mother's white Tacoma. "Trusty Rusty," she called it. The one Jimmy's father had left her nineteen years ago, weeks before Jimmy and Charlotte's birth, when Magnus the Mysterious had left on foot to buy cigarettes and never came back. Alice hadn't understood it. They were having twins, so why would he leave? And even more mysterious—why would he leave *on foot?* She had heard of "walking out" on someone, but it seemed crazy in a literal sense. Ain't no buses in Thunder.

No, Jimmy wasn't dreaming. He was wondering again why his father had left, and why he had left on foot. Why nineteen years before the twins were separated, the parents had been separated, and the brand new truck that Magnus's company had bought for him would remain inexplicably with his mother, who now rode in it with her son back into Thunder, looking rattled out of her mind.

And even though the sky was much bluer, and Jimmy was sure the world was hiding something, the pain in Jimmy's right hand told him that he was awake. His mind was sore, as if reverberating the ache in his hand, creating an echo and absorbing the bounce back. His right shoulder was badly bruised from landing on it in last night's flying attempt to put out his hand. His face and arms were scratched up, and worst of all, his hangover supplemented his body wherever pain fell short, crippling his stomach. His eyes hurt, too.

Think you're dreaming? Yeah, dream on. You're in Trusty Rusty. That leopard print seat cover and pink fur steering wheel is your mom's. He hadn't checked when she picked him up, but he was sure that if he looked at the back of the truck, he would see the bumper sticker. The bane of his being. The thing that he and Charlotte had dedicated their lives to take down. It was faded, almost out of existence, but it still read:

PRAY MORE
WORRY LESS

"Ma, are *you* ok?" Jimmy asked. He automatically sensed a reaction radiating from her. She always got disappointed when he asked her stupid questions. Here it comes: *Why do you make me go out of my way to tell you my feelings when you already know exactly how I feel? Do you like hearing me complain that much? What's wrong with you? Don't you go to Columbia? I swear they musta switched your entrance exam with someone else's by accident, the poor sono-fabitch.*

But the shift in Alice's expression was not one of strained disappointment. It was pity, as if she knew that *he* didn't know what he was asking. *Ma, are you okay after Charlotte's freak accident?* No, that was not the question. Something else had happened. Something else *was* happening, and Alice knew it. Her facial shift only proved it. There was something that Jimmy didn't know about, and his own mother couldn't tell him. Not now, anyways. Something big was happening in Thunder, but Alice couldn't articulate it.

She drove on, and the road never bent, as they headed for Thunder.

11

L ANG FIELD WAS forty-five miles northeast of Polacca, across Navajo territory, in the eastern part of the Arizona Hopi reservation. From there, if you drove thirty-six miles directly north on Old route 28, you would find Thunder, which sat on the Navajo-Apache border, with Navajo to the northwest and Apache to the southeast.

In the center of town there sat a barren dirt courtyard, home to the town's gatherings, showdowns, and holiday festivities. An adobe wall, about four feet high, corroded by time, ran a soft diagonal through the square. This wall divided the old natives' territories, but these days, the square was mostly populated by kids, and there were no territories.

The courtyard, known contemporarily as Apavajo Square, was the center of town. It was the hangout and the meeting spot, and one of the only places in Thunder where one might happen upon some company. Otherwise there was the bar, or the church, or the Stop-N-Shop.

The Thunder shopping center was northwest of Apavajo Square. There you'd find the package store, a RadioShack, the Dollar Store, a J.C. Penny, and the Stop-N-Shop. South of that was the Green, a small floral roundabout with a general store and the big white church. East of Apavajo Square, about a quarter mile, you'd find the bar, aptly named *The Bar*. There was no other in Thunder, so there was no need to specify. Still, it was known among locals as *The Hole*. Of course in Thunder, there were only locals.

Aside from Old Route 28 to the south, only one other road traveled in and out of town. To the west, off Route 160, about fifty miles northeast of Tuba City, a small, unnamed road snuck off to the east, between the eggplant-colored buttes, eventually sniffing its way up to Thunder. The locals had a name for this road, too: Copperhead Canyon. "Bring lots of water, plenty of gas, and don't get eaten alive," they'd advise, tongue-in-cheek.

Thunder was established in 1862 as a nickel-mining camp, discovered by lost travelers who'd been attracted by the peculiarly shiny mountain caps. The cost of nickel was so great that by 1870, Thunder had a population of over four hundred. The mines expanded and franchised, leading to more mines and eventually a town. The Nickel Rush had begun. By 1880, nearly two thousand people had migrated to Thunder. By 1890, three thousand five hundred. Thunder homesteaded people from China, the Netherlands, England, Cornwall, and France. But in 1896, the price of nickel suddenly dropped. "Fell off the map" is more like it. The mines were no longer economically viable, and the townspeople hung up their hats and picks and pioneered on. *Quickly*. By 1898, the entire town of Thunder had evacuated. Every last person gone.

The lost travelers had come up with the town's name after their second night in camp. The faces of the mountains, tear-streaked with nickel, flickered in the moonlight like titans crying in the dark. It looked to them like lightning, and they worried with their traveler's superstition. Seeing lightning and not hearing any rumbles or booms was like dropping a penny down a well and not hearing it *plunk* at the bottom. It was unsettling and creepy, so they gave the name Thunder out of respect and fear.

12

JIMMY SOON DISCOVERED that Alice didn't need to explain anything to him. The earth spelled it out for him in caps.

Fifteen minutes into the drive, Jimmy started to see strange, ghostly shapes on the horizon, directly towards Thunder.

Was that smoke? he wondered. *Was it burning? Or was it coal-colored whirlwinds?*

No, that would not be possible. The hardpan was a multicolored vista, like tie-dye. Whirlwinds in these lands were luminescent, like psychedelic specters of mythical rainbow beasts. No, it was not whirlwinds. It was dark smoke. More fire was ahead, and his hand was still screaming. *Fire! Yeah, fire, motherfucker. You like that? I own you motherfucker!*

How much of Thunder was burning Jimmy could not tell. The Galls seemed to be about two miles ahead; maybe they could see farther. Jimmy's green eyes narrowed to slits. He breathed erratically, through his nose.

Then Alice began to talk.

PART
TWO

13

BUSTER WELLS HAD been a handsome fellow before his house fell on him. Very well built, he'd never scrambled for attention, and he was smart. He'd always told it like it was, never using gaudy exaggerations or ornaments in his speech. Similarly, he never wore jewelry. He didn't strain himself to be normal either. He was just Buster, through and through.

In high school, about fifty years earlier, he'd been the star quarterback for the football team, in addition to being an A-student with barrels of friends. He never got in any fights.

Buster had moved away from Thunder when he was sixteen, off to junior college with a football scholarship. He left after one semester, having been expelled for drinking a beer in class. When his parents didn't take him back he enrolled at West Point, a military college, where young men studied the governing body of the military and became soldiers. He got in with another football scholarship. Buster had thought he was quite an athlete, but the scholarship was really just a front for recruiting students when enrollment numbers were low. In fact, the football team at West Point was kind of a front too. They only played six games a year with neighboring colleges.

The entire campus was architecturally phenomenal: bleak, straight-edged, and massive. The buildings were painted a serene, steel grey, almost transparent, like an invisible starship. Surrounding the campus, a glorious green forest.

To the east of the campus was a slate black cliff side, with the

Hudson River of New York below, where the most strategic battle of the Civil War had taken place.

Everyone on campus always wore a uniform, even when they slept. Light grey and angular—talk about school spirit! Ironically, the United States' top military college had the worst football team in the whole northeast. Worse than Purchase, worse than Bard. No one knew how that was possible.

While enrolled at West Point, Buster ran into a few of the wrong guys. He was younger than most of his classmates and more than a little naive, yet he was socially acute. He started a small drug network, involving people he'd met on weekend trips to the city, friends back on campus, and a few strangers but mostly friends of friends. His grades went south as he began a study in drugs—using and abusing, dealing, and discovering all kinds of things about himself. He wove it into his schedule, as he dealt on campus to the other soldiers.

Eventually he graduated from West Point. The Vietnam War hadn't escalated to more than a rumor at that time, and no one was talking about a draft. But before long, Buster was a lieutenant on his first mission to Saigon. Call it another football scholarship.

He had heard that soldiers got into terrible trouble with drugs in Saigon, and he was thankful for his knowledge about them. He was safe. Safe from that guerrilla warfare. That sneak attack.

Buster was dishonorably discharged from the army in 1970, eight months after he started serving. He'd been caught by his superiors selling heroin to the other boys, and he was later charged with conspiracy and a slew of international misdemeanors.

But then his career really took off.

He moved to Phoenix, where he started from scratch. He used his wit, his good physique, and what had remained of his observation skills to join a drug cartel coming out of Juarez to Phoenix, skirting the hard-ass cops of New Mexico along the way. Buster felt like a quarterback again. Someone gave him the package, and he gave them the yardage.

Buster kept his job with the company for thirty years. His experience and his awareness of death eventually hardened him. He'd become extremely well-trained, as if he had graduated West Point three times and served in four wars. His hearing and vision had become better than average—he could fight without blinking, and he could shoot a P-90 machine gun like a German sniper.

After thirty years, Buster became head honcho, the Godfather to this nameless, invisible family. He was heavy and severe, like a Mexican Viking. He should have worn a heavy crown, but instead he wore a huge, intimidating mustache. And mirrored sunglasses. The rest of his face never moved, even when he spoke. Buster's metamorphosis had completed.

On his sixtieth birthday, Buster informed the other honchos that he would retire from their company. He'd been suffering from heart palpitations and lung failure, among other things. He hadn't joined the cartel on the road in almost ten years. He kept to Phoenix, Buster's "territory." But now he was done with that, too, for his health. He would retire with a fortune stashed away in his 401(k), which was a four-hundred-and-one thousand cubic-foot vault containing only cash. The smell inside the vault was an intoxicating money stench.

They let him go. They let him walk away in peace, out of respect, and Buster retired to Scottsdale, a rich little city outside of Phoenix. He lived in a large house on Camelback Mountain, just outside the city, el ranchero style.

For ten subsequent years, he lived his life as it should have been lived all along—quietly, away from any cutthroat institutions. Away from uniforms, superiors, and rocket launchers. Just

Buster of the mountain, observer of nature. This was his fourth and favorite career. Buster in the moon. Eating with a spoon.

Buster was seventy-two now. Still intimidating, still heavily mustached. His home on Camelback Mountain had remained in solitude. In 1986, that part of the desert had become a national reserve, protected from zoning and future developments.

It was his mountain.

He had his women on his mountain. He'd always loved women, and his thirty years in the secret militia had made him extremely lonely over the long term. Not to mention how lonely the army had made him. He'd had limited contact with the world outside of his confined life, and he'd had few "real" women, as they called them in Saigon. Working seven days a week in a small environment could make a man crazy with lust, in a bad way, in dangerously selfish way. He'd had whores, lots of them, and he still had them now and again.

When he'd moved to Phoenix back in 1988, he married a woman named Esther Forsythe. They had a child, a girl. They called her Jackie Wells. But Esther left him and took the baby when he told her the story of his life. He believed they were still somewhere in Arizona. She never asked him for any money. She must have had a thing against blood money.

Buster never told anyone else the story of his life. He kept that book closed, for private viewing only.

Buster let loose his seventy-two-year-old moan. He was ready for bed, all the caffeine from the day having drained from his body. He no longer used drugs, but his brain had been fried and rewired by the continuous influence of drugs. He was a weirdo now, with weirdo infrastructure and a brain that might as well have come from a Dr. Seuss jam factory.

"Kelsey," he said. "Kelsey, fetch me my slippers." His voice sizzled like hot oil, clean and lightly accented like a half-Mexican. His bones cracked and creaked as he moved. Even speaking would pop a joint somewhere in his body. He looked like a skeleton, too, except for his head, although when he wore sunglasses it was easy to mistake his eyes for dark empty sockets.

Kelsey was his companion for the evening.

Buster was naked and love spent, his mustache bathing in the moonlight. "Fuck," he mumbled, reflecting on the night's events. Seventy-two and still able. Amazing.

He rolled his wrists in slow circles, cracking every joint in his hands, wrists, and elbows. "You need to go, Kelsey," he said.

Kelsey sauntered over with his slippers, and he sat up reaching for his robe.

"Thanks," he said. "You know, let me tell you something. You make me feel naked in the jungle in the sun. Like I'm at war in the jungle, and suddenly the war's over, and all the gooks are gone, like… just gone, and I'm there, naked in the jungle in the sun, and I'm safe. Fuck, you make my nose smell gardenias and wild cats. Kelsey… you're fucking great."

She kissed him on the mouth and slipped away gracefully, never to be seen again by old Buster Wells.

Buster sat still on the side of the bed, trying to warm up in his robe and slippers. In a few moments he would be comfortable, but for now he just sat there trying to radiate, dreaming, and at total peace. He felt good. He had his heart palpitations, lung problems, two replaced hips, full body arthritis, cysts on his liver, but otherwise he felt really great.

He reached for a glass of brandy, the first and only brandy of the night. He sat back down on the bed with the glass, done at last.

As Buster sat there, looking out of the large picture windows into the night, with the full moon reflecting off his tarnished soul, he felt eternal. He thought back on his life, as he had every night. He thought about every little baby step from a straight-A niño to a drug cartel's hammer smash head honcho. Even though he was an asshole and a murderer, he never forgot where he came from. Good old Thunder. Home, home on the range.

Suddenly he heard a terrible crash. It came from the bathroom, twenty feet from him. He pulled himself up from the bed, glass of brandy in tow, and slowly crossed the room to the bathroom door. His body sounded like a crackling fire.

The door hung partway open, and he could see that the room looked different, new shadows and light in the narrow space. He pushed the door open, and a surge of fear lit up his back like grass-fire.

The whole ceiling had fallen over the bathtub, huge chunks of drywall scattered around it. He looked up to see two large ceiling beams standing at terrifying angles, looming over him. They looked like intruders from another world.

His initial fear subsided enough for Buster to think clearer. *Why* was he afraid? He was never afraid; his nerves had been sanded away years ago. He wasn't even afraid of death—he'd literally written it down on his bucket list. So why was the sight of this structural malfunction rooting him to the floor? His crotch was numb. He felt as if he had woken up in the night to find two raping thieves standing over him, grinning.

Buster stepped into the bathroom. He could smell the plaster that had disintegrated all over the floor. He peered into the tub to survey the damage, half expecting to find a meteor or a tablet with the Ten Commandments lying in the center of it. Or a baby alien, glowing. But he saw nothing but spent ceiling. Pieces of his house in his bathtub. He looked up. Another wave of fear. Within the pipes, stone, and wood something moved. There were things in the ceiling. His demons. Shit, there were so many of those bastards that they'd formed an army, and now they were coming for him, to finally claim him and drag him to hell.

As if responding to the crackles coming from Buster's body, the ceiling released a loud *SK-KACK!* as a pipe fell, breaking open a smaller pipe underneath it. Water burst out, spraying Buster in the face and scaring him almost unconscious.

In his robe, he looked like a Mexican wizard, a spectacular magic spell backfiring in his face. He yelled and spun on his heel. He meant to bee-line for the door, to run out into the master bedroom, safely into the moonlight, but he didn't make a single step.

He spun right into one of the fallen beams, staggering backwards along the side of the tub. He fell hard. Water sprayed and sprayed. He touched the side of his head that felt warm. His right temple had gashed open, and blood flowed out. He tried to pull himself up, the crackle of his joints sounding like a wet popcorn machine.

Struggling to his feet, Buster knelt beside the tub and tried to catch his breath. He imagined he looked like a man at a funeral, weeping over an open casket.

Then the whole ceiling came down. With a deafening crash, the bathroom was obliterated, Buster and all.

In his last moments, kneeling at the tub like a churchgoer deep in prayer, Buster managed one last, clear thought: *Please God, watch over my soul. Please provide beer for me in Heaven. And please watch over my daughter, Jackie, whom I wish I had gotten to know better.*

The boot heel of God came down swiftly, crushing Buster Wells like a bug.

If you dug, you might find his mustache somewhere at the bottom of the rubble.

14

ALICE DREW A deep breath, suspended it, then let it out. It was the first human thing she'd done since she'd met Jimmy twenty minutes earlier, and he was greatly relieved.

"Strange shit's goin' on here, Jimmy. I don't know how to explain it. I don't think anyone does. Things are happening all over the place. Thunder's pretty much gone crazy."

She looked over at Jimmy, and for the first time she noticed his hand. He was clutching it at the wrist, as if trying to stop blood from flowing. She saw it, looked back at his face, then decided to ignore it for the time being. "Last night people started disappearing. Like they'd go out to buy beer or something, and then they don't come back. You can hear phones ringing, all urgent in the night."

Jimmy said nothing.

"Also, last night the Gibsons' pickup ran off the road with the whole family in it. Everyone one of them died. The Tuckers all died in their house, and no one knows why. The three marshals died in the police station—same mystery, though I'm not particularly sad to see those guys go. But we don't have no cops anymore, and I guess that's bad. Jesus has a plan for all this, I know. But I can't imagine what it is."

"Mom," Jimmy started, but then he found that he couldn't finish. He looked down at his hand, then returned his gaze to the windshield.

"Four houses burned down around dinner time last night. I

think one of the houses was Mrs. Dee Dee's, your teacher. Then I got the call from the police about Charlotte. Around ten-fifteen last night. Georgia came by, though I never rang her up. She just came, and I couldn't turn her away. I was gone, you know. Beside myself. I just couldn't believe it! None of that other shit mattered—the *weird* stuff. Only Charlotte."

"Mom," Jimmy began. "I'm so sorry." He scratched his right palm with his left thumbnail. "But this is nuts. Like... are you being for real?"

"Then at around eleven," she continued, glancing at Jimmy but ignoring his interruption, "the gas station blew up, killing the sheriff and three other people. It's like the end of the *world*, Jimmy, and it's only happening in Thunder! Know what happened after the gas station blew up? A blackout! We ain't had no power since!" Alice pressed her lips together in a tight frown. Her grief and confusion strangled her, and her own words confused her even further.

"We ain't had working phones since last night. When you told me what time you were coming into Lang, the phone clicked off, like someone knifed the line. It was scary as hell—I had to look behind me! And Sally's freaked to hell 'cause her husband and son went out this morning to try to get radio reception and never came back. She's freaking out, Jimmy. There's no calming her down.

"Jimmy, Thunder ain't pretty in a time like this. Aside from what I've seen and heard, I ain't seen too many people around. I think they're all disappearing. And there's been rumblings," she continued. "It's these little tremors. They feel like earthquakes. I guess they *are* earthquakes. They're fuckin' scary.

"And then *Charlotte*, my Jesus. Holy God, *Charlotte! A fucking bus, Jimmy!*"

Alice's bottom teeth jutted out in a strained grimace, which meant she was within an inch of losing her mind.

"But Ma, Charlotte wasn't *in* Thunder," Jimmy said, desperately.

"Now Dessy got a call last night, too. Around ten. Her boy Richard was murdered in the street. Thing is—Dessy's boy wasn't in Thunder neither. He was in *Bermuda*, doing a study thing! Richard said it was the most peaceful place you can imagine. That everyone's a friend in Bermuda, and not on a computer, but like real life friends. There's no such word for strangers; everyone's just nice. No one ever gets murdered on the street in Bermuda!"

"There's pirates in Bermuda," Jimmy said. "Lots of pirates." He didn't know why he'd said that. He had read that there were pirates in Bermuda, but not lots of them. There weren't lots of *anything* in Bermuda. It was twenty square miles, within thousands of miles of open ocean. Bermuda was like Thunder Island. It was even protected by a barrier reef. The only way to safely reach the shore would be to follow the lighthouse. You would have to follow the swatch of light in the water as the lighthouse keeper guided you. In the old days, pirates ran Bermuda. They would lead the ships right into the reef, crashing and sinking them. Then they'd boat out and loot the ships for all they were worth. This was how Bermuda had sustained its supplies. This was their trade.

There were still bandits running around on Bermuda. Descendants of the pirates. And they *looked* like pirates—dreadlocked, striped shirt-wearing hoodlums with no underground to call their hood—

What the hell was he thinking about? Pirates? Charlotte was dead, his mother was spiraling in shock, and his home town was disappearing with everyone in it.

He was suddenly reminded (by his hand, of course) of the fire last night at The Dockside.

Holy God, was it meant for him? And Chester?

They had leaped out of the fire, and what had happened since then? Nothing?

His twin sister... Jackie Wells... Everyone was going down

around him. Everyone except for a few, including the other ten people on the airplane. The last airplane.

The stewardess! Had she died somehow? Just like that?

Thinking about the stewardess in her blue mask, seeing her one minute until the next minute she was gone—it all hit home for Jimmy. Reality washed over him like ice water.

But Jimmy didn't let his mother on to how spooked he'd just become. Nor would he show how badly his hand was hurting, or how heavy his sadness for his family felt. He froze inside with these things, alone.

"That's not all Jimmy," Alice said. "I mean, this is going to sound really weird, but I've been having... No, this is going to sound stupid." She pushed her greying hair back with her hand.

"Just say it," Jimmy said. "It's okay."

Alice looked at Jimmy, taking a moment to glance at his hand again. "Okay, shit," she said. She looked in her rearview mirror. She was either buying time so she could string her thoughts together, or she was checking to see if someone was following them. "I've been feeling these kind of heat flashes lately. I feel like something's here in Thunder. It's like a heat on my skin. I just start heating up real bad. It feels kind of like when I come indoors with all my coats on, and I can't take them off, and my skin starts burning. And I think it has something to do with all the nasty stuff that's been going on."

Jimmy watched her face flush red as she spoke.

"Actually," she continued. "Now that I say it out loud, it sounds—"

"No I get it," Jimmy said. Then, when he saw her apprehension he added, "I feel like everything's clearer. Bluer. Magnified somehow."

"I Iuh, yeah. I guess," she said. She pulled out a pack of Benson & Hedges. Alice didn't smoke anymore; she'd kicked the habit when Charlotte and Jimmy had gotten accepted into college, but she never got past that last part, the oral fixation. She would never put a toothpick or a dumb lollipop in her mouth, so she kept the cigarettes around, and stuck one in her mouth to calm herself down from time to time.

There was a monster here. A real monster that no one could see. It was moving around, and it was making people disappear. And they were now heading straight for it. *Pray more, worry less*, Jimmy thought, and he wondered if his mother was worrying less right now. It was hard to tell.

"Now tell me something," she said. "What the fuck happened to your hand?"

15

HELL FINN WAS a horrible, insane man. Always had been and always would be.

He believed that the world had done him a great slew of injustices, that it had intentionally dealt him shitty cards, starting with his parents, then his school, then his hideous face. He was unrelentingly bitter. He ate loathing, and he shat revenge.

Originally from Las Vegas, Finn had left his home when he was thirteen. He dropped out of middle school that same year, and for a while he walked around with a piece of paper in his back pocket. It was an affidavit from his old principal, stating that young Finn "does not play well with others." He used it as his ID, his sarcastic membership card to this iniquitous, ill-willed world.

Shortly after, Finn disappeared. No one saw him for two or three years. When he eventually turned up, he was something of a celebrity in Vegas. At first, they called him "Gilbert Grape," a reference to a fourteen-year-old retarded kid with a dirty face from the film. He wasn't really retarded, but whatever drugs he was taking were messing him up fast. Eventually he became the "Tropicana Psycho," who threatened and screamed at everyone and slept everywhere. He was a sunburned skeleton, and sometimes when he slept, he looked like nothing but a laid out pile of cheap Walmart clothes.

It wasn't long before Las Vegas turned Finn into a textbook meth head. Twitchy, snaggle-toothed, and completely self-obsessed. He stole; he attacked the tourists; he even killed three or four people over the years. These murders he had no memory of. He couldn't even confess to them believably enough if he were tried in court. He only remembered crack. And meth. Everything else was too cumbersome to carry around.

The air in Vegas was lethal in large doses, especially with a head full of meth. Temperatures climbed as high as one hundred forty degrees, and it was as it was as dry as the moon. Not to mention a secret altitude of two thousand feet that would get you every time.

You would see Finn on Tropicana, screaming and pacing, searching for his lost something-or-other.

If you were driving, and you were unlucky, he would run out into the street in a crazy curve, yelling at his demons, blind to the traffic.

Call him bipolar, give him Asperger's, say what you will, but at the core of it all, Hell Finn was evil. He was the wrong answer to everything living. He could reverse your bowels simply by walking past you. He would kill his own mother if he ever saw her again.

And he was always armed—armed and paranoid.

One day, men in suits grabbed Hell Finn and threw him into a van, tactical-style, then drove him to Thunder. They took Copperhead Canyon, only a five-hour drive from Vegas to Thunder, if you use sirens.

Finn was put to work in a mountain mine, lifting beams, cleaning caves, janitorial work.

He was a nauseous mess, coming down off alcohol and meth. He vomited up weird stuff in the dark brackets of the mines. His hair started to fall out. He would find clumps of it where he napped, or in his food. Each day the sickness worsened.

Finn always chalked it up to withdrawal. He enjoyed crack for its mild withdrawal symptoms, but in his latter years he had started a crossover, involving meth, heroin, and riots of alcohol.

Withdrawal, yes, it was easier that way. It helped him get through his days. It was also a sign of progress, not degeneration, and that was something. That was better than thinking there was another presence in the mine *making* him sick. Something hungry, lurking in the dark drifts. No, that would be far too spooky. Withdrawal sounded better.

How about radiation? That should have been the first thing he thought of when the sicknesses had started to spread. But it never even crossed his mind. He never surmised that he might actually be getting nuked down here, and that was why he'd been grabbed off the street, and why he wasn't paid for his labor. No, Hell overlooked that idea. Chalk *that* one up to withdrawal.

Nightmares consumed his life. He never got well, just sicker. He bled out of his orifices. He thought his conditions were a result of drug damage, and he told himself that he would heal. *Just a crack,* he would muse, and then he'd laugh a short, lonely laugh.

For two years, he worked down there in the mines. He didn't see many people. He would go hours at a time without any light or company. He moved around in the dark, sweating and mumbling, and he *loathed...*

Finn had created an image of himself in his mind. A sort of character to be his id.

This character was an apocalyptic gunslinger, with a huge rocket launcher in one hand, and a combination shotgun-Desert Eagle in the other. In his fantasy, he blew away everyone he saw. He did it like it was his job. He would blast and blaze until he had successfully obliterated part of the world. The iniquitous, scheming, conniving, unjust, hateful, evil world.

He was never allowed into the town of Thunder. He wore an electrical collar that would kill him if he stepped foot outside his confines on the mountainside. His territory, he called it.

Then one day when Finn was down in the mine resting, lamps off, thinking about the apocalyptic gunslinger, he drifted off into sleep. When he woke up, everything seemed peculiar to him. He put on the lamps and looked around. The equipment was there, all the tools and the work in progress. But he heard no sounds, no distant voices.

Curious, Hell ascended to the mountainside.

Everyone at the site was gone.

He walked back to the camp to find everyone there gone, too. The whole project appeared to have been evacuated.

Everything electrical was powered off, even the lights. His dog collar was dead, and although he was almost too nervous to try, he stepped outside his territory, and he did not die.

The open air had never smelled so sweet. It was different on this side of the line somehow. And the setting sun, Hell could almost smell that, too. The sky was huge and all kinds of blues, lightly spotted with the happiest little clouds.

He began to walk downhill. It would be just a short stalk down the mountainside to the center of town. With two tree branches, one in each hand, and a grey plastic collar around his neck, Hell Finn descended into Thunder.

When he got to Thunder, Hell Finn lurked in the shadows. Like the dark mines, shadows were his home.

He stayed invisible to Thunder, mostly. When he was somewhere public, he was pleasant, and people eventually got used to seeing him. Owning only four teeth was not unusual in these parts of Arizona. In fact, he fit in pretty well. No one ever got his first name. No one got to know him. No one saw evil, even when they walked straight out of church and spotted him at the general store. They would spend an hour in there, yelling about sin and demons and hell, and then they would walk right out the front doors into the green, see Finn, smile, and wave. No one ever learned of the seething—the *vengeance*—that boiled just under his surface.

While his body sauntered through the drug store in town, his mind lingered on his gun room at home.

For six months, Finn practiced and mastered hating everyone in Thunder.

16

ABOUT TWO HUNDRED people had gathered at Apavajo Square. All were scared, confused, and dazzled by the sunshine. Some held bibles, most were obese, and more than a couple appeared to be drunk.

It was two in the afternoon, and John Lajon and his girlfriend, Sarah Simonez, had taken the lead. They were both wearing white tank tops, shorts, combat boots, and leather jackets, facing the crowd like a two-piece production of *Grease*. It was a cold day in the desert, and the sun was blinding.

A young girl in the crowd spoke up. Her name was Cherish. She was nine and small for her age. "How come you guys wearin' the same clothes?" she asked. "Are you like, the *Bobbsey* Twins or something?"

John and Sarah didn't look at each other. For once, they didn't care what they were wearing. "What do you know about the *Bobbsey* Twins?" John said. "When were you born, like 2016?"

This was good, John thought. The crowd seemed okay with a bit of humor, and that was maybe the first step towards getting back to normal. Cutting through this tension. John wanted more of this sort of crowd. Dumb and easily entertained.

He continued: "They still got *Bobbsey* Twins, shit. At the end of the world, when all communications are down, you still got *Bobbsey Twins*. How do you like that?"

"How come no one's come to rescue us yet?" someone cried. Others replied with low mutters and shuffles of agreement.

John looked startled. "Now listen," he said, although he had no idea what he was going to make them listen to. He shifted on his feet, realizing that he had absolutely no leadership skills.

Sarah stepped in. "Check it out," she began. She glanced at John, then glanced at his outfit, disapprovingly. "Some of you have been contacted by police departments outside. This means they'll come visit us once they realize they can't reach us through the phones anymore."

A couple of distracted murmurs, mostly in agreement, shuffled through the crowd.

"We can all expect some help, when people from the outside arrive." she continued.

A couple more audible agreements.

Sarah shot one more glance at John. "Let's all just take it slow for now. We're country folk. Don't get too quick. People will be showing up real soon, so let's make this town civilized for when they get here."

Enough consent to call it general. Enough to keep a pulse going.

Another voice spoke up, even smaller than Cherish's, and a little scratchy. "Is Charlotte dead?"

It was Chuck, the little Davidson boy. Sarah knew him because Charlotte had babysat for him before she went to college. Chuck was eight years old now, almost old enough to fend for himself. But that didn't give him a reason to be out here all alone. His parents didn't seem to be with him; Sarah couldn't see either of them anywhere in the crowd. Chuck looked tiny without them. In a filthy, oversized Diamondbacks jersey that had once been white and purple, he looked like he had been zapped with a shrink-ray gun.

"I Ii, Chucky," Sarah said. "We'll know—"

"We will know more about the Johannsens when Alice gets back. She's getting Jimmy from the airport right now." John took a step closer to Sarah. She took a tiny step away from him, almost imperceptible.

"What if they don't come back?" a man said. But before John or Sarah could answer him (who said they knew *anything*? And who put them in charge of this craziness?), another man spoke up, with a far more important question.

It was Lyle Greenleaf, the man who ran the Train Car Diner. He was old, long, and misshapen. His arms, which were blemished and covered in burn scars from sixty years of deep frying, seemed to hang all the way to the ground. His bright blue eyes and white hair made him appear ghastly, semi-opaque in the February sun. He was half man, half spirit. He looked to Sarah like a man at the end of his rope, as she imagined most ghosts look, worried, helplessly searching for a way out of their world and into the next.

"Wudder we s'posed to do about our businesses?" he asked. "I ain't got enough generator to run the rest'raunt."

People murmured in agreement, as if this little epiphany had never occurred to them. What would they do about food? With the gas station gone, they wouldn't have enough fuel to run the generators in the grocery store or their homes for more than a day. The other businesses in town would have to close shop indefinitely.

Sarah spoke up at once: "We will have to pool our resources the best we can. We can close most of the establishments in town, leaving only a few places open for shelter and accommodation. If we keep open The Hole and the Stop-N-Shop and the church, we can move all of our generators there, and we can maintain power for a week or more, I'd say. We'll need to move supplies from the general store, rearrange the town a little bit."

The people stared back at her dumbly, the sun shining crazily in their eyes. A woman holding two bibles raised her hand. "I have to go to the bathroom," she said. The crowd understood her predicament, and they consented with her audibly.

We're doomed, thought Sarah, as she looked out at the town folk. They should be in their homes, with their bibles in one hand and their TV remotes in the other, waiting for the power to come back on, beer hats draining through rubber straws like sand in an hourglass. In a crowd, they were utterly useless. John, too. He was useless. Unless you consider online dating in a town with six hundred people in it to be "useful."

This was going to be a long bitch of a day, and Sarah Simonez would be hoisting a lot of slack before it was done. There must be someone in this crowd who could help, someone with half a brain. Someone other than John, who was like a brain dampener. If she could get a group together—eight or nine Thunderians with half a brain each, it might mean hope for everyone. It would make this town functional. She needed some kind of staff she could delegate to, some kind of committee. With that, she might actually be able to secure what was left of the town, to come to a logical course of actions, to eventually get help, and to restore everything back to normal. Eight heads, half a brain in each. A committee. They could even call themselves the CIA, if they so fancied.

But for now there was just Sarah and John. John stood six feet off Sarah's left, not close enough to back her words up, but not far enough away to deny accountability.

Mick Benson, the retired sheriff, was also in the crowd. Though he was senile as a fish, he knew every road and soul in Thunder. He would come to their aid and help delegate. That sounded like half a brain to Sarah, and that would do well enough to start.

While Sarah and John surveyed the crowd, they wondered who in town had not showed up to the meeting. Who was off somewhere else, and what were they doing?

Stealing all the town's gas?

"Who's good at making lists?" Sarah called out, a ninety mile-an-hour question in such a crowd. "We need to take inventory on this town, the generators, *and* the people! It's the only way to make shit make any sense."

She was right, of course. If they didn't know who was here in the courtyard, and who was off doing whatever else, then they would have too many rumors demanding investigation. They wouldn't be able to organize the town well enough to feel safe, wherever safety lay, if anywhere in Thunder. If they didn't keep an inventory on the whole town—nine hundred people as of yesterday—then they would be as lost as stray dogs. They needed to know who was where, who was dead, and who was missing. And they needed to be sure that certain tools and tractors could be found, should the need for them arise.

The nights froze in Arizona at three thousand feet. Thunder was at five thousand feet. It would be more efficient to keep a couple of small buildings heated than to try to heat all of them. That meant that life would not go on as usual for them. No pretending this wasn't happening.

It was time for Thunder to pull up its socks.

"I'll make a list," Mick Benson said. The old, senile sheriff, reporting for duty. Seventy-six and taking names. Good. This meant the committee was beginning to form.

"I'll help him," said a woman named Laurel Beckhoff. It sounded to Sarah as if these were the first words this woman had ever uttered in her life. Her voice was cracked and squeaky, like a tiny, rarely used bicycle. Laurel Beckhoff was a mousey woman of about forty-five. She had lived in Thunder her whole life, except for one semester abroad in London. She never imagined that she might be destined for something great. Now, suddenly, she'd found courage, and she had purpose, and with no family—just a lost daughter in Los Angeles from whom she never heard—she felt as if fate had risen to claim her, to become a new Laurel. *Very good,* Sarah thought. That could potentially be number four.

Who else? Sarah thought there must be another group somewhere across town. Or more than one. Why weren't they at Apavajo Square? It had been the center of town since before white people had claimed the land. And now it had come to this crowd. One guy was wearing a beer hat. He had forgotten he had it on, and no one had informed him.

"This is good—see? We're gathering intel now. It's not so hard." Sarah continued. "We need some gas for important missions. Missions like getting barbecues and copious amounts of food. We should also scout for other survivors so we can bring everyone together later today. Can anyone afford a car?"

"There are loaded vehicles at the police station," Sheriff Benson chimed in.

"What's copious?" someone else added.

"I can go down there and grab a few vehicles with my buddies." A young, glimmering man had spoken up from Sarah's left. Servil Carlsberg was his name. He had the look of a med school student. Focused on the good, the solution, as if he'd spent his whole life reading a textbook, learning everything but experiencing nothing. He wore nerdy serial-killer glasses. Another able man. And he had two buddies with him.

"How come you guys get all the cars and gas and stuff? What's the rest of us s'posed to do? Just stand here and freak out?" The woman who spoke hadn't even looked at them—she just stared off into nowhere, talking to no one.

John spoke this time. "Go to The Hole. Drink some beer and stay put. We will bring supplies there. And more beer."

John Lajon, Sarah Simonez, Mick Benson, Laurel Beckhoff, Servil Carlsberg, and his two buddies had formed the new government, as far as they knew. The Seven of Thunder.

Before they all broke, Sarah spoke up once more: "There's one other thing we all need to discuss." She smiled to herself—just a flicker—at the thought of calling what they were doing "discussing." When she had their attention again, she went on. "I've heard talk about some strange people being seen around town. Like foreigners. Can y'all raise your hands if you've seen 'em?"

Four people raised their hands, slowly. Only one of them spoke. It was Cherish, the little girl who knew about the *Bobbsey Twins* books.

"Yeah," she said. "They just be sittin' there, or walkin' around like they live here. Only I never seen 'em before, not in my whole life. They dress like us, in overalls, and they don't have haircuts."

The people in the crowd didn't understand. It was like delivering terrible news to a field of cows. Their baffled faces made them look like the butt end of a practical joke, as if they weren't sure how badly they'd been had, or who was laughing at them, or why.

"One of them I saw sitting on the Davidsons' porch," Cherish continued. "Just sittin' there, drinking a beer this morning like it was nothin'. Pretty sure he looked at me. But he ain't no Davidson though. No, sir."

The boy, Chuck Davidson, was on the other side of the crowd, but he didn't appear to be listening. He was looking to the south of the Square, shifting his weight, as if what he was seeing made him nervous. Sarah and John both noticed his odd behavior, being the only ones facing the crowd, but they didn't see what Chuck saw.

Suddenly, a wind picked up.

It was a cool wind, so smooth that it seemed to refresh the crowd, Sarah and John included. It blew away some of the tension and fear, but it had exposed a feeling of sadness and nostalgia.

A wave of dust blew up on the northeast side of the crowd. It crashed into the wall next to a woman, sending dirt up in a spray.

The woman threw her hands up to cover her face. Her right hand had been resting on the old wall, and she threw a small pebble that was stuck to her palm down her throat. She gagged and threw her body onto the ground in a jerk reflex, landing on all fours, heaving. Her eyes popped out and her jaw wrenched itself open. She looked as if ready to plunge her arm down her own throat into her lung and pull the rock out herself. But she didn't; she couldn't. She just stayed down on all fours, her face locked open as wide as it would go, not breathing. The color went out of her face. Two townspeople tried to help her up, while a third and fourth videoed it with their phones.

The breeze rolled by again, as if to say, "You're welcome."

And that's when Hell Finn showed up.

17

"HEY FUCKFACES!" Hell shouted, approaching quickly from the south end of the square. He was wearing a black trench coat, arms thrust inside, and a black cowboy hat, tipped back. His face had split into an eerie grin, four teeth boasting like diamonds.

No one responded. They looked at him dumbly, as if he were a walking television.

"Yeah, *FUCKFACES!*" he screamed. "That's what you all are! This here's a stickup! I'm taking you fucks for everything yer WORTH!"

Faces in the crowd livened from blank to bewildered, as they lamely looked at each other. *Is he talkin' to you? No? Maybe you?*

Suddenly, a low rumble thrummed in the ground. It seemed to Finn that it had started at his feet and rippled outward, through the square. His smile faltered. *That's fucking weird,* he thought. But he would waste no time. He had a scene he needed to get through, and earthquakes were not in his copy of the script. His rage had been aging for too long already, and the cops were dead. This was his time.

He whipped the guns out: two shotguns, one in each hand. In his right was a Tactical Police Shotgun, and in his left was a sawed-off 20-gauge.

Hell broke loose. The first explosion made the whole crowd jump as if they were at a rock concert.

A relentless storm of bullets ensued: *BLAM! BOOM! BLAM!*

BOOM! On and on. No one could hear the screams under the thunder of the shotguns.

Silver hailstorms spattered over a hundred people, shoving them, ripping their ears, scalping, halving noses, excavating eye sockets. Excavating their sanity.

Then Finn threw down the shotguns and pulled out a huge Desert Eagle, Dirty Harry style, to trim the edges. Stragglers, people who'd spread to the outside of the crowd, trying to flee, were shot down at once.

The woman who'd had to go the bathroom ran straight north. Finn decapitated her with a 50-caliber shot. Her head seemed to evaporate, and she dove forward as if into a swimming pool. Her shoulders hit the dirt soundlessly. She urinated, pale jeans darkening, then the beige hard pan. Finally she was still, spread-eagle on her stomach, headless.

John and Sarah were able to duck straight through the center of the crowd and jump the wall in time. It was four feet high, good cover. If they ran east from where they were now, they would get tagged for sure. So they crouched there and covered their ears. Cherish was there, lying on the ground with her hands clutching her ears, rolling from side to side. But she didn't appear to be hurt. Just very dirty.

After the revolver was spent, Hell brandished an automatic rifle. A Heckler & Koch MP5. He was elated now—doing productive work. Obliterating crowds felt wonderful, almost numbing, as if he were high on crack.

A man wearing an American flag bandana and sunglasses had brought a gun of his own. Surprisingly, he may have been the only one. Or at least the only one who got a chance to pull it out. He fired one round, missing Hell Finn, wide on the right. "Aw, f-*fuck*," he choked, his voice quivering, his hands quivering worse. The scene was too amazing. Too horrifying. He was as weak as a sound wave and in no condition for shooting, ironic as that might have been. He fired another round, and it hit the dirt, next to Hell's foot.

The automatic rifle went off.

It cut through the crowd like a laser. Wherever there hadn't been blood before, now there was blood, the foray of bullets casting bodies to their final positions, piling on one another. The MP5 had one hundred rounds and took nine and a half seconds to unload.

The man in the bandana was perforated across his torso, thrown onto his back, bullet holes hissing steam into the air like a spirit escaping.

The woman with the rock in her lung was still choking on the ground, no longer breathing. Her face now looked oddly bluish amid all the red. But at the end of it all, she survived.

Finn decided it was time to go. To continue with the plan. Now was the time to steal some stuff. But not here. Anyways these people had nothing on them. Except for blood.

He ran south, back from where he'd come. He threw two grenades back towards the square, where survivors had started to walk around with their fingers in their ears, heads jerking uncontrollably from the haunting echoes of gunshots in their heads. He pulled the pin on one grenade, then pulled the pin on the other, tossing them over his head like a double high five.

He ran to the edge of the square.

BANG! And then, wait for it... *BANG!*

Six more people were killed. And four more were injured.

Finn grabbed the best car he could find. A Jeep Wagoneer with wood siding. He peeled off and was gone, headed to search the town's homes for useful loot. It was time to collect his reward for having been God's laughingstock all these years. His paycheck.

After the dust had settled, the blood beginning to dry into the earth, the Galls and the Johannsens showed up.

18

CHESTER'S FAMILY WAS small, like Jimmy's. But unlike the Johannsens, the Galls were close, like a tight-rocking three-piece band.

Chess's father, Vincent, was a particle technician specializing in extraterrestrial materials, like meteors. Before moving to Thunder, he'd worked in the Houston Space Control Laboratories. He'd lived in Sugar Land, Texas with his family.

Vincent had been offered a very well-paying job in a rather poor small town—Thunder, Arizona.

Well, the job actually took place in a small facility in the foothills, outside Thunder to the east. On the surface, it looked like a small cluster of construction trailers. They stood together at random angles between the small mountains and huge piles of gravel. A private road ran out to the facility, clearly marked with a bullet hole-riddled sign that read, "PRIVATE ROAD—KEEP OUT" affixed to a heavy steel gate. The construction trailers housed laboratories, and the facility was known by its employees simply as "Fontaine."

Of course, the small cluster of buildings was *only* known by its employees.

How the Thunderians throughout history had never discovered these buildings was a mystery. The gate was impossible to drive through, but easy to climb over. Still, the desert was wild, and the thousand feet from the gate to Fontaine deterred wanderers with huge insects and glaring holes in the earth, sickening buzzing sounds, and spider webs the size of Joshua Trees. Out there, it was best to stick to the roads that were somewhat paved.

Vincent moved his family—his wife Juniper and his son Chester—to Thunder in 2007, and they lived in an unassumingly fancy house on the edge of town. It was single story, brown with white trim on the outside, but the inside was high-tech, with all the amenities—a scientist's house.

To Jimmy, the Galls' house was ideal. He privately coveted Chester's family. Their televisions had remote controls. Chester had his own phone line. There were times in Jimmy's life when he, Charlotte, and his mother didn't have a phone at all.

But it wasn't the technology that spiced up their household, nor the cleanliness and sturdiness of the house itself that Jimmy fancied. It was the love. It was the way Chester's father kissed his mother, as if they were still on their honeymoon, twenty years later. It was a happy family, and positive energy gleamed on every cupboard, countertop, and closet door.

Jimmy's house was the opposite. It was depressed, quiet, and cramped, with little hot water and no snacks or sugary beverages. The house seemed to face the wrong direction, and it stank of old cigarettes. Benson & Hedges Menthol, ultra slim. A redneck smoke if there ever was one.

Alice horded things, and she was obsessed with kitsch. Small artisan crafts, bobble heads, and Jesus figurines cluttered every room.

Magnets covered every surface of the refrigerator, holding old photos of Alice and the twins. No photos of her husband—not on the fridge, anyway. The magnets themselves boasted of the shittiest places in America. Places like Gonzales, Texas, or Gila Bend, Arizona, and some unincorporated township in New Mexico called "Candy Kitchen." No need to specify what kind of candy they were cooking there. The Candy Kitchen magnet held up a photo of Jimmy and Charlotte as kids, playing in a kiddie pool in the front yard. Jimmy was splashing Charlotte, and she was in mid fall, almost upside-down, screaming. Half of the photo was blurry, and Jimmy knew why. It wasn't because it was 2005, and the Fujifilm two-megapixel camera was running rampant. It was because, in those days, Alice would slather herself in Crisco cooking oil when she went outside to get a tan. It got on everything she touched, and she must have touched the camera lens when she was taking the photo.

In his earlier youth, Jimmy had secretly wished that he could go to sleep a Johannsen and wake up a Gall, in the Gall's house, with no cigarette smoke, no bobble heads, and no souvenirs from Candy Kitchen.

When the Galls and the Johannsens arrived at Apavajo Square, the smell of blood and gun smoke still hung in the air. They had heard the gunfire from a distance, but it had ended long before they reached the square.

Finally, Jimmy thought. *I can thank the state for speed limits.*

But what began as relief turned quickly to horror when he actually saw the bodies. They were scattered everywhere, overly detailed, too real to comprehend. The Galls and the Johannsens slowed their pace with each step, until they were barely making any distance.

On the west side of Apavajo Square, three large stone statues huddled together. They were statues of a Navajo family in full Navajo dress. Underneath the statues, twenty-two shell-shocked Thunderians stood trembling.

Of the forty-somewhat survivors, half had scuttled off, splitting from Apavajo Square like water from oil.

When the Galls and the Johannsens were about halfway down the square, John Lajon called out to them.

"STOP!"

They stopped. After a moment, Jimmy broke the silence. "John," he said. "What the FUCK?"

"Just meet us at the church!" John shouted. "At six o'clock tonight! I told the others! Now, LEAVE! JUST GO AWAY!"

Jimmy and Chester were friends with John and Sarah, but they met no friendly greeting today.

All the survivors held their faces with their hands. They looked like they were digging at their minds, trying to suppress their consciences from exploding. Their fingers all pushed and pushed, forcing their brains to stay still. *Fuck, if I take my hand away, my brains will blow away, blow away, with the rest of the town's brains, up, up and away!* These people couldn't wrap their minds around witnessing a hundred of their townspeople blown apart in front of them. The carnage was too much to bear.

As the Galls and the Johannsens turned to leave, Jimmy understood that this was the most horrible thing that any of them had ever seen. Alice would never get over this. Perhaps it was better that they were turned away; any length of time spent here would guarantee madness for all of them.

The two families headed to the pharmacy to collect burn treatment supplies, then to the Gall's house to regroup.

19

T HE CHURCH IN Thunder was very simple and lacking in any
gaudiness. It was painted pure white with white pews, like
the Mormon churches in the neighboring state of Utah. The
church boasted one stained-glass window near the apex of the
roof, and all the other windows were large and open to the mountains beyond. The hardwood floors were clean and bare. With no
artwork or candles to adorn the interior, it looked more like a large
dance studio with some benches. One could imagine figures in
there, muscular bodies filling the space, rolling and lifting,
writhing and falling, the waltz of Michelangelo's *Purgatory*.

The reverend would have liked very much to see that. He was
more like a quirky small town artisan than a priest. In fact, Reverend Cal Foster was without a doubt the most unusual priest in
Arizona. He wore a white cowboy hat that matched his God collar.
And he loved to rhyme. He thought rhymes and puns were pure
and Godly.

"He turned the piazza into a human pizza!" The reverend
exclaimed. "*Eeeevil's* his name, and death is his will! He'll line us all
up in a cue to kill!" Reverend Foster was not standing at the pulpit, but on the floor with the rest of the people.

"Yeah, yeah, he'll toll your soul like a *troll*." Sarah Simonez
rolled her eyes. "This is *real*, Reverend. We need to think clearly.
Stop with that, already." She was perched on a pew, on fire. Figura-
tively speaking.

Other people nodded along with Sarah.

It was six o'clock, and there were only twenty-nine people in the church.

Mousey Laurel Beckhoff and ex-Sheriff Mick Benson had gone around the town, making lists of those who were still alive, or said to be. Now they were back at the church. There were one hundred and eighty people still walking and talking in Thunder, as of 4:45 p.m. today.

Jimmy and Chester joined John and Sarah at the pew. The four of them sat precariously on its high edge, like actors posing in a corny musical. But instead of bursting into song, they turned to ask the people around them for their names and their recollections of the last twenty-four hours.

Chester's parents stood in the back of the crowd, offering comfort to a few people. They had brought waters, a six-pack of Cokes, and three beers.

Chess sat next to Jimmy. Both had their right hands wrapped as their elbows rested with purpose on their knees.

"Oh great, more *Bobbsey Twins*." Chester looked down. A little girl with a yellow perm had ended up in the cast of characters on the pew. "Hi, I'm Cherish. I live around the trailer park."

"What's up, Cherish? I remember you." Chester said. "Welcome to the party." He gave her a fist bump with his left hand.

The sky was a melting layer cake of red, butterscotch, and blue. In a few moments the whole town would be shrouded in darkness.

"Did you guys see what happened at the square before?" asked Cherish.

Chester didn't say anything.

"No," said Jimmy. "We didn't see anything. We actually came here from New York." He looked briefly behind him, laying eyes on his mother, then turned back to Cherish. "How old are you, little friend?"

"I'm nine. I'm old for my age though. How about you?"

"I'm nineteen," Jimmy said. He suddenly felt heavy and failed, his energy starting to fade. He wished he could share this with his twin sister. But she was gone somewhere, missing, and he was here, confused. What was he even doing here, among the people he had worked his whole life to throw over and leave? The people he thought he'd never see again after he left for college? The only person abandoned here was himself, walked out on by his other half. Was this the other side of death? Was this a stress fracture in the apocalypse? Were they waiting in line for life's refund slip?

Chester piped back in. "Same," he said. "I'm also nine."

They had generators. They had gas. Without many people around, they had more than enough power and supplies to last them a long while.

Twenty-nine people. *Twenty-nine fucking people?*

John Lajon spoke loudly, as if he were the president of the universe, jerking Jimmy out of his thoughts. "It's ten minutes after six, so let's try to start the meeting. Anybody have anything they'd like to address? Reverend?"

Sarah rolled her eyes.

The reverend looked startled, then began moving towards the pulpit as he composed himself. "Well, yes, I think we should begin with a prayer for the dead," he said. He looked to the group and found no objection. "Just a starter-prayer, and then a moment of silence, while everybody's souls are still fresh."

Jimmy looked at Chester. *Fresh souls?* Chess chuckled, picking up on the thought. Chester knew about the reverend's idiosyncrasies. His parents laughed about him sometimes, Vincent calling him "River Cal," a joke name derived from "Reverend Cal". The nickname meant nothing except to belittle the priest and maybe equate him with a small-time revival tent minister.

When he was younger, Chester pictured crazy old River Cal traveling along the Colorado River, venturing from town to town, setting up tents like a traveling salesman. Only instead of selling vacuum cleaners or lightning rods, River Cal sold *imagination,* delivering sermons to a crowd of thumping, screaming simpletons, making sure to add as many absurd visuals to his stories as he could, so they could really *see* the truth of God. It didn't bother Chess, and Jimmy saw that as part of his optimism. If people wanted to devote their lives to these fairy tales, well that was their prerogative, just like Chester dedicating his studies to nuclear science and banging chemistry teachers was his.

Jimmy trusted the reverend about as much as Chester trusted the nuclear power facilities—that is to say, not at all. *Pray more, worry less.* His mother's idiotic bumper sticker was the perfect example. To Jimmy, that was religion boiled down, distilled into four words. *Jesus's responsibility, not mine.* So was this Jesus's responsibility? The town of Thunder, sliding off into the imaginary sea? Somehow, Jimmy didn't think so. However, he welcomed a moment of silence for Charlotte and the others.

When the prayer ended (Reverend Cal managed to rhyme "deceased" with "feast") and the silence was complete, Jimmy opened his eyes.

What he saw before him sent gooseflesh all over his body. He hadn't noticed before, but Cherish was the only child in the church. All the other kids were missing.

Thunder had never been full of children—the elementary school had only thirty kids enrolled—but it still shook Jimmy. He was looking forward to seeing Charlotte's little friend, Chuck Davidson. He liked that little dude. After the reverend thanked everybody for their silence, Jimmy began to speak up. But before he could, Cherish, as if reading his mind, beat him to it.

"Reverend Cal, where are all the kids? And where's Chucky? I ain't seen him since the gunfight in the square." She was still filthy from rolling on the ground during the shootout. Jimmy could picture Cherish roaming around the town like a detective, searching for kids. She would rather investigate than go home and shower. Jimmy liked that. But if he had known she'd be dead by sunrise, he might have preferred she showered. Then at least, he'd know she went out clean.

Reverend Cal replied, "Well, Cherish, they're probably with the others."

"Where are the others?" Cherish belted, several octaves higher now.

"*Who* are the others?" Jimmy added. It was the first time he'd asked a priest anything since he was ten years old, when he'd asked Reverend Cal to please leave him the fuck alone.

But before the reverend could reply, the church dimmed, then fell completely dark. It was like some giant hand had reached up and pulled down the sun. Where it had just recently blazed through the western window, there was nothing but a burnt orange sky emitting no light. Jimmy had seen an eclipse before, on a solo trip to Georgia a few years back, and this was that same surreal experience.

Suddenly, everyone in the church became delirious, as if they had taken a small dose of some hallucinogen. Cicadas and night bugs began roaring their nightly chorus, and in the distance, Jimmy could hear wolves.

"What in the ever-loving tarnation?" Chester said, in his thickest Texas accent.

"What time is it?" someone said. Jimmy realized how dark it was in the church—he couldn't see who had just spoken. There had never been a generator there, and no one had thought to move one in.

"It's the end of times," another townsperson said, and Jimmy knew *that* voice. It was his mother's. She had come up next to him when the church went dark, and Jimmy could see her in the dimmest light. She was clutching a bible and two hymnals to her chest. Her greying hair shone like nickel in the dying light.

"Now, everybody stay calm," the unmistakable croon of Reverend Cal begged. "Just stay where you are; you're safe in here. This is God's house gosh darn it, and no way that demon is getting in here! God will give us the light! And He will lead us all to safety! And burn that Satan-loving, evil, walking tragedy to the *ground*!"

"You're damned right!" yelled Alice, and a few others hawed in agreement. There was some low chatter, mostly people asking each other what was going on, when a low rumble rolled across the church floor. It was short, only three seconds, but another followed shortly after, a more invasive shudder that made everyone yell in surprise. The window to the west cracked—a sharp line slashing up the diagonal with a loud *CLICK!*

The group fell quiet.

Another earthquake. But it didn't feel quite like an earthquake to Jimmy. Not in this context. It was more like an aftershock, or an echo. An awareness or signal of some kind. Jimmy suddenly pictured the idea of a *pre-shock,* a warning of some kind. He couldn't deny the feeling that the worst was yet to come.

Ten seconds passed. Then Chester spoke up again, slowly. "Just an idea," he started. "How do people feel about The Hole? Like, booze and cheeseburgers, and a comfortable place to sit?"

They didn't need any convincing. The Hole had beer and warmth. God's house was welcoming, but food and electricity was better. They could invite God along with them. He could protect them from there. Surely, he was capable of that.

"You can bring your hymnals if you want," said Jimmy, eyeing his mother, surprising himself with his lack of sarcasm.

The crowd headed out of the church, with some carrying flashlights. Jimmy and Alice were the last to leave, and as they turned to close the church doors behind them, they saw something that made them freeze in their tracks. A squirrel and a raccoon were standing on their hind legs next to each other, looking up at them. They looked like a calendar photo, standing right in the middle of the doorway, as if to say, "Come back again soon! And let us know how that recipe turns out!" Jimmy and Alice looked at each other, then back at the animals. But instead of bursting into laughter, they slowly pushed the church doors closed, hiding the animals within. Then they turned around, closed their jackets, and walked into the darkness.

PART

THREE

20

FIFTY-NINE PEOPLE WERE alive in Thunder.

They were all at The Hole, dimly lit by lamps fueled by the generators. The rest of the town was draped in darkness, the moonlight shielded by a black sheet of clouds, a ceiling that stretched over the mountains in all directions like plastic wrap.

The fires from the last two days had been out. It was as if the town around them had faded into oblivion, leaving only The Hole.

In the front of The Hole was a large veranda with two picnic tables and some benches. The tables held ashtrays big enough to eat lunch in. One could light his face on fire and put it out in these ashtrays.

Mick Benson, the retired sheriff, stood in the doorway, leaning on it to ease his back. He held a long barrel shotgun, pointed to the porch like a cane. His shirt sleeve on the arm that held the gun was rolled to the wrist, exposing thick white arm fur over long-forgotten ghosts of tattoos.

Kevin Halloway stood with him on the other side of the door, facing out. His young hand clutched a .38 revolver.

They stood like blind knights defending a king's quarters. They could only see as far as the end of the parking area in front of the bar. Beyond that there was only darkness.

There was a line they couldn't quite perceive, just beneath their conscience, somewhere in their peripheral. They squinted to see this line more clearly, but to no avail.

Soon the two sentries started to feel a kind of vagueness in themselves, as if their present lives were nothing but mere memories—photographs they'd seen in the past. They felt the weight of everything in their lives suddenly lifted, and the sensation terrified them. It felt as if their lives were disappearing, as if they were becoming ghosts. There was nothing in the darkness, not even them. And their hearts quietly wailed with an emptiness as dark as the night.

There was no light on the veranda. The generators were in Servil and his buddies' hands, and they had not yet gotten to powering the porch light, reserving the power for the refrigerators and the grill and bar back first.

They had candles, a lot of them, but Jimmy had advised everyone against lighting them. They thought they should stick to only lighting cigarettes, for now.

Inside, the bar was crowded. The Hole was one large U-shaped room, with a grill to the left from the entryway, followed by a bar which wrapped around to the left, to the other side of the U. On that side of the room was a red pool table and some card tables. The sheriffs never complained about the card tables. Probably because they sat down at them sometimes, on their off days.

Straight to the back and outside was the patio, a vast area with beer troughs, an outside bar, picnic tables galore, and Chicken Shit Bingo. There were a hundred places to sit and drink and look at the mountains. Except for tonight. The evening was so dark the townspeople couldn't see into their own beer.

No one was on the back patio. Vincent Gall and Reverend Cal Foster sat in the doorway. They had each pulled up a chair and sat there, blocking the entrance. Nothing could get inside through the back without going through Vincent and Cal. They were the door. They each held shotguns.

"You know something, Reverend?" Vincent said. "I've never

seen anything like this before. I work with materials, you know. Earthly, and like meteors and stuff. You see, it's like there's a substance here, like a... like a *thing*. I can feel it vibrating, like some kind of layer of quartz. I can *feel* it... I can almost see it."

"I hear what you're saying." The reverend spoke softly, humbly. "It's something I can see, too. But not... really." He straightened up. "You know, I believe it's pure evil. This is what evil's face looks like, up close."

Materials, Vincent thought. *Nuclear materials.* This had to do with his work in Fontaine, somehow. His secret work.

Reverend Cal, as if reading Vincent's thoughts, continued. "Nope, I'd say you're wrong there, son. This here's the wrath of the devil. You have no grounds on which to say you can see dust that you cannot see. That's not fair to me. You see, at least my theory has a purpose. My principals are equipped with lessons."

The old priest-and-scientist routine.

"But I *can* see it," Vincent argued, almost under his breath. He made no effort to sound convincing. He backed off at Reverend Cal Foster's denial. He concentrated on his thoughts, convinced that there was a *name* for this. And a concrete explanation.

Chester and Juniper walked over to them with a bottle of Wild Turkey and some hot dogs. Chester was sneering from the pain in his hand. The five Advil he'd taken seemed to have no effect anymore. The pain had outsmarted it. His expression went unnoticed by everyone, for they all felt pain, and they all felt overwhelmed. If this were an orchestra of pain performing a symphony of sorrow, then Chester was playing the part of the blistering hand, way in the background.

"Here's to all the wolves," he seethed, and took a sip from his glass. They sat down quietly at a table nearby. They watched. They waited. They ate.

John Lajon and Sarah Simonez were at the bar inside, drinking Flagstaff Lagers. Their commanding time was over. They had their relationship to work on now. And beers, as long as they were still cold. And after all, they were only twenty, not yet of legal drinking age, so drinking at The Hole was awesome for them. They were getting drunk like adults, something everyone needed to do at least once before doomsday finally came for them.

Jimmy and Alice were in the area by the pool table. It was more brightly lit, and the red velvet of the table offered them comfort. In fact, almost everybody in the bar had gathered by the dim light in this half of the room.

Alice was quiet, still overwhelmed by the death of her daughter. She held only one bible now, her thumb stroking it absently as she stared off into space. Jimmy wanted her to say something. He was nervous, and he was certain that the guy Finn would be back. He could feel it in his tired, oversensitive bones.

Still no word on his first name.

Well, Jimmy thought, *at least we'll go out with a good view.* He liked the lamplight in here, and the smell of burgers and hot dogs going on the grill, the world spiraling in like an iris.

Jimmy turned to his mother. In a soft voice he asked her, "Ma, why do you think this is happening?" She didn't respond. Alice's pride in her son lay in his ability to reason. Ridiculous stray comments peeved her like crazy. Jimmy saw Chester at the back of the bar, and he wondered if maybe this was part of Chester's perennial theory—radiation. But radiation doesn't make gas stations explode and people disappear. *God* then? "Ma?" he said again. "Do you think God did this?"

Alice didn't look at him, but a tear slid down her cheek, and she appeared to be fighting off dissolve. *Yes, maybe God,* Jimmy thought, but they weren't being punished. Why would they be?

They were nobody, here in Thunder. The innocents of the world's innocence. Why not Candy Kitchen, for Christ's sake?

As far as anyone knew, this wasn't happening anywhere else in the world. Considering how substantial this wreckage was, it seemed to be contained in Thunder, with no evident threat to spread. So why here? Yes, the phone lines had died with the sunrise, mysteriously. Was that a miracle only God could perform? To Alice, that was a reasonable deduction. But to Jimmy, it was preposterous. Alice then spoke the weirdest words he had ever heard her say.

"Maybe it's God, but it's more complicated than that," she said. She continued to stare at nothing perceptible. "Maybe God and the devil are fighting, and humans are suffering, like... collateral damage. Maybe there is war here, but we can't see it. Everything just looks brighter, and, you know, *clearer.*"

She said "clearer" as if it were code for something. But it was quite literally true. Everything had looked brighter and clearer that day. And Jimmy had heard people commenting on it. But now the sun was gone. The day was gone, and the only thing that was clear was the darkness. Crystal clear. Freaky, purple darkness.

"I'm going over to talk to John and Sarah," Jimmy said. "Come with me, Ma."

Jimmy got up, walked over to his mother and kissed her on her head. She stood up slowly and looked at him. Jimmy felt his heart swell, like a bed sheet in the wind. But he didn't cry. His emotions counterbalanced quickly and with grace. He squeezed both of her hands, then took her into a long hug.

Jimmy and Alice went to chat with John and Sarah for a bit.

Then they visited with the Reverend and the Galls out back.

They wanted to know who'd had the opinion around here.

21

So they'd all gathered at The Hole, everyone except for Finn, who was rumored to be both alive and dead. But they had lookouts for him. Dark watchmen, embroidered in the night, like black oil on black oil. The townspeople knew that Finn did not kill everyone in Thunder, and they also knew there was something way beyond Finn that was reaching them now. But Finn was still out there, and that gave them a center of gravity, something to pivot on, a hinge on which to lever their nearly nonexistent collective wit.

Lyle Greenleaf was manning the grill, his long, scarred, hairless old arms flipping burgers and multitasking. He looked half squid, half man. In the low light, his blanched arms lopped over the grill, and his legs pulsed hydraulically under his white apron.

Laurel Beckhoff and little Cherish were behind the bar, serving drinks. Dave and Deer Man, the original proprietors of The Bar were gone. They had been there last night, when tragic news had started to simmer and then boil all over town. They'd been there, open late, when the gas station had exploded, and they'd been there when the blackout hit. They closed shop after the blackout, and no one thought they had seen them since. But Cherish had seen them, although she hadn't recognized them at the time.

She'd been walking through town, a few hours before the incident at Apavajo Square, and she saw two men who looked asleep, or passed out drunk, between two small houses.

It was just after seeing that creepy man in overalls drinking beer on the Davidsons' porch. These two *borrachos* had been behind a cluster of metal garbage cans, and Cherish could only see their legs and boots. Their pants seemed baggy, loose, or half-undone. It wasn't unusual for someone to half-lose their pants before passing out drunk. But for fear of embarrassment, Cherish did not wander over to investigate them.

The two drunks had been Dave and Deer Man from The Hole. They had snuck behind someone's house for a little late night nookie, sexually charged from the blackout and the danger. Homosexuality was a crime in Thunder, so they had to get intimate behind trashcans or in their own home. But the blackout was romantic, and the peril of death erotic, so the two men chose behind the trashcans in the night.

Dave had had a brain aneurism when Deer Man put his hand down his pants. He flung his face up to the sky, screamed holy sacrifice, and collapsed, just like that.

Deer Man took his hand out of Dave's crotch and froze there for a moment. Had someone heard that scream? It sounded as if a train had run right between the two houses.

He should run, *now*, he thought, before he was spotted and accused of murder. Or *worse,* homosexuality. But he didn't move. He looked at Dave and was shocked to see the strain that remained in his dead face. Then his own brain exploded. He collapsed right on top of Dave, and no one ever saw them again except for Cherish, in passing.

So Laurel Beckhoff was behind the bar, a tiny thing who had never spoken to anyone in her life, a gopher of a woman, pouring drinks at The Hole.

And Cherish, although she was shorter than the bar and couldn't really see who she was serving, kept up the pace underneath. It was The Hole's busiest day of the twenty-first century, and she was a very nimble beerslinger in a very needy bar.

❖

Mick Benson and Kevin Halloway were still on the front porch at twenty minutes past nine. The sounds of cicadas, the wind in the sparse trees, and the far off coyotes were much louder than usual—nature reaching an all-around wail.

"Now where'd everybody git off to?" Benson asked. He was looking to the porch deck and up, then back down again, as if he was not sure where he was. He was using his shotgun as a cane, and Kevin wondered if the old sheriff even remembered that it wasn't a cane, and that it was a shotgun.

What kind of a question is that? Kevin thought, eyeing the old man.

"Uh, Lord knows, Benson, but a lot of people are dead, like really dead." Kevin faced straight ahead, eyes tracking horizontally about a hundred degrees, back and forth like tiny security cameras. Black on black.

"Oh really?" Benson said calmly. "And you?"

"No, Sheriff," he said. "I'm fine."

"Yeah, I know all about that." Benson smiled, as if agreeing with Kevin's opinion. "Now... Where'd everybody git off to?"

"I dunno, Sheriff."

"Huh. Strange, isn't it?" Benson scratched his hairy wrist and looked down at the deck. Then he looked up again. "Now I have one question. Where'd everybody—"

"What the fuck is that?" Kevin stood up, but before he could get his balance, old Mick Benson lumbered up and walked straight off the porch with his shotgun leveled, pointing straight ahead. He went down the three steps without looking, perfectly.

Barely visible, a man stood at the back of the parking area.

"Put your hands in the air! Who the fuck are you?" Mick Benson was now back on duty. Apparently, he was less delusional while engaged in police activities. Kevin continued to look around, stepping to the edge of the porch, scanning for others. Some people in the bar stepped toward the doorway at the sound of the commotion, but no further. They were not interested in getting shot up by Finn again. They were all Finnished up.

"I'm one of you—don't shoot! I'm from Thunder! My name's Dale Howard!"

Benson walked a third of the way out in the parking area, about a car's length. "Come closer. Slowly."

Dale walked slowly with his hands out. It was melodrama, really, but the whole town buzzed with it. Here the air was different, and the nature sounds were much too loud, and this man did not look familiar.

Old Sheriff Benson knew every man in Thunder. Dale Howard wasn't one of them.

He circled around the man and stood behind him. "Get yer ass movin'," he said.

Vincent Gall came up to the front of The Hole to meet them, leaving Chester, Juniper, and the Reverend to watch the back.

The new guy looked at Vincent as he walked through the front door. "Hi," he said softly, winking. Then, to the rest of the crowd in The Hole, he said, "I'm Dale Howard. I live on the hill. You guys open?"

22

DALE HOWARD SAT on the stool inside the front door of the bar. The bouncer's stool. It was just before the grill, on the left as you walked in. Sheriff Benson stood almost directly over him, leaning on the threshold, a shotgun's length away. Kevin stood in front of the doorway, holding his revolver in both hands, barrel pointed at the floor. Vincent stood on the other side, inside, completing the square.

Behind Dale was a tall cupboard rack with grill supplies, buns, and towels and things, next to a small deep-fryer, and then the grill, where Lyle posted up, all white and ghost-like. The way he'd appeared in the Square this afternoon. *Haunting.*

But now he was grilling, bouncing like a normal short order squid-man cook. John Lajon gazed at him from the other side of the bar. Squid-man was like an eye magnet. All in white, and in the lowest of low bar light. It was as if he were the only one in his world, his hot dogs his haunt, and he would stay like that forever, grilling ecto-dogs for no one, bouncing, buoying, like a squid-ghost grill man.

Vincent's gun was pointed down; he was in no mood for a strange accident. The world was off balance, and he could not guarantee to maintain his own. He had drunk a good portion of that Wild Turkey, too.

There were four people sitting by the grill, while others stood farther off, totally still, facing the stranger who was sitting in the bouncer's stool.

"You walk here?" Benson asked.

"Yes, sir," he replied. He seemed friendly.

"From the hill?"

"Yes, I reckon." His eyes flickered with doubt. An audition face. Was he acting like an idiot as a disguise? The hillbilly from the hill?

Then Vincent Gall spoke. "*What* hill?"

Dale looked from Benson to Kevin then to Vincent. He surveyed the bar, delicately. It was as if he had never seen this place before. *Trustworthy eyes, and he doesn't drink.* In the desert, that's at least one red flag.

But Dale didn't seem concerned about blowing his cover; perhaps he was ready to show what was underneath.

"I'm not from Thunder," he said at last. "I lied about that. But I mean you no harm, and I can explain it."

Tension filled the tavern. Of course he didn't mean no harm. There were at least four guns pointed at him.

"I'm a stranger, and I mean to tell you what I know."

There was a long, hungry silence. The only sounds were of fat and onions hissing on the grill and the low, distant rattling of the generators.

"Where'd you come from, Dale Man?" Sheriff Benson piped up, his shotgun propped on his hip, pointed directly at Dale Man.

But Dale Man didn't answer. He pretended as if he hadn't heard the sheriff. "Everyone who has ever been to Thunder is going to die. Or be transported to another world where there is little oxygen, and you will die there quickly. I'm here to... Well, I *was* here to supervise. And collect data."

Brief terrible silence. The generators growled on like a ring of coyotes.

Kevin Halloway was the first speak. "You said everyone who's ever been to Thunder?"

"Yes, sir," said the stranger.

Kevin continued: "So how come you don't disappear yourself? Or die or some shit? What are you, immune? You got a pill I can take and a ride outta here, doc? I'll ride with you, man. I'll be your shotgun, or your thirty-eight, you know?" He gestured vaguely with his revolver. Kevin was going a little bit crazy. Perhaps trading crazies with Mick Benson.

"No, young man, it's not like that. I am going to die, too," Dale said. "I know this. If I *didn't* know this, I definitely wouldn't be here right now. Seven of us are dead. There's just me left. I'm the last... stranger."

"So how come you don't just kill us all now and take a little vacation while you still can?" Kevin asked.

"Or why don't you just take a little vacation, and *not* kill us?" Cherish added. They looked over at her, dirty face peeking at them from behind the bar.

Dale looked at the guns drawn and people facing him. All were meters in the red. "I can't kill you guys. That's ridiculous. There's just *me*. Anyways our weapons stopped working hours ago."

Vincent Gall glanced towards the grill. Lyle the Squid was there, but he was fidgeting with the knobs, having a bit of trouble.

"Who do you work for?" Vincent asked.

Dale looked at Vincent. His disguise suddenly looked like a cheap Halloween costume. So *fake*, so totally half-assed and unrealistic. What a joke, this guy. Then he spoke.

"I work for the same people that you work for, Vincent."

23

J OHN LAJON SQUINTED at Vincent Gall, Benson, and the stranger from across the bar. He was enjoying the show, his fourth beer by far the best one. But his attention shifted when he heard Lyle muttering strangely by the grill. John couldn't tell what he was saying, but it sounded something like "commie fuck." John looked at the cook and saw just how overwhelmed he was. His movements were indignant, energy nearing outrage. He was dropping food on the floor and getting confused about his grill knobs, all the while cussing nonsense under his breath.

John shuffled over towards the grill. He left Sarah on the far side of the U.

"You all right, Lyle?" he asked. But Lyle seemed not to notice. The guys crowding the doorway were focused only on the stranger.

"Lyle?" he repeated.

The old grill-master twisted around and looked at John. He rubbed his left arm and whispered, "Bedtime for Lye-Lye," then froze, his face twisted up in a wolfish grin that didn't look remotely happy. He stood there in silence for a moment, and no one spoke. The men at the door turned and looked at him.

"I can't feel my arm," he said, his grin turning to a sneer. "It ain't there." Then, as if confirming this, he said, "It ain't—it's gone! It's gone!" His right hand went for his heart, clawing at his soft, blankety skin.

"My heart!" he screamed, stumbling backwards. He thumped

his chest with his right fist, and his left arm shot out for support, plunging into the deep fryer.

The pungent steam shot up out of the vat, and all at once, Lyle got the feeling back in his arm. He flung it out of the fryer, fanning the crowd in an arc of boiling oil. Everyone screamed. Lyle yelled something incomprehensible: "Heg-g-gee!" He lopped flat on his back on the floor, convulsing, pulsing, slowing.

Push! Kick start yer motor, Lyle! Push!

Everyone was screaming, in panic and in pain, for there is no pain eviler than a grease burn, and these guys were positively *splashed.*

Vincent Gall brought up his gun in reflex, confused and drunk. He shot it off and blew up the grill, propane tanks and all, along with half the bar.

One third of the tavern had been blown away, tossed to tattered flames that disappeared in the quickly freezing night.

The survivors were exposed like wolves in a den, clustered and looking out at the darkness.

24

FIFTEEN PEOPLE HAD been killed in under four seconds: Vincent Gall (Chester's mysterious dad), Dale Howard (the stranger), Lyle Greenleaf (Squid-Man Ghost Grill-Master), Kevin Halloway (revolver kid), Laurel Beckhoff (mousey woman with a bastard daughter in Los Angeles), John Lajon (unworthy boyfriend), Senile Sheriff Mick Benson, and eight others. Deadily-Doo-Dah, all of them.

Ten of the survivors fled in their cars after the explosion. Their taillights seemed to fly fifty feet or so into the night, before winking out into nothing. The stranger's news that these events were only confined to Thunder gave them hope of refuge somewhere else. But most of the survivors stayed around The Hole, hoping the storm would pass somehow.

Twenty-three people remained in the bar.

The temperature had fallen below freezing and was still dropping.

The sounds of cicadas and wind grew more intense. At times the noise seemed to fade or diminish, as if their ears were losing power, then it would amp back up, like tuning to a clear radio station, a frequency more powerful that its static margins.

All the heat in the bar had been lost at once. They were now, effectively, outside in the plummeting temperatures.

No one spoke. Life seemed to be slowing down rather than speeding up.

Would anyone connect Vincent Gall to the stranger? Did anyone even moderately intelligent *hear* what the stranger had said? If so, how long before they, and everyone else, turned toward Vincent's family—Chester and that sweet woman, Juniper—in search of answers? Would they become scapegoats? Or would they be labeled spies or witches of some kind? Surely they'd stumbled upon a supernatural presence here, and a whole lot of confused townspeople were eager to point fingers at someone, *anyone*, if it would help give them clarity. So how long before the remaining survivors all went ballistic?

Chester rushed toward the explosion from the back of the bar, leaving the back door unmanned.

Jimmy, Sarah, and Alice had been all thrown backwards from the blast, onto the floor. Alice was passed out, clutching her bible.

Jimmy and Sarah propped themselves up to their elbows and faced each other. But that was as far as they could move. They felt as if they had been struck down to the ground with sledgehammers.

25

COLD HAD PUT its boot down.

The remaining Thunderians huddled bear-like in the nook of the tavern. Half of the U-shaped bar had been blown apart—the half that had once featured the grill.

Jimmy sat behind the red pool table, which had slid five feet towards the wall in the explosion, and which was now black instead of red, black as everything else. His mother huddled under his right arm, looking at his blistered claw.

Some people went to their cars to get blankets and clothes. Some never returned.

Now Jimmy and Alice sat facing out, feeling their pupils dilate in the dark, feeling them in their heads. Cold arms and legs and stretchy pupils in their heads. This was the end of their world. The strangest of fellowships in the most distant of places. This was the edge of reason, the cornerstone of faith, the end of hope.

26

R ED AND BLUE lights flickered across the mountains. The road
seem to twist and drop like a strobing footbridge. Hell Finn
and the sheriff were dark in the luminescence, almost invisible, the
only people around for miles.

"Let's see your license and registration." The sheriff was heavy-
set and slow, by the look of him.

Under the black cowboy hat, Hell replied, "I ain't got none."

The sheriff took a step back. "Step out of the car now, sir."

Finn stepped out of the Wagoneer and stood by it with the
door open. The wind blew in all directions. He looked totally law-
less in a long black trench coat, and a black cowboy hat—no need
to mention the scary teeth.

"What's your name, crazy?"

"My name's Hell Finn."

"Your *name's* Hell Finn?"

"Yes, sir."

"Your first name is Hell? Don't fuck with me. What kind of
fucked up hillbilly name is that?"

"It's German. It means bright and lively." He'd barely made it
out of Thunder, a few miles to the west, past the mouth of Copperhead Canyon. Only minutes to Tuba City.

This cop was alone. He started to move his hand towards his
Motorola CB clipped to his shoulder. But Finn opened his trench
coat and drew his .44 Magnum straight to the sheriff's chest. The
handgun glinted festively in the flickering lights.

BLOWIE! to the chest.

"Owie! Owie!" echoed across the desert.

The sheriff flew backwards, feet lilting into the air. If he had not been wearing a flak jacket, the bullet would have gone through him without tossing him so far. But his jacket had absorbed the bullet and transformed it into something more like a race car at full speed. Ten of the cop's ribs were crushed to dust. His heart exploded. He landed dead in the dirt, two arms, two legs, a head, and a bag of dog meat holding it all together.

Hell slid back into his Wagoneer. He could have taken the cop's uniform, if for no other reason than to look less unusual. But he kept his own clothes, because they were so goddamned comfortable.

With a few diminishing flashes of red and blue light, Hell Finn was gone from the scene.

27

T HE SURVIVORS AT The Hole (which now quite resembled a hole) still huddled, but they were much weaker now, fatigued, and much, much colder.

Servil Carlsberg spoke up from somewhere in the wreckage. "They got an earth cellar here. It's small. And it's pretty warm in the winter. We should all go down there if we want to survive this. I think."

Silence. Undertones of rising hope.

"How do you know this?" Jimmy asked.

"I spotted it when I was hooking up the generators. I even kinda checked it out. It's warm, and it'll fit us tight, but we can fit."

No one seemed particularly enthused about this. Alice was awake, curled up on the floor, clutching her side. Jimmy didn't know it, but he guessed she had broken one or two of her ribs.

She did not want to be in the earth cellar.

"I'm not getting buried alive, dude," Jimmy said. "Don't mean to steal your thunder."

Servil narrowed his eyes at Jimmy, the way one does when another makes fun of him. He spoke up again, more certain this time. "Well, I'm going down there. It's warm, and we will very likely freeze up here... and more people is better, I think. To keep it warm."

Jimmy rolled it back. He spoke respectfully, careful not to flourish or exaggerate his words. "I think we might need to go out to our cars to keep warm. We might even be able to sleep in them.

Anyways, we'll be above ground. As for the earth cellar, I'm not really sure the earth is our friend right now."

"Cars aren't our f-friends either, Jimmy. You could freeze… in your car," Chester chimed in. "The earth c-cellar is the only option that doesn't have c-certain danger. Out here w-we… can die." He shivered hard, clutching his mother, who reciprocated. His Chesterly optimism had gone.

"What's dangerous about a car?" Jimmy asked. "We can leave the keys in our p-pockets." He was ready to carry his mother out to the white Tacoma. Trusty Rusty. The pickup's seats didn't recline far, but it would be much better than shivering on the floor with three broken ribs. "I'm g-going," he said.

Jimmy stood up, collecting his mother, who yowled in pain.

A few other people started to gather themselves as well. Talk started up about the earth cellar, warm yet ominous.

It took only one minute for everyone to decide. They had been out there in the cold for almost an hour, and they understood now that they couldn't survive any longer like this.

Half of them went out to their cars. The other half went down to the earth cellar.

28

Sarah Simonez had come to the tavern in John's car. John was now spread across the ground like red toothpaste, and she had no desire to search what was left of him for the car keys. Five minutes earlier she had hated him, even in the face of her approaching doom. But now she was sinking to the floor, which seemed to rush up at her from miles away. She'd been cleaved in half in a flash, suddenly heartsick to the point of nausea. Shivering, she peered into the darkness where the wall had once been. Then, picking herself up slowly, she walked out into the parking lot to look for an unlocked, vacant car.

She found the sedan next to Alice Johannsen's Tacoma unlocked and crawled inside.

After some struggle, Jimmy was able to get his mother in the passenger seat of her truck. He closed the door and went around to the driver's seat.

He got in the cab and locked it.

The only sounds were Alice's staggering breaths blending into nature.

Ah, shit, where is everybody? The more alone Jimmy felt, the more jittery and nervous he became.

Chester, Juniper, Cherish, and the reverend had gone down to inspect the earth cellar. Perhaps they had made the better decision.

It was freezing in the car. None of the electrics worked, and their blankets seemed totally useless.

The two of them stared at the windshield. It looked to Jimmy like a television in its off position. Alice began to doze.

The rain started to fall. *Pet! Pet. Pet pet!*

Suddenly, Sarah hammered on Jimmy's window, making him jump. Her eyes were bulging, and she was yelling. Jimmy opened the door and slid over towards his mother, making room for her.

"Come in, come in!" he said.

"Oooh, fuck. Thank you!" she replied.

"Yeah, totally," he said. They tried to settle, but they were trembling too much. Especially Sarah. They were grateful to have each other's body warmth, and they rubbed each other awkwardly, favoring their injuries. Alice was still dozing. She had taken no notice of Sarah coming in.

With no bucket seats, the three of them were able to sit close together and keep the cab above fatal temperatures. Jimmy imagined the burn on his hand shedding warmth into the cab.

"Thank you so much," Sarah said. "I was so cold. I thought I was going to d-die. I s-started to panic! Thank you!"

Jimmy turned to look at Sarah, but she was almost completely invisible to him. They might as well have been in a nickel mine. Sarah was nothing but a cheekbone and an eye in the dark. He had saved her life. This was what the life he had saved for her looked like. A crescent edge of a young face, thankful in the dark. It was the smallest thing in the world, and it was perfect.

"I'm sorry, Jimmy," she said. "When that first rain hit, I got so scared, I—I don't even know why—" Panic started to rise in her again, and Jimmy put his hand on her knee.

She softened, starting to pull herself together. "It's okay," he said. "We're safe in here. As long as an airplane doesn't fall on us or something."

But he didn't believe that. They weren't safe. No, Jimmy hadn't felt anywhere near the ballpark of safe since he saw Jackie Wells running to the ice basin with her hand on fire, twenty-four hours ago.

29

THEY DIDN'T TALK much, there in the Tacoma, and when they did, they spoke in low whispers, so as not to wake up Jimmy's mother, who might have been sleeping for her life. They let her rest. They didn't know what else to do.

Jimmy and Sarah still could only see a faint outline of one another.

The rain started coming down hard. Then, torrentially. It slammed and punched the truck, making it tremble. The clouds loomed at ridiculous closeness, spraying the truck in blasts.

Then the hail came, first pea-sized and then near cinders. Within the truck, it sounded as though kitchen knives were slamming down, pounding and shredding every surface of the old beast. The knives became hatchets, axes, then rocks the size of bobcats. They pounced and exploded into earsplitting titters.

"What are you going to do if you survive?" Jimmy yelled over the thundering hail.

"I'm gonna work with animals!" Sarah replied. "What are *you* going to do if you survive?"

Their voices grew loud and desperate as the world around them battled, louder than any gunfight, louder than any war. Jimmy saw a piece of hail the size of a boat falling to Earth, just near the open wall that used to be part of the building, The Hole. How had he seen *that,* in the utter darkness? Lightning had begun to pop, illuminating unimaginable things. It hung in mid-air, as if resting on a pane of glass, and the next instant he heard an explosion of sound, as chunks of ice blasted across the car lot. A piece shaped like a surfboard sailed through the passenger-side window, missing Alice's sleeping face by inches. Whatever heat was in the cab vaporized at once.

It was a stop-motion film after that. Arctic, dreadful polyrhythms. Angry music. Cubism. It was Braque, maybe even Picasso.

Jimmy must have dozed off or slid into some outlandish hypnosis.

The hailstorm hadn't ended, though it had subsided. Now, globs of ice were spitting out of the clouds, then shattering on the ground like glassware. Trusty Rusty, and everything surrounding it, was in shambles.

Jimmy rubbed his eyes. His right hand pained him awake. He saw the world around him covered with ice. The cars looked like great luminescent insects in the flickering black night.

He looked to his right, towards his mother. Was she still sleeping? Where was *she* in all this?

She was frozen to her seat, dead.

Alice's mouth was open, drawn down, her eyes drawn up in a horrible Jesus-Christ-on-a-cross expression. Large gobs of ice hung from her nostrils, pointing down like tusks of some ghoulish walrus. She was the ugliest Jimmy had ever seen her. She didn't look as if she'd died sleeping. She looked like she had been cleaved in the stomach with an axe and then flash-frozen.

Jimmy did not know for how long he'd been unconscious. It must have been just after ten o'clock when they'd gone to the car. The color of the night indicated that they were still nowhere near morning.

Alice looked like she had been dead for hours.

His heart sloshed. He felt fear and woe in great waves, churning around him like flotsam.

He turned to Sarah. Maybe he could stick his face in her breast, and then wait out the rest of his life there; that would be the most sensible thing to do. But when he turned to his left, panic threw a plastic bag over his head.

Jimmy's legs straightened, sending pain everywhere. He was trapped inside the truck.

Sarah was dead, too. And she looked as if she had been *eaten* by the cold. She was sealed to the seat and stuck to Jimmy's clothes. Alice was stuck to him, too. Jimmy spasmed, their clothes crackled off his, and he kicked and elbowed the ice away.

Then he reached for the door by Alice, to his right, but the seam where the door met the frame of the cab was covered with a hard, bulbous web of ice. It sealed the door with molecular power. The door to the left, by Sarah, had met the same fate. He couldn't get out. The windshield was marbled but still mostly in place. The truck was a hollow block of extra-strength ice.

Before he had a chance to rip the duck feather skin off his face in fear, he heard a sudden *BANG!* and the Tacoma was thrown in the air, an easy four feet, maybe five. All at once, loud roars, like foghorns, consumed him. The car launched, and in the light of electric sky, he could see other cars suspended in the air. Like photographs, cars and trucks were strobing off the ground. It looked like illustrations in a children's bible, fake and terrifying.

He realized in horror that it was an earthquake. Alice and Sarah's bodies cracked free from the seat and clumsily battered Jimmy as he screamed. They unwound his mind in a matter of seconds.

He dedicated himself to opening the driver's side door, past Sarah's stiff, dancing body.

Jimmy thrashed about like an enraged monster, the force around him so deliberate, so violent, that he cried. He imagined a devil shaking a door handle, trembling with rage, unable to open the door, shaking, screaming, turning all evil inwards towards this door, and the door was Thunder.

After fifteen seconds, the earthquake stopped.

Cars and ice chunks were scattered everywhere.

There was silence then. Not even nature sounds.

The door frames had cracked back into their functional states. Jimmy stayed where he was, caught between the two dead women. He didn't want to leave the truck. He would rather be buried alive with two horrible corpses than go out there looking for a new car, blind in the frozen darkness and scared beyond reason.

30

CHESTER WAS IN the earth cellar with fourteen other people—a small, crowded after party to the chaos earlier in the evening.

They had lit a few candles, and they could see well enough. It was plenty warm for everybody, despite the thermal demise outside.

The earth cellar was cube shaped, with no floor apart from the hard earth, and low, filthy beams for a ceiling. It had nothing in it at all—no food storage, no supplies. It was as quaint and cozy as a spider's asshole.

A minute passed before the townspeople noticed the white sacks hanging from the ceiling, like myriad golf balls. Now they all were in focus, dangling all above them but not moving, as still as cat eyes, predatory but in repose.

Cherish stared back at them. "Fuck," she whispered, cutting open the silence that had blanketed them for the last minute or so.

Two cellar doors opened upward atop some stairs in the corner, then closed heavily. Everybody had come inside, except for the eight or so who had gone for their cars.

The candles burned...

"Those things are freaky," one person said. There was no guessing to what she or Cherish were referring.

"Yeah, they're actually bugging me out," another person said. "What is this? Fuckin' *Aliens*?"

Then someone spoke up who Chester didn't recognize. It was a woman who looked to be in her thirties. She had yellow crimped hair and an oversized Christmas sweater that read, "KEEP CALM AND FOLLOW THE REDNECK." She wore blue eye shadow over hollow eyes, and by the look of her, she was probably from Thunder. She looked like an older version of Cherish.

"This is a nightmare," she said. "This is a chase nightmare. We're all sleepwalking! These are night stunts! We could kill each other! This is dangerous!"

Chester didn't know what this woman was talking about, or what "night stunts" were. But after she calmed down, everybody else seemed to calm down. And for the first time yet, the people under the earth cellar doors quieted, feeling somewhat connected. Chester could feel a low buzz of supplicating awareness.

The golf balls on the ceiling, looming like white scrotums, threatened everyone. They all watched them for a moment, then thought it better to look away, to watch the candles instead. Their imaginations were beyond lucid right now.

They started to hear some rain. Fat rain. *Pit. Pit. Pet.*

The Reverend spoke. "Heavenly King," he began, but his voice trembled with uncertainty. "Send us an angel, or... anything." His white cowboy hat levered upwards, aimed at God. But he couldn't meet God's eyes when he spoke.

They all stood in silence, in the candlelight, squashed together like cargo on an old slave ship. Thirty minutes passed, and the earth cellar grew warm.

Then the nests started to move, vibrating, then shaking.

"Fuck me!" Cherish cried, as she grabbed the pant leg of the person next to her. It was Chester, and he put an hand on her shoulder, giving her comfort, also taking a little.

A large man in the center of the room yelled, "I'll get the door!" He shoved easily through the crowd. His name was Errol Speck, and he knew that now it was *his* time to help. He was the biggest man in the room.

He moved straight for the doors in the ceiling as everyone else turned their attention back to the hanging sacks. They were still closed, like garlic bulbs, and about a quarter of them were moving. The sacks emitted a sound, almost like sizzling. But the sound was soon drowned out by the rain outside, turning to hail, and a total bitch of an ambush, by the sound of it. Chester could barely keep his eyes open, and he flinched from every arhythmic impact.

Four seconds passed, and then the people turned their heads back towards Errol, towards the doors. It would only take him four seconds or so to get—

Suddenly, there was no Errol Speck. He was gone.

The people took no time to think about his absence. They surged for the doors. Some actually got their hands on them when a boat-sized block of ice sent them all swiftly in concussion back down the stairs. Backs twisted, and some sprained in multiple places.

It became harder to see, as some dropped their candles, darkening the room considerably. With sudden horror, Chester saw there were fewer people down here, maybe ten instead of the initial fourteen. The air had thinned, and the temperature had dropped. People were disappearing around him. He remembered hearing the stranger say that they'd be transported to a world with little oxygen, and they'd die quickly. It seemed unreal, unbelievable, yet all too terrifying.

Two candles were picked up off the ground and relit. Chester turned back to the spider nests. He watched in horror as the nests boiled open, spilling baby spiders to the floor. Each membrane contained hundreds, maybe thousands, of tiny, aggressive cave spiders.

Vincent had assured Chester in his youth that cave spiders were not deadly when found alone. But in large groups, the spiders could be deadly. When in the tens of thousands, their venom would eventually become corrosive, dissolving flesh into nothing, leaving black craters where flesh used to be. Chester had heard about people found in mines and earth cellars face-down with what looked like a model of the Grand Canyon in their backs, rainbow colors and all.

The spiders were spreading out everywhere.

People stamped and danced all over the place. The den looked even more like some sick after party, only now the hallucinogens had kicked in, and everyone was dancing like no one was watching.

Even the reverend seemed to feel as though no one was watching.

They ran out of energy quickly. They sat on the ground with their backs against the walls, exhausted, nearly paralyzed. Chester surveyed the scene. *Ten of us, now,* he thought. *But they're blurry.*

They no longer worried about the cave spiders; they had all been bitten dozens, perhaps hundreds, of times, so now they sat slumped haphazardly on the ground. Baby spiders flowed directionless in silence. They skittered over their legs and hands, some up over their faces and into their scalps.

The noise outside had receded, leaving only sporadic shatters and slamming sounds, random chunks of ice, like dreams falling from the sky in pieces.

31

Hell Finn streaked across Copperhead Canyon like a comet strapped into a Jeep Wagoneer with wood siding.

"Aaaahh," he breathed, drawing it out, feeling the wind in his gums.

He loved this new idea of making the world less claustrophobic.

The Wagoneer was alpine skiing, gliding gloriously upon black snow in the night.

He could see the lights of Tuba City ahead. He flushed with excitement. He drove as fast as he could. In a few moments he would slow down, but for now he pushed it as far and as fast as it would go.

"GET YOUR UMBRELLAS READY, FOLKS! ITS A-COMIN DOWN' HAAARRD, TONIGHT!"

As he began his final descent into Tuba City, Hell felt his destiny rising inside him like a mushroom. It felt wonderful, the psychological walls surrounding him collapsing as he grew into a giant version of himself. The shadows, to which he had been confined his whole life, were beginning to fade into light. He was free of the mine sickness that had once crippled him. Free of the hard drugs that had once bound him. And free of the shadows that had *possessed* him under lock and key for all these years.

In simpler terms, he was free.

As Hell approached Tuba City, he came upon some gas stations. He rolled casually into the second gas station that presented itself to him. Dino-Soar, it was called. Self-service, that'll do.

As he pumped gas into the Wagoneer acting as casually as he could, he noticed something going on by the far side of the station facility to the right.

Two men were having a heated but quiet argument in the shadows, out of view of the security cameras. One of them had a long red ponytail, and the other one wore a backwards baseball cap and stood with his back to the wall.

Oooohh. Interesting, Finn thought, smiling.

They were waving their hands at each other. They both looked scared but pretending not to be, and Finn knew that scared people were the absolute most dangerous. *The best kind,* he thought. Anything was about to happen, Hell could tell. Hell could see that shit a mile away, and it made him weak with happiness. *Let the bad times roll.*

Aw, Jesus Christ, this day is amazing! It's like I died and gone to heaven!

Hell found his bearing, leaning on the car. He checked his guns: one Magnum, one Glock, and one shotty on hand. The Magnum was *in* his hand, and it had five shells in it.

It ain't un-leaded, but it's enough for both of them, and to blow this whole place to gas station heaven.

He slinked, and he watched. He hated these fucking guys. With their apartments and shit. Their hand gestures poking and looping. They were so *confined,* so stuck in this paper-thin cage of non-threatening gestures. Hell saw right through them.

It wasn't long before the action started. The red-haired man on the outside contracted, throwing an uppercut right into the other man's face. It connected under his jaw with a high-pitched *click,* and the man by the wall's head flipped backwards like a balloon, smacking the back of his head into the wall. His cap flew off, and he fell to the ground at once. He rose for a moment, halfway to his knees, and the red-haired man pulled a handgun out of his waistband and shot him in the chest.

Smoking coffee burst out of the kneeling man's back. He fell backwards to the ground and lay lengthwise along the angle where the pavement met the wall.

The red-haired man saw Finn and swung the outstretched gun in his direction. He wore narrow, oval-shaped glasses that glared reflections in the fluorescents. He had a confused expression on his face, as if he didn't know what he was doing. When the glare slid off his spectacles, Hell could see his eyes. There was no cognition in them. He had the expression a dog has when told to shake before its master.

Hell took one slow step to his left, revealing his shotgun on his hip, pointed calmly toward the red-haired man. The man lifted both his arms, turned in a circle with his hands up in the air, and said, "Okay, okay!" as if caught in a game of hide-and-seek. He looked like he had been zapped by a confuse-ray gun.

This ponytail guy is nuts! Finn threw his gas handle back into the pump, keeping the shotgun trained on the stranger. He kicked his car door closed, started walking towards him, and said, "Inside." His four teeth gleamed in his wiry, coal-stained face.

They walked toward the entrance of the station. The strange murderer led, and Hell Finn followed.

Inside, the man flipped the "OPEN" sign on the glass door to "CLOSED" and then shut off the outside lights and the sign.

He didn't shut off the pumps.

32

CHESTER LOOKED WEAKLY to the reverend, who was loosely propped against the wall of the earth cellar. His breathing was jagged, and he otherwise didn't move at all. The backs of his forearms were on the ground, palms facing up, his legs out-stretched in a V. His white cowboy hat, still shining in the candle-light, now pointed down towards the floor. To his left lay Juniper, and to her left Chester. To the Reverend's right was Cherish—the filthy, craterous, but still breathing remains of a nine-year-old girl whose last words had been, "Fuck me."

Across the room and in front of them was what remained of the door in the ceiling. It was smashed up and dashed to the stairs by a titan's fang of ice.

To their right, on the other wall, lay Servil, with his nerdy serial killer glasses, and four others.

Three of the candles had burned out. Only two remained, and they only had a half hour or so left in them.

Chester was covered in sores and black, bloody holes. He could see that some people had considerable lesions. Nobody could move.

Then a sudden pain erupted inside Chester's abdomen. The poison had found its way into his stomach, bursting like a volcano. He tried to vomit, but only a red string of slime came out.

Someone across the room joined in on the experience. Then a third. Chester thought he may have gone blind for a few seconds. *Candles can't go out and then light themselves back up again...*

The venom of the cave spiders seemed to exact many vengeful symptoms upon its victims as it flowed through everybody: waves of nausea, extreme stomach cramps, blindness, schizophrenia, and, of course, the constant corrosion of flesh. The earth cellar was now a dungeon.

Then all at once, the reverend pushed himself up to sitting, with his back against the wall. His eyes were open wide and suddenly clear. He had a huge hole in his neck that started above his collar bone and ended at his jaw. *Wasn't his jugular somewhere in there?*

He spoke loudly and clearly. He had an eerie, possessed-by-God sound to him.

"When I was a boy, five years old, my father and I went to Laguna Beach." The reverend was no longer breathing irregularly. "This was in the sixties, and there were sharks there in the sixties. My father had said, 'Now, Cal, don't go out past the breakers, all right? There's sharks out there,' and I said, 'Okay,' and I went running into the water with the rest of the people."

"Next thing I knew, the whole beach was running to the water, screaming and yelling and swimming towards me. I got grabbed and swam to the shore, where my father stood confused and terrible-like. When James Foster got mad, he would sort of implode; it was pathetic. He was so embarrassed that he lost his little boy in front of everybody, poor guy—he lay down and put a newspaper over his face for five minutes while his numb-nut son scared everybody in Laguna Beach. Oh, he was so mad, and he said 'Calister! Calister, why'd ya do that? I told you not to! There's sharks out there!' And he was imploding fast. 'I wanted to meet the sharks, Father,' I said."

Then the reverend tipped his white-hatred head back down again. He chuckled. "I wanted to meet the sharks, I said."

And then he passed out. Or died.

Chester briefly tried to imagine what kind of craters were forming under his own clothes. It was a terrible thought, but a logical one. He looked around. Others were passed out or comatose or dead. His mother was alive. And Cherish was alive, although only barely. Her fingers were moving, and she appeared to be looking at him.

Chester tried to turn his head away, but he couldn't. He managed to shift his gaze up to the ceiling.

He heard a strange noise coming from the doorway. He moaned, "Yeah" as if to acknowledge it, but he couldn't really see what it was. His vision was too blurry. It almost sounded like... Digging.

Were they being rescued?

They were being rescued!

Chester wanted to smile but found that he wasn't capable. He was paralyzed. Then he realized with horror that it didn't sound like digging at all. No, it was too weird. Not human—too fast. It was more like... *sniffing.*

Oh dear God—

The ice in the doorway started to chip and fall away, and then Chester saw a paw.

In the very last of the sputtering light, three large wolves snuck down into the earth cellar. They went for Cherish first.

Chester's eyes were locked on the ceiling, but he could hear them. They sounded like they were enjoying themselves. But the wolves never got to their second course, which would've been Chester's mom, if his science was right. Juniper was the only other female down there, and Chester believed that they would eat the women first. Instead, he heard a pulse-breaking eruption, and everyone was tossed in the air. Chester slammed into the wall in front of him, and the world went black.

It was a box of spiders, humans, candlesticks, and wolves, shaken vehemently by some screaming devil.

Everyone in the cellar died in the earthquake, including the spiders and the wolves.

33

ELL FINN PULLED a six-pack of Steel Reserve's from the refrigerator and sat down with his new favorite person. His red ponytail was greasy, and he wore dark grey fatigues with no name embroidery.

"What's yer name, buddy?"

The station manager looked at Finn in the fluorescent lights and grimaced. He looked down at the counter instead. "Name's Meatface," he said.

"Your *name's* Meatface?"

Finn looked at the man. He pulled a malt beverage from its pack and opened it. Then he took a long drink and put the can on the counter. "All right, good enough," he said at last.

He put his guns away. He was sitting half on the counter and standing on one leg, while Meatface sat in his clerk's chair on the other side. Finn could see that there were no more weapons around, and decided he'd truce the guy for the rest of their beers. Meatface drank very slowly and looked at Finn.

Finn put an empty beer can on the counter and pulled another one from the ring. "I'm going on a little road trip," he said. "And I would love it if you came along."

Meatface spoke like a man who didn't know what he was talking about. "–Wh-why the hell would I go with you? I mean you seem fun and all... but hey, where you goin' anyways?"

Hell knew where he was going. "Vegas." He grinned.

"Oh shit, man. I ain't never been to Vegas!" Then he softened. "No, I can't go with you, bro. I got a fambly I gotta take care of."

"No you don't, *bro*. You're a wanted murderer." Finn took another long swig. "And, you're a ruthless fucking *beast!* I saw what you did back there, fucker. It was *awesome*. I like you very much. Yer kinda like me."

"Listen, sir, I have no idea what happened back there. All I know is that wasn't me! It was the weirdest thing! I was just talking to Robinson like I always do! I like that guy; he brings me pot. Then you showed up in that... that fucking Wagoneer, and we watched you get out of the car, and next thing I know, we was arguing about something, and then fuck, like a spark went off and I—I wasted him somehow!"

They looked at each other, Hell smiling crookedly, Meatface utterly unsmiling. "That wasn't me, man. I swear!"

Hell finished off his second Steel Reserve and placed the empty can neatly beside the first one. Then slowly, indulgently, he pulled a third can from the ring. He had been drinking for five minutes.

Hell cracked it open and continued. "Well I have eyes, Meatface, and I say it *was* you!" He took a drink and composed himself. "My name's Hell Finn. I'm going to Vegas. Now grab your bullets and a bunch of cigarettes and get in my car. You're gonna be my buddy."

"No! What the hell, man?" Meatface protested.

"No questions anymore!" Hell stood up. "You're my buddy! We've been joined together by the *devil* or some shit! *Fuck* your family! Get yer shit together!"

Hell went to the fridge for more beer. Some roadies. "Anyways," he continued. "You can't be as angelic as you say you are. Your name's Meatfa—"

He turned back to Meatface and froze, eyes bulging under his waxy hairless brows.

Meatface's red ponytail was standing straight up. His eyes were shut tight behind his oval-shaped glasses, as if he were warding off a gritty wind. Then his clothes started to billow upwards.

Meatface disappeared. He seemed to expand like a soap bubble, then pop into absolutely nothing.

Finn dropped all the beer on the floor and gasped, stumbling backwards. He checked his pockets but had no idea why. Everything was still there, but Meatface was gone.

He snatched up one of the six-packs he'd dropped and a carton of Marlboros from behind the counter, then ran out of the station.

34

EVERY WINTER, THE entire world's population of Baikal Teal flew south out of Siberia, migrating towards Southeast Asia, in search of food and warmth. Often, they would miss their destination and continue to unexpected land. This was due partly to the winds, which could carry the duck-like birds off course, and partly to mob mentality, which, with four-hundred thousand small birds, can be extremely irresponsible.

If they missed their destination, they would sometimes have to travel thousands of miles across entire oceans, before they found the next available land mass on which they could settle. Some years they'd been spotted in the most unexpected places, surprising people in Italy, in Kenya, and even in the American Southwest. They could travel for up to a month as far as halfway around the earth, darkening one sky at a time.

As the first light materialized over Thunder, like a prehistoric dreamscape, the Baikal Teal arrived. All of them. The entire world's population in a single flock.

The birds hit the ground like feathery brown snowballs. They bounced off everything, slid on the ice, then settled, burying Thunder in a slushy depth of ice and dead birds.

And this was how Thunder, Arizona would remain, until it passed out of existence forever.

35

*F*UCK, *TALK ABOUT better and better! Could it be that I've gotten my wish!? My SUPERPOWERS?*

Hell Finn was driving fast, unaware of himself. He had forgotten all about Thunder. Now all he thought about was home. He was going to get all the Tina in Vegas.

And now... this other thing. *The ability to make people disappear? Did that guy just poofity-pop because of ME?*

He believed it, yes, sir. And in a way, it was true.

HELLL FINNN, THE WORLD'S WORST SUPER-VIL-LAINN! YEEEEE-HAAAAWW! TREMBLE! TREMBLE AND RUN!

Hell Finn drove on, but he did not stop in Tuba City. He went directly to Vegas.

36

JIMMY DIDN'T EXACTLY wake up because he hadn't exactly been sleeping. He had lost consciousness, but he couldn't remember waking up or opening his eyes. Or why he'd woken up. He had no memory until now. He was barely alert, and he did not feel like he was in the same place. He took an embarrassed moment to take in his surroundings. Then he reached over Sarah's frozen corpse and climbed pathetically down from the Tacoma.

Jimmy looked east. The sky was finally beginning to blanche. In a few minutes it would be sunrise. But for now it was still mostly dark and cloudy. He couldn't tell how much he had slept.

Welcome to the world of the living, he thought, grimly.

He quickly realized how difficult it was to walk out there. The ground was uneven, and there was black slush almost up to his ankles. He was relieved to be out of the truck, though. It was still cold outside, but it was bearable. Better than before. And there was that almost perceptible light that would soon break into dawn.

The cars were scattered about the parking lot like discarded toys. As Jimmy slid around the nose of old Trusty Rusty, touching the body that had once had white paint on it, he noticed that both headlights were gone. The grill was twisted and hanging off the front like a stroke victim's frown. He looked down: slush and smelly ash up to his wet ankles. Pieces of the tavern, glass, and... dead birds? *Eugh! Awful!*

Jimmy found some unlocked car doors and was able to collect some jackets and things. He found a pair of dry work boots, and he tied the laces together and slung them over his shoulder. Then he climbed onto the top of the tallest truck, a Ford F-250, and waited.

The darkness was thinner now, the world just barely visible. Beyond the parking lot where vehicles lay scattered and flipped about, Jimmy saw nothing remaining of his hometown. A fine dark mist stretched out in all directions.

Jimmy stayed on top of the truck until full daylight came.

He saw no people and heard no sound but the sighing breeze.

By the end of that morning, Jimmy hadn't died, or gone to another world where there was little oxygen. The ground was finally dry enough to walk on. It was difficult, swamp-like, and Jimmy had to jump puddles and zig-zag to get back into town. There was slush everywhere, tinged pink with the blood of birds. The birds themselves were haunting—a million eyeballs seeing nothing.

PART
FOUR

37

Dani Beckhoff was at the shoreline of her dream. She smiled and thought hazily about falling in love while being asleep. How wonderful she felt. Smelling the bed comforters, cool and slightly damp with sweat. It smelled so good in the morning. Ah, she would lie in this love forever.

Then she sat up with a start.

Shit! I'm late!

She felt her lover leave her forever.

Dani was damp and flattened by deep sleep. Her eyes were gummy, and her black hair stood straight up in the back.

She scrambled to throw on some clothes, dimly remembering the way her man had looked at her in the dream, as if he knew they would be torn apart forever. Their worlds would never join a second time. But she was grateful for that moment of happiness, even though she would never see him again, *and* it made her late for work. She had fallen deeply in love, behind closed eyelids, and now she felt like she was on top of the world, albeit slowly descending back to reality.

She took a two-minute shower. She had to shower and blow dry her hair if she didn't want to look like a monster at work. In the shower, she thought about his hair. His dream hair. The third minute was free, so why not?

Dani walked outside, stepping off her sleepy Echo Park apartment steps and into the land of real life.

Goddamn, she was going to be late. She had never been late

before. Dani was a stage manager at the Music Center downtown. Stage managers were *never* late.

Dani's car had been in the shop since the day before. Los Angeles without a car was enormous and confusing for people who were used to driving their own cars. But Dani was lucky, and she found a cab easily on Sunset.

"Hi," she said as she got in the car. "I'm going to the Music Center downtown, please. I'm in a bit of a hurry."

He took off. "What building, miss?"

"Dorothy Chandler. Take me to the corner of First and Grand. Thanks."

Dani sat back, uncaffeinated, embarrassed. *How are some people late all the time? It must be so stressful!*

But soon she was able to relax and feel the cool, February morning air coming through her window. Dani loved Los Angeles in the morning. She was crazy about the smell. So far it was a great day for smells.

Another cab pulled up next to them at a red light on Sunset. "Excuse me—where's the entrance to the 110?" the other driver asked.

"It's back behind you, a quarter mile," said Dani's driver.

The other cab sped off without so much as a, "Thank you."

The cab driver spoke. Dani could tell by his ID that he was from Morocco, and he spoke Arabic. He might have lived in LA longer than her, and she'd lived here for nine years.

"People in this city are so rude these days," he said.

"Yeah, it's not like it used to be," Dani agreed.

"I've lived here for twenty-two years. People have never been this rude. After 9/11, it was better, but now... shit, I tell you."

"I agree," Dani said, and she did agree. She thought that people should be much nicer in general, and it bothered her.

"Everybody blaming everybody," said the driver. "Anger. Racism. The Arabs never killed anyone. The Christians never killed anyone… The Muslims, they never killed anyone. So why all this hatred, here in LA? Nobody is hurting *anybody*."

"You raise a good point, sir, and I share the same sentiment." Dani liked this guy so far but could do with less race-talk in the morning.

He paused and then spoke again. "Everybody knows the Jews kill everyone. They are the killers. Not the Christians. Not the Arabs."

"That's not a very nice thing to say," she said. "I'm a Jew, and I've never even *met* anyone who's killed anyone." Dani remembered what she just thought about being sweet and played it pleasantly. *Be extra nice,* she told herself. "You have your facts wrong, sir, and you shouldn't be talking about such things with your passengers. Now just get me there fast, please… I'm late."

She looked at his face in the rearview mirror and imagined that it was her own face. She squinted her eyes and forced her brain to understand that this was *her* reflection. She admired his eyes, as if they were her own. She grew excited for his nose. She thought this face was much more beautiful than the passenger in the back. And then she snapped out of it, delighted by that cool, trippy effect.

They stopped at another red light on Figueroa, and the driver turned around and said, "I'm sorry, miss. I just know what I know. I don't mean *you're* to blame. I just mean the Jews. You're a nice girl, but Jews are killers. I know. I know."

"Even if you *do* know, which I'm not sure if you do, respectfully, you should keep your mouth shut while driving with me."

She thought of her mother then, and she suddenly felt guilty. Why did she feel guilty when she thought of her mother?

Good old Laurel Beckhoff. Mousey, alone, and in Thunder.

The driver, still twisted in his seat, looked at Dani sympathetically. He opened his mouth as if to argue his point further, but instead the strangest thing happened.

In the back seat, she expanded. Except expanded wasn't the

right word—more like inflated. She clenched her teeth and shut her eyes, as her shape started to swell. Her black hair began to stand up. Then she opened her eyes and disappeared completely.

The image of her open eyes was the last thing to remain of her.

Cars started honking their horns ferociously.

The cab driver was glued to his seat in fear, and in rapture.

38

ERROL SPECK STOOD, looking up at a night sky thick with stars. He had been running to the cellar doors not one second before. And now he was here. The starlight nearly blinded him after the dark of the earth cellar.

It was beautiful at first, but he could sense horrible things in the distance, just out of sight. He felt as if he were being watched with eyes drawn open as wide as they would pry. *If this is a dream,* he thought, *it is sure to become a nightmare in no time at all. I can hear it in the underscore.*

The stars were huge. They created a spider web effect across the sky, which churned above him at slow, varying speeds, leaving the ground behind. There was no moon in sight. Nor was there a single cloud.

Where in God's name am I? he wondered.

He suddenly realized that the air was not right. Not right at all. But instead of panicking, Errol grew curious, and he started to walk around. As he moved, he became weak and slow. Before he could understand what was happening around him, his mind went weak as well. His hearing diminished, and the world fell totally mute.

Errol couldn't detect any smells either. With that, his memories, and his sense of presence became displaced. He had heard once that the sense of smell was the most lucid sense, and he'd never quite comprehended that. But now, without a single smell in the air, he fully understood. He had lost all comprehensive association. Without smell, he barely knew who he was.

Of course, he didn't know *where* he was, either. Nor would he; he wouldn't know where he was even if he had his sense of smell *and* proper oxygen levels in his brain.

The stars above him burned by the billions. They shone down, and the light dashed off the black dirt, rotating as if thrown off a thousand disco balls.

An image of a tiny planet, one much smaller than Earth's moon, flashed across Errol's mind. It was an illustration in his imagination, something like *Le Petit Prince*, although Errol had never heard of *Le Petit Prince*.

He was able to come up with one thought, however. It was a strange one: *If night is as bright as day, then what's the* day *like?*

But Errol knew that he would never see the light of day, no matter what planet he was on. No matter how healthy he had been ten minutes ago.

Now he was as high as a kite. Stoned like the Grateful Dead, and equally as out of tune. Whatever oxygen had been in his brain before was now burning up, leaving an ashy paste in its wake. This brain soot was killing him, sending his identity to the four winds.

His knees gave out. He collapsed into a Muslim prayer position. It would have been a painful drop, but Errol felt almost nothing in his body.

The sky continued to rotate. Errol looked up dizzily and watched it turn. He felt as if he and this tiny strange planet were falling, sliding. *Drowning*.

The view in the distance was the worst part. Jagged mountain peaks tore across the sky like teeth, alligator jaws biting the bright sky open. This view seemed to spin the universe in two directions, creating vacancy over the horizon. With the sky in its crooked rotation, the mountainous jaws appeared to be opening and closing at the same time.

Errol clambered back to his feet, using old scraps of magic that became will power. He began to walk again, though it wasn't really a walk—it was more like a leg moving exercise.

He struggled forward. He felt as if he had swallowed sleeping pills. Each step started at the beginning and ended at the end.

When he saw the body of the Davidson kid—*Chucky,* he remembered—curled up dead under the mountain scape, he finally began to panic. He took in a huge involuntary breath, but his lungs didn't fill up with air. Instead they jammed up in his throat, stuck like an elevator. Then his lungs fell back into his chest uselessly. There was pain in there. His heart spasmed, then shot a double jolt of adrenaline through his limbs.

Rotten blood shot through his system like brake fluid. He collapsed again, at first to his knees, then all the way down, sending starlight off his muscular crescents like powdery snow. His face hit the ground.

Errol Speck lay on his stomach in the black dirt, head turned sideways, allowing him a small amount of breathing. His one above-ground eye remained dimly aware, wandering like a mollusk.

In that eye, he saw the woman Dani Beckhoff appear, confused but sober, touching herself with her hands—her abdomen, her jeans, looking around comprehensively at first, then confused, eventually distant, and finally dazed and sedated.

At Dani's appearance in this bleak, jagged black landscape, Errol rolled over and released what was left of his life.

The stars overhead consoled no one. They draped across the sky like a banner, shining with intention, constellations spelling out claims with wordless promise: The cosmos will live on forever. With the glorious limn of a teenaged genius god. Worry not, Master Speck. You are no longer essential. And don't worry about that cellar door. They all died in there. But the mountains are taller still, and the seas are deeper so.

39

Nuclear fallout resided for two generations in the mines of Thunder. Slowly over time, it dissolved holes into the earth. But they weren't the holes you would imagine, and not in the earth you'd imagine either. It was Earth's *dimension*. The realm seen as real life—Mother Nature's flesh—had corroded like the flesh of a cave spider's victim.

As the radioactive atmosphere matured, it spread, crawling out of its lightless cave, towing death and chaos from realms that existed beyond our own into Thunder. Like a family of barn swallows, it simply moved into the barn, and the barn was Thunder. Destruction moved in from the realm of evil, freezing, torching, and stealing everyone in its path.

In the time it took for the radiation to complete its burrow, from 1963 to 2021, people studied the strange mines of Thunder. Fontaine was established in 1963, and since then added it had been added to and built upon, growing from one trailer to six. Scientists moved in and out. Not many, only three or four at a time. But their research accumulated. Vincent Gall had been one of them. Dale Howard had been another.

They had men working for them in the mines, misfortunates recovering rock samples and reinforcing the walls for safer explorations. Men like Hell Finn, with no advocates or objectors. These men were called "moles," for obvious reason. They were outcasts, criminals, and often homeless. All the moles died. Most within a year, some within as little as a month. That risk had never been explained to Finn up front, but to be fair, he'd never asked anyone about it.

Perhaps it was the company that started it. The execs, who had forced all these men into working for them as moles for all these years. Maybe those guys threw a kind of rope, a safety line of evil into the portal they hadn't known they created. Or maybe it was the idea itself, testing radioactive weaponry, for the sole purpose of war and destruction. Perhaps they'd built an express track to the realm of death itself, and the realm of death offered return service, dark ghost trains in the night, shuttling hourly.

Meanwhile, the fallout lingered. And in the end, forty-eight years later, evil found its way through the portal. The secret doorway that only radiation from man-made weaponry could forge was unlocked and then opened.

PART
FIVE

40

COPPERHEAD CANYON, EIGHTEEN miles west of Thunder, intersected with interstate 160, which began at the northeast rim of the Grand Canyon and journeyed northeast through Tuba City and beyond. The nights out there were exactly as bleak as the days.

Navajo territory. Before that, shamans and cavemen. Before that dinosaurs.

Now there was a new native to the land. Evil.

The sun came up confused on the morning of the twenty-fifth. The blue air seemed to melt away in its embarrassed red glow. The Painted Desert whispered rumors, bits of stories that had floated over the planes in the night.

The cacti were stiff, watching each other with large, sidelong eyes. They spoke of nothing. The Yerba Verdes and Joshua Trees cast occasional glances at each other but otherwise pretended to be invisible. Every rock seemed to possess its own opinion. The flamboyantly colored sand looked as if it secretly contained bodies, quiet corpses hidden just beneath the surface. The boulders all faced the other way, flushed with subdued distaste.

The sun was bright but also suspicious. It glared down at the land, as if to discern the mystery of this oddly sublime picture.

The Navajo came out of their homes one at a time. They cooked their food and set up kiosks for Grand Canyon tourists that might wander out their way. They began to look for old dinosaur tracks or bones that may have eroded to form during the night.

It had been a brutally cold night. And the earthquake had woken up the whole camp. It sounded like an explosion, followed by an exodus of giant, stampeding reptiles.

41

HELL FINN SKIDDED along the north rim of the Grand Canyon. He was almost to the junction of 89A that would take him through the Kaibab Forest, tearing ass north into Utah. After that, it was only a simple free fall southwest into Nevada, and the big fat lap of Las Vegas.

He felt the chilly breeze in his gums. His black cowboy hat sat beside him, with plenty of room in the passenger seat. His Magnum, still mostly loaded, lay beside the hat. Finn's hair wiggled out behind him as he drove, like thin black cobwebs. He was only thirty-three years-old, but his hair was that of an elderly man's, like mummy hair, and it matched the mere scaffold of the body that wore it. His eyebrows had fallen off, leaving his eyes like barren, empty graves. This gave Hell's face an opened, hungry look. A headlight on the road to mischief.

"Yes," he muttered, as the junction swirled off to his right. It fell out of view behind him.

Only a couple of hours to go.

Hell thought back on Thunder, savoring the bloodbath in Apavajo Square. He was proud of it. All his life, Finn had wanted to create carnage like that. He would've regretted every last day he hadn't tried. *Might as well get it done*, he thought, and he had gotten it done. Extremely well, he thought. Much better than he had expected. It was like all them in the square were *destined* to die. Doomed or cursed or whatever.

He was their curse.

Bloodbath. Massacre. A smile boiled up in his face, showing a bit more tooth. *It was like an orgy,* he mused.

Did he want more? Yes. Shit, he needed more. He felt the icy, empty morning air on his face. He thought of all the crystal in Las Vegas. And in that cold morning air, a hot twinkle of anticipation bloomed in his stomach, radiating through his guts.

He was the *new* Hell Finn. Free of his bonds, and he could have anything he wanted. He grinned as he drove. It was an obsessed, gummy grin. His four teeth glinted in the moonlight, like a rat behind a steering wheel, chiseling his way to the good stuff.

With his thoughts of Vegas, Finn's mind started to drift toward his past. He thought of home as a real place—perhaps for the first time. His high school. His elementary school. His *parents.* They were still there, as far as he knew. And everyone he knew, fading all the way back to people he barely knew, and things he barely remembered doing. Hell Finn had once been a child in Vegas.

Now he was a wraith, moving north along his warbled road, entering the first pines of the Kaibab Forest.

The bluish light of early morning appeared suspicious to Finn somehow, and he immediately sobered up from his daydreams. He mumbled something. Then suddenly, he couldn't focus on the road. The Goddamed forest was distracting him! It was so sudden, so green. Finn couldn't remember the last time he'd seen a tree taller than eight feet. And now there was an army of them. Pine towers, unrolling all around him. Beyond that, green echoes as far as he could see.

He switched on the radio and turned it up to full blast. The moment the sound hit his ears ("Stop!" by Jane's Addiction) it all hit him again like a cannonball.

The loins. The lust. The upper-stomach tightness. Suddenly wanted flesh again. Red, bloody style. He wanted to kill, more than ever.

He pictured a map—the parts of the map he knew. If he had

thought of it, he would have looked for Meatface's phone, and he might have had a map with him now. Or that dead guy, Robinson's. He certainly wasn't using his. But Finn remembered some parts of these roads. He knew he would hit 89A at Fredonia, then buttonhook west, and the 15 should be right there to take him south to Vegas.

So let's see, he thought. *What do we have coming up along the way? Colorado City? Fredonia? Hurricane?*

He turned down Jane's Addiction, so he could think.

Hurricane?

Wouldn't that somehow fit the theme? Then, for some reason, he thought of enchiladas and realized how hungry he was. He had been running around all night. As he looked down at his emaciated body, Finn realized he hadn't eaten in a week.

Enchiladas it is, then.

He twisted his spine in a circular direction, stretching the little muscles. He wiped his dusty face with his clammy hand and took a deep breath. All his normal pain and anger fell back in its proper place, and Hell was commanded once again by psychotic hate.

"Aaahh," he muttered, and it turned into a belch. He pulled out a fresh Marlborough, let it dangle in his gums for a minute, then lit it.

Hell was almost relaxed when he spotted something curious about a mile off the road—a small corrugated tin shed, and the sunrise hit it just so that it glowed fiery yellow, stinging his eyes. It was far away, but it almost blinded him in that moment. Hell didn't take his eyes off it. He popped the clutch and coasted down the hill for a moment. As the Wagoneer slowed, his stomach pressure intensified, so much so that by the time he stopped the car completely, he felt as if he might explode. The shed shone at him like a laser pointer.

Hell threw up the brake handle and popped the driver-side door open.

Frosty pine needles welcomed his feet. He could smell them, and they crunched lightly under his boots like gritty kisses.

42

Tʜᴇʀᴇ ᴡᴇʀᴇ ꜰᴏᴜʀ people inside the shed: Yuri Pitzkov, Anders Lund, The Skull, and a bloody, blubbering man tied to the floor.

The former three were mercenaries, and their objective was almost complete. EVAC was on the way, expected to arrive in less than three hours.

The Skull was in charge, but her authority was wasted on these two men. They weren't real military. They weren't even German. They looked good enough—Yuri had all the gear and guns required and a black goatee. His eyes were blue crystal, and his bald head shone bone white and looked bulletproof. Anders was tall and blonde, the image of a proud Swedish infantryman. But The Skull thought there was something off about her subordinates. Something a little loony. Anders was gay, which made The Skull uncomfortable, and Yuri was just... too much. He had his carbine rifle, standard issue, but he had stenciled Putin's face on the side of it. Well, at least Yuri had balls. And he was Russian, which meant he could follow orders.

She was ready for EVAC and for this weird operation to be over.

"You gotta tell that story again, the one with the dresser," Anders said, holding yesterday's newspaper, open to the horoscopes, and he waved it at The Skull. "Boss, you are gonna die when you hear this story. This is a great story."

"Don't laugh, Anders. It's my life." Yuri spoke through a dark green afghan. Even through his tactical gear and parka, he felt the cold of the shed.

"Dude, come on—it's just a story!" Anders reasoned.

"It's a story about my wife."

"Ex-wife... Look, I'm sorry." Anders flicked his hand again, this time at Yuri. "It's a funny story though, hilarious actually, and you can't blame me for laughing. That's not fair." Then he returned to the horoscopes, as if he had moved past the conversation already.

"I'd like to hear *you* tell the same story, asshole," Yuri said.

"I said I'm sorry." Anders lowered his paper and smiled patiently at Yuri, as if to say, *I understand you, brother.* It was his way. His spiritual, botanical, numerological way.

The Skull fidgeted with her walkie-talkie. She had already cleaned her bandanas and reorganized her duffel. She always wore her ponytail tight, and it never seemed to need retightening. She was barely interested in what Anders and Yuri were saying. They were fruitcakes, she assumed, probably assigned to her by accident. Unless this whole mission was a wash, nothing more than a four-day scout. That all depended on the man tied to the floor. He would be the one to assign their purpose.

"All right, fine," Yuri said. "But it's true, boss. You will have no choice but to love this story." Yuri took a drink of coffee and screwed the cap back on the thermos. He looked at Anders and The Skull. He smiled at Anders, as if to say, *no hard feelings.*

Then he adjusted his utility belt, sat cross-legged on the floor, and pulled the shemagh scarf off his face. After a moment, when he had the group's attention, he began to tell the story.

43

THE PEOPLE WHO knew Yuri Pitzkov would say he lived the lives of a dozen men.

He himself would say the same thing. And although Yuri was only forty, he had traveled to over two hundred different countries, and could speak eleven languages, each fluently. He had always been able to speak these languages. It was as if Yuri had been born from eleven different mothers.

That wasn't far from the truth.

Among a traveling circus, known as "Circus Circumference," Yuri was born in a boxcar. His mother and father were both flying trapeze artists. His mother, Irina, would perform her daring act while she was nine months pregnant with baby Yuri.

Unfortunately, Irina broke her neck and died shortly after Yuri's birth. The adhesive spray she'd worn on her ankles was of a new brand, one to which she and her husband were not yet accustomed. They'd tried it once, and it turned out to be not reliable, resulting in Yuri's mother's death.

So Yuri grew up with his enormous Russian father, Oleg, but everyone in the circus raised him. Acrobats, animal tamers, riggers, and clowns from all over the world. They spoke to Yuri in their native languages. Usually they spoke to each other in English or Russian. English was the "official language" of the touring company; although, the Russians and the Ukrainians would never learn it. Because Yuri had been brought to them before he could speak or understand anything, they all spoke to him in their own tongue. This became normal, and a little bit amusing, and it continued well past baby Yuri's first words.

Yuri was adored by the good people who raised him. They were worldly, and they were kind. They raised Yuri in a world that was their own: chartered by train tracks, rotating on a schedule. States were footsteps, national borders were doorways, and the sun rose and fell in their blood the way nature preferred—reflecting off a steel rail.

Yuri's big father, Oleg, also taught him Polish, his *actual* mother's tongue.

Yuri traveled with Circus Circumference for sixteen years. Then he split, side-stepping the train rails, never to return.

And this story—the one with the dresser—wouldn't begin for another twenty years, when Yuri Pitzkov finally decided to settle down.

Twenty years later, Yuri married a small blonde woman named Ufe from Germany. She spoke only one language, and Yuri loved that about her. Hers was the only language he wanted to hear. He loved her perfectly.

He worked in a brewery, and they lived together in Munich. Eventually, Yuri came to believe that his destiny was to live a simple life: in Munich with his wife, a small house, no kids, making exquisite beer in a generic factory. He never imagined that he would be part of a small intelligence militia, telling this story to a scary frail woman named "The Skull," and Anders, for Christ's sake, in a shed in Utah in the middle of nowhere. But here he was, nonetheless.

Anders, he mused, and smiled to himself. *God bless him.* You never know who your life mates will be when you first meet them.

44

"WELL," YURI BEGAN. "My ex-wife, Ufe, turned out to be too good to be true." His accent was thick and unspecific. "She was gorgeous, for starters. Sympathetic, young. Had lots of actress money. But she wasn't insecure or self-obsessed like most actresses; in fact, she was quite service-minded and almost *too* nice.

"Her family had been Nazi folks—by default, she always said. Her grandfather went to prison many times for impersonating Hitler while he hammered together the walls of the ovens. Ufe mentioned that quite often, as if bringing it up would absolve him, or whatever. Ufe felt a kind of moral debt and regret from her family history. So much in fact, that she was always involved in some form of community service, charity donations or some crazy social penance of some sort.

"It's funny how one generation can be black as obsidian and the very next white as snow. Maybe it's a flip flop. Or reverb. Maybe it's random. Sure, I believe apple trees can bear oranges. Why wouldn't I?"

"Yuri, why are you telling me this?" The Skull interrupted. The man on the floor uttered a wet cough, as if in agreement with her. "Anders," she said. "Put the sack on his head." She looked at Yuri, but she waved a negligent hand toward the man lying on his back, near the corner of the tin shed. "See if he'll sleep some more."

Anders did so, efficiently.

"What was I saying?" Yuri asked. After a pause, and without an interjection from The Skull, he carried on. "Ah yeah, the story of the dresser."

"My wife was really amazing, that's it. She always said the right words, she cooked great, and she let me work my regular job at the brewery, even though we could both retire comfortably, a couple of thirty-five year-olds in the luxury of a super-modified renaissance village, no problem. But she asked that I only work four shifts a week. A man's gotta work, I said! For his sanity if not for money. And four shifts a week was fine with me.

"When I was at work, I could honestly say that I had no idea what Ufe did with her days. We can never imagine our wives without us, right?"

Yuri started to laugh, then abruptly stopped. A sour expression crossed his face. He seemed to turn his gaze backwards, toward the past. The others could see the focus knobs, turning like cogs in his mind.

45

Yuri's wife, Ufe (pronounced *Oof!*), was sitting in the parlor of her tall, medieval looking house, cheerfully sorting through the day's post. The unexpected bill didn't worry her in the least; she had enough money to pay the whole town's bills by accident and never notice. In fact, the crisp purity of these unopened envelopes felt like money in her hand somehow, and not the other way around. She wished she could have more luxuries and, consequently, more bills to reiterate how well she lived.

Her bare feet kneaded a soft leopard skin rug, which still had its head. Its eyes had been chemically sprayed to shine. It faced the front door, almost squarely, but tipped slightly off into the parlor, to not appear too sentient. The cat's skull nested within its head. Inside the skull were six gold bars.

It was old Jew's gold, three kilograms of it. Almost two hundred thousand euros worth. Her family had found this small fortune in a metal box near the train tracks outside of town. The box was nowhere to be accounted for. But the gold was right there in big cat's head.

Across the room, the European Semifinals were happening on TV. Ufe had the volume up.

She didn't care much for football, and she couldn't care even less for *watching* football, but her husband had choreographed a small bit for tonight's interval show. She'd told him that she would watch it, but sometime between absentmindedly turning on the television and sorting through the mail she'd forgotten. Her paranoia, like a muse, fluttered in and began to inspire her, eventually coaxing her into a trance. She was always thinking about Yuri. About his trips. How he didn't seem to want to sleep with her anymore. She missed the interval show while in her trance. She had been wondering who Yuri's mistress could be. She was sure he had one. One, or more than one. *Two*, maybe.

But she was wrong. Yuri just flirted a lot and received letters from girls in different languages that, when translated poorly, could be incriminating, and for Ufe, slightly maddening.

And when the mind became occupied with possibilities, it found that anything and everything was possible. The universe could do whatever it wanted. There were no rules in the imagination. Nor were there always facts. Ufe never brought her concerns up to Yuri because she really didn't have any reason nor any facts to bonk him over his head with. Only old letters that she had read in secret. Letters she didn't know how to read, translated in shoddy form by her phone.

When Ufe was sure she didn't have any more mail worth opening, she stood up and crossed the room to her grandfather cuckoo clock, still holding the small stack of envelopes in her hand.

The grandfather cuckoo was the house's main event. It was structured on the far wall of the parlor. It went right up the center of the wall, towards the apex of the house's lofty ceiling.

If Carlo Collodi's Master Antonio had sold his magic firewood instead of giving it to the puppet maker Geppetto to make Pinocchio, his house would have looked like this: Nuremberg chic with a fireplace big enough to park your car in. He would have had a big lynx named Fritzov instead of a peon house cat named Figaro and a miniature reef shark in a tank, instead of a stupid goldfish.

Yuri Pitzkov did not like his wife's collection of rare animals. He believed the big lynx belonged somewhere in the foothills of the German Alps, where he'd come from. And as for the Chompster, well he belonged on the shores of some perverted scientist's forgotten dreams. Yuri got along with the animals well enough, but he believed that if you wanted your money to eat and breathe, you must give it to a friend or something. He didn't even like the cat skin rug, and yes, he knew what was inside its big head.

But Yuri did love the *clock*, the grandfather cuckoo clock. He was very much into craftwork and design, and he brought this passion to his beer-making. This clock was three meters high, with an exact replica of the Munich Glockenspiel on top. It had two tiers of revolving figures that danced and acted out scenes from the middle ages. The first tier had two concentric rings that revolved in opposite directions, forcing the figures to interact. There were knights jousting atop horses, buglers that deafened the jesters with their horns, and flag fliers that sometimes blinded the saints with their banners. On the top tier, mustached men danced and twirled in a circle. It looked to Yuri as if it had been crafted in another world.

It mesmerized him, and he could look at it for long, meditative periods of time—although he didn't really look *at* it; he rather looked into it, somewhere into that fuzzy depth where his gaze would bathe for a while, and he would see things in his mind. Things other than jesters and buglers and knights clashing forever.

And then the bird would shoot out, breaking the air like a pistol shot. It would soar a third of the way through the parlor's space, scream *KA-HOOO!* and slip backwards into the clock, into that strange world where it lived. Every hour.

It also had a "do not disturb" feature, so you didn't have to hear the ruckus all the time.

The clock got more attention than the Chompster, the lynx, and the cat skin rug put together.

As Ufe crossed the large room to the clock, she aimed her attention out the window for a moment, to the front of the house.

She narrowed her eyes to be sure. No, there was no one there.

46

T HE MERCENARIES LAUGHED and grinned inside the shed. *Story time with Uncle Yuri.* Even The Skull had started to pay attention. They all knew something wonderful was about to happen, a grand unfolding of serendipity and plot.

The Skull picked up her walkie again and slowly scrolled through the channels just to make sure. But no one was online. She put it down, smiling calmly at Yuri, seemingly relaxed. She laced her fingers together, her grey business suit still smooth and wrinkle-free under her nylon parka.

After a brief silence, they heard a weak moan from the man on the ground, muffled by the sack.

Yuri waved his coffee thermos at them. "So at the time," he continued loudly, as if to claim their attention once again. "Ufe was home doing her thing. I was actually at the football match in Munich. I was a circus choreographer for a short bit, and I had some guys doing a gig at the European Semifinals—Anders, here was one of them. It was like a 'Munich Local Arts' thing.

"And strange shit started happening. It started there at the match, as Anders will tell you. But it has to do with my ex-wife, too. I promise.

"So, Ufe's at home, doing nothing. And I'm at the match, like forty miles away…"

47

"R*AGAZZI... PRONTO... IN cinque, quattro, tre...*"
Marco had Anders's weight centered on his back, balanced, and gripped tight.

The rain came lightly, stippling their naked bodies. They were cold, but even worse, they were unrehearsed. As usual. The first thing Marco became aware of was looking directly into the camera. He was at the center of the world—the European Semifinals. It was Italy against Ukraine, in Munich. The red eye above the lens of the Steadicam erased Marco's mind completely, just before it blinked off into a blank matte camera.

Well, these things never go as you plan them anyways, he thought, with some courage finally turning up. *They'll probably stop us halfway through, like always. So let's just do the opening and go home.*

But he knew. He knew they couldn't end the number until the stage manager said they could end the number. They couldn't stop until they were told to stop. They were the entertainment, and the little red lights on the Steadicams would alternate accusatory angles until they felt like finishing. The pressure of live television was strangling him.

Or was that Anders, on his back?

Anders didn't give a shit. He'd been up partying and drinking all night long, since yesterday. He smelled like old rum and cokes and looked even worse. It was four in the afternoon, and he still hadn't opened his suitcase; it was by the door in his hotel room. Anders didn't give a shit. Anders was barely here.

Well, there's only one way we can go... Marco understood everything at once.

Left!

He slowly shifted to his right foot, levering their weight onto his knee, which creaked in protest. He slid his left foot out to the side, cutting a wave of cold rainwater up off the grass. They were moving now.

Marco thought, *This ground is impossible. Mud grass. Shit...*

And yet it got worse. Almost as soon as he started moving, Marco began to feel as if he had filaments attached all over him by fishing lines. He began losing his breath, and he couldn't balance properly.

Anders, meanwhile, was loving it. He was in a half-trip, performing that last bit of the previous night's booze away. It was a perfect feeling: being able to focus, to balance. To feel your core. The rush of live performance felt like riding in a space shuttle as it broke through the clouds and then the atmosphere and eventually into outer space. Fuck Anders. Yes, he could do it. He could do a lot of things; he was very well trained.

Marco started to feel as if he were dancing on puffy crash pads, the kind that pole vaulters use. Then he started to see them—black porto-pits under his feet. *Impossible,* he thought, but he continued anyways.

Anders dug his fingers into Marco's face. His hands fastened on Marco's temples and nose. A hard thumb sank painfully into Marco's right eye socket.

Then Anders started climbing up Marco like a cat. Up and up he clambered, pulling Marco's hair, digging his right knee into his shoulder.

Marco tried to balance Anders, high stepping and crossing his legs to stay upright.

A fall will NOT happen.

What is going to happen?

Anders then pulled the clouds down from the sky. He climbed up Marco so far that he grabbed the clouds, and they came down around Marco's eyes like a low hat, blinding him.

Now there were clouds in the stadium, and the alternating red lights of the Steadicams loomed like demon eyes in the fog.

Marco fell to the grass.

The fishhooks in his body pulled him in different directions, but Anders's weight pushed him down. He landed on his back in the wet grass, and Anders came down knees-first on top of him. Marco's back seized up, like fingers in the back of his ribs clenching. The weight forced his breath out of him, and his will to stay upright died at once.

A zombie popped out of the fog, to his right. Followed by another, behind it.

A third zombie, and then a fourth. They were all around him now, seeming to notice him. They didn't notice Anders or the camera guys or the thousands of people in the stands, but they noticed Marco Valoso, and they began their irreversible shuffle towards him.

All that Yuri Pitzkov saw from where he sat was two men—*his* two men—in a dramatic entanglement. They started to move, with the lights shifting, and they looked pretty good, and the music was loud enough. It had started rather well, Yuri admitted to himself.

Then both went down. Anders landed squarely on top of Marco's upper chest. It looked like a sparring blow, one of the finishing variety. Anders rolled off quickly, and Marco laid on his back with his arms and legs up in the air, waving them like seaweed, and then he passed out. Anders bolted upright and surveyed him, then knelt at his side. He didn't know what the director and the cameras were doing, but he didn't care. He thought he had killed his partner!

Back in the coach's office, Marco slowly came back to consciousness. Before he opened his eyes, he knew he was in trouble. His neck had been badly sprained, but not broken. The pain saturated his throat and neck. He lay on the floor in a semi-daze, trying to focus on the pallid grid of the drop ceiling. He felt as if he had been struck in the neck with a sledgehammer while two grandmothers yanked at his ears. *What happened?* he wondered. Then he remembered fishhooks in him, and zombies coming to pull him apart.

Was that a hallucination? Or some kind of dream? What happened to the performance?

He had no fear of zombies. Or fishhooks, for that matter. Marco's only living fear was that of failing performances. And lasting neck injuries. Marco thought for a moment, lying on his back. He tried to remember what had happened. He'd been at a gig, he knew. An awesome one. European Semifinals, in... at first it didn't come to him. Then he remembered: *Munich!* Yuri's hometown! Yuri and Anders had been there. Yes, Anders had been a lazy shithead, and Marco had been upset about it. Then during the show, some kind of attack had almost killed Marco. Something had happened.

As he lay on the floor of the coach's office, he tried to replay the sequence of events. But his thoughts were jumbled, and they scattered like rats every time he heard a sound. He felt a swelling, like a scream in his head. It sounded like a waterfall being turned on and off. Marco slowly realized that it was the crowd outside. The game was back on, and it was a tight one by the sound of it.

Marco closed his eyes and prayed. He was an Italian Catholic, after all. As soon as he got through the good part of the prayer, he heard a familiar voice—Yuri's, with its loud, non-specific accent. As a wave of crowd noise receded, Marco opened his eyes. He found he couldn't turn his head in any direction.

Yuri's voice became clear. "Is there anything you need, bud? Can you move? Are you ok?"

Marco blinked twice in slow motion. In his own way, he was checking his brain for damage. "Whiskey... In my locker," he said. A tiny fishhook of a smile pulled at the corner of his mouth.

Yuri shoved through the blue door of the coach's office, leaving a wary, unhappy crew of people inside. The medic was with Marco now, and an ambulance would be here in a moment. Goddamn, this was awful.

One of the walls in the stadium's labyrinth was lined with beige, built-in lockers. Most of them had large, white name tags for the performers and staff of today's event.

Yuri felt heavy for losing his best guy, Marco. This would reflect very poorly on Yuri's reputation as a choreographer, but that didn't concern him too much now. Not compared to Marco's wellbeing.

This was humiliating for everyone. Actually, "humiliating" would be an understatement. In front of the entire world, live, in *high-definition,* this situation was downright flattening. All three of them had become the subject of international laughter. They were the *real* halftime show; the rest of the interval was spent replaying the fall with various commentary in myriad languages. Yuri would have understood many of these languages. But instead, all he understood was ridicule—and regret for not having demanded royalties for his dancers. The number of times they replayed the blooper on television was just plain stupid. You would have thought they'd opened a McDonald's on the moon.

Yuri walked along the wall of lockers, thinking about the simple and honest pain of a circus fall. The kind of snafu that had killed his mother. The stark job-related horror. It was foolish, abusive, and *whorish*.

This is what happens to people when God gets drunk, he thought.

Yuri trundled along the wall, ashamed and, admittedly, a little afraid, until he found the locker labeled "M. Valoso" and opened it.

He yelled, "HUP!" and jumped backwards. He stared at the open locker with his hands up, almost a fighting stance.

He realized he was looking at a bird claw. It was long and hairy and hideous. And it smelled; Yuri could almost feel it in his nose. Not strong but not weak.

He reached into the locker and touched it, curiously.

48

Y URI'S HEART WAS hammering. He had not been expecting this. He had been expecting whiskey and clothes. Not this *thing*. But really, why should it startle him? Sure it was weird and a little scary looking (as if it wasn't dead but only sleeping), but it was still just an object; it might not even be real. It might be a fake bird claw, just a figurine. No different than a skull or a Buddha. Or a book-end for some gothic kid's bookshelf.

But the *smell* was what made it real. It smelled like bacteria and formaldehyde. Yuri knew Anders was into crystals and astrology and other slightly occult things, but Anders couldn't be into this. The guy showered three times a day! Yuri pictured Marco giving this thing to Anders as a gift, and he laughed. The look on Anders's face, a man who'd grown up on *Will and Grace* and knew the exact amount of protein he consumed. That was a face Yuri would pay to see.

He thought of Ufe, feeling guilty for even *looking* at this aberration.

Yuri realized that he had been holding his breath. As he righted himself, he smelled the corpse-hand-thing once again and wished he was anywhere else but there. Naturally, he thought of home. That old Nurenburg Chic. The grandfather clock. He imagined unlocking his front door and walking in, into the smell of the house, knowing Ufe was there, small and warm and waiting for him. He could almost smell her, as he walked into her aura. He could feel her in his skin. Now, he *could* smell her. A nostalgic pang chimed in his stomach.

He wished he could be there, at that special moment, opening the front door.

And suddenly, all at once, there he was.

His right hand turned the doorknob and shoved it open.

He burst into his foyer, sweating, shocked from the sight of the claw in the locker, not yet startled by the sudden change of atmosphere.

The world slowly changed around Yuri. He felt a quaking sensation, and strips of the wall where the lockers had been started dropping. The world became the texture of fabric, and it fell away in ribbons, like a photograph through a shredder. Behind the lockers, he could see his living room. He started to feel the warmth of it. Now he could smell it.

Ufe was in the parlor, halfway between her chair and the grandfather cuckoo. Her back was to the wall, arms straight out as if holding an imaginary door closed. She gaped at him in horror, envelopes scattered around her on the floor.

49

Bᴀᴄᴋ ɪɴ ᴛʜᴇ coach's office, Anders was sitting next to Marco, feeling guilty and ashamed of himself. He wasn't sure what he could do to help Marco. He felt alone. He didn't have a liaison or presenter with him. No manager. Anders was now alone in Munich, and he didn't speak a word of television.

He left Marco and went out to the hallway to find Yuri. Or at least find the whiskey.

He didn't find Yuri. But he did find a closed locker with a name tag on it that read "M. Valoso." The boss was probably in the bathroom down the hall.

One locker, halfway down the hallway, stood open, and an upsetting smell, almost like rotten hose water, not strong but not weak, emanated from it. Anders ignored it.

He opened the locker that supposedly had Marco's name tag on it. He did a double-take, not recognizing the bag as his partner's. But he saw a bag, some whiskey, and a name tag that with his name, so he didn't think much of it. Maybe Marco got a new bag. He grabbed the bottle of whiskey and the bag of clothes, glancing again, furtively, at the open locker down the hall.

After a moment of hesitation, he began to walk towards it, curious about what might be inside. The smell coming from it repulsed him; it reminded him of when he would walk by a hedge and smell a dead animal rotting in it. Dead animal smell—awful, even worse than a room full of neglected, worn football uniforms. But this smell was not *so* bad. It had some charisma, he supposed, like the charming welcome of hose water on a hot summer day. If something was dead in there, perhaps it was a tiny mouse atop a stack of brand new books.

He reached the opened locker and froze.

Anders felt a pang in his stomach, similar to what Yuri had felt. He almost dropped the whiskey bottle from his right hand. He pulled himself together with urgency and stumbled back.

He saw a gym bag, purposefully squashed into the locker. It was dark blue, Adidas, and utterly normal. On top of the gym bag, a little fallen to the right, between the bag and the wall of the locker, was a severed claw from some kind of monster, or prehistoric-looking bird.

"Oh, shit," he said, drawing a long, slow breath, despite the smell. He rose to his tip-toes and snuck backwards a few more feet.

Then he took a swig from the bottle he was holding, capped it, and brought it all back into the office, leaving what was in the locker where it lay.

If Marco was happy to see Anders, he didn't show it. Perhaps he *couldn't* show it.

"Where'd you get *that*?" he said, gesturing toward the whiskey bottle. "Big one." Marco lifted his right arm off the ground, gesturing toward the whiskey bottle.

Anders didn't know how Marco couldn't recognize his own whiskey bottle, especially since he had sent for it in the first place. But placing that thought aside, he stepped forward and handed it to him. He didn't know what to say.

When Marco seemed satisfied, not making any further requests but rather lying with his eyes closed in discomfort again, Anders grabbed his own bag and went back out to the lockers.

He was going to look at that claw again.

50

"*WAS... SCHEISSE!*" UFE screamed. Yuri's face was like hers, open-eyed and dazed, his black hair a mess atop his head. They stared at each other with the front door wide open.

The television was speaking, and Marco and Anders's blooper was cycling on. Yuri heard one of the commentators yell, "Oof!" when the fall happened, and Ufe blinked.

"*Wo ist ihr auto?*" she said, glancing out front, through the parlor window she had looked through a moment before. *Where's your car?*

51

ANDERS LEFT THE coach's office and went back into the hall-way. There he stopped for a moment, looking towards the locker with the claw in it. It remained open and unattended.

He adjusted the gym bag on his shoulder, ran a hand through his bristly blonde hair, and sighed. His shoes were the only things to be heard beneath the distant, undulating roar of the crowd. They clacked slowly down the hall, and he was there again, facing the dead claw. The scent emanated from it was faint and yellow.

Yuri was still nowhere to be seen.

Anders thought he should throw the claw in the trash. He didn't really know why. But when he checked the locker door for the name that was taped to it, he froze in disbelief.

"M. Valoso."

At that same moment, Anders saw the claw again, four talons curled in a sort of human gesture, leaning off the bag. It was nes-tled into the wall of the locker, and it seemed to be pointing at him.

Anders was struck by a moment of clarity. He knew this gym bag. *What's blue, Adidas, and Italian all over?* He sometimes had said that to Marco. How he loved Napoli and low fashion. He checked the name tag, and sure enough, he was right. It was big and laminated, like his own, and it had a photo of Marco's face on it.

The claw pointed at Anders, as if to say, "*You* know what's going on here!"

Anders grimaced at the display and brought the back of his hand to his mouth. He needed to do something now—no one else could. *Shit,* he thought. *Marco's paralyzed, and Yuri's probably off yelling at the production team about it. And now there's a severed body part between me and Marco's gym bag, and it reeks like nothing I've ever smelled before!*

He was alone. He heard the noise of the game upstairs lull then swell like a dark storm.

Then Anders got an idea, and it made him laugh. The sound was strange in the empty hallway, but Anders felt better already. He might not be alone after all. He went down the hall to the men's bathroom, pushed the door open and called, "Yuri?"

There was no answer.

"Boss?"

Okay, maybe he really was alone. Anders let the bathroom door fall shut and went back to Marco's locker. The claw had rolled over onto its back. Before it had pointed at him, saying, "You the man." Now it offered the same gesture, but upside-down. Now it was saying, "Come here."

Anders stepped forward, forgetting that he was a germaphobe. It stank, but Anders found that he kind of liked the smell after all. He didn't feel alone anymore, and he was grateful to the hand for that. *Did he just call it a hand?* It was a *claw*—nothing with scales and old feathers has hands. It was a claw. Or a foot. It was not a hand.

He drew a line down its palm, slowly, with his index finger. Then he gripped it in his own hand, as if to shake on a business deal.

Anders un-shouldered his gym bag and put the claw into it. Then he grabbed Marco's bag and slung it over his other shoulder, when a few glass airplane nippers clinked together. *Wrong fucking*

whiskey, too, he thought. He walked briskly back towards the coach's office.

He had the right bag now, but he didn't feel any better about Marco. He felt responsible for clobbering him, and the more time that passed, the more foolish and ashamed he felt. He wished for Marco to be all better.

He wished that more than anything.

52

"MY CAR, IT'S... I guess it's at the arena?" Yuri said. He couldn't believe where he was. He looked at his hands, then around the entryway of his house. His eyes fell upon the cat-skin rug, and he gasped. At first couldn't tell what was wrong with it. Then it was obvious. Its head was missing.

"Stop," said The Skull. She was paying attention now, her walkie-talkie all but forgotten on the floor. "I'm hearing two stories at once. Yuri, what is this all about?"

"I'm getting there, boss," he said, smiling. "I promise."

"Get there faster. The sun is up. We have work."

"Yes ma'am," he said.

But he knew he would keep her interest, no matter how long he took to tell the story. He'd sunk the hook, and The Skull couldn't wiggle it out until it was over. Yuri was sure.

Before continuing, Yuri gave Anders a woeful look. It was quick, but The Skull was able to catch it. Anders only smiled. *I know*, the smile said. *It was my idea that you should tell it.*

"So," said Yuri. "Ufe looked at me so accusingly that I actually felt *guilty*, like I had blood all over my hands or something. I'm serious. I'm standing there in the entranceway, with my wife in the parlor gaping at me, and I felt guilty! Like she had been right all along! Right about something big! I couldn't—for the life of me— think of what that was."

"Wait, hold on!" Anders interrupted. "The claw!" He looked to The Skull. "Yuri, explain to the boss that Marco *had* this claw before."

The Skull looked at both of them like they were crazy. She blinked at Anders and made a slow winding gesture with her hand: *Go on.*

"He brought it with him," Anders said. "He got it in a package from some Navajo man in Arizona when he was traveling across the U.S. Marco said he was like a warlock or a shaman, I think. Anyway, this guy says that he put a spell on this mummified rooster claw. That for a short time any man could touch the claw and be granted one wish. But the wish would cost an enormous amount in karma, 'for fate cannot agree to be willed,' he said. 'Wish well or wish null.' Marco didn't believe him, of course—although he is superstitious. Or at least, he *was*."

"Yeah," Yuri said. "*Now*, who knows? He's either dead or extremely superstitious."

The Skull stared at them both, not believing. She began to make her finger-twirling gesture again (she loved to give commands without speaking), when Anders started up again.

"Get this," he continued. "Marco didn't open the package until he got to Munich. No wonder he was trembling like he'd been before we went out on the field. Something was happening to him. Marco's not typically a worrisome guy; he's strong—he's from fucking Naples! But he was acting weird and nervous during our warm-up, before we went on. He wasn't stretching like he normally did. And *when* we went on, he disappeared. I've never seen him like that. It was like I was clinging onto a tree with no soul in it. Clinging there, like a dead tree, and I was trying to hang on while it moved... Eugh, no wonder! The claw had done something to him! It was really ugly, and it smelled bad, and it changed him somehow. I guess because he made a wish, or something." Then Anders blinked, realizing he had just interrupted *his* boss, stealing part of his tale. "Sorry, Yuri. You got a funny way of telling stories. That was pertinent."

"Anders, this is a story about my ex-wife," said Yuri.

"Yes, it is, sure," said Anders.

"And the dresser," reminded Yuri.

"Yes sir," said Anders. Then he turned and winked at The Skull, his boss's boss.

Yuri continued. "So apparently Marco opens this thing, this *package* at the game, and doesn't tell us. And then all this weird shit, as I've said before, starts happening to us. To me and my wife and to everyone."

The Skull was straight-faced, watching the two men patiently, sitting on her flight case. She still didn't believe them. But she liked the story nonetheless, partly because it seemed to be going somewhere good, but also because it took place in Germany and had it Germans in it. She thought of Anders as a German, too, even though he was Swedish. He had lived in Munich (where he'd met Yuri), and his accent was good, so The Skull respected him. She watched the two ex-circus performers-turned-mercenaries with subdued amusement. In her crisp grey suit and perennially tight ponytail, she very much looked like she was their boss.

Her boss, "The Brain," was as obscure as the devil himself—no one she knew had actually met him; it was almost as if he didn't exist. But he was known to have eyes and operations everywhere. No one knew how many, but they were mostly Germans, and they worked happily for him. The Skull, Yuri, and Anders were a small satellite of an operation, mostly reconnaissance, floating out there in the sprawling roads of Northern Arizona and Utah.

The Brain had sent The Skull and her guys on a simple capture assignment: four days, planned and supplied, in which they would locate and detain Magnus Johannsen. They were free to ask him questions if they spoke only about Thunder, Project Fontaine, and

Magnus's son, Jameson Johannsen. Time was limited, and any information regarding what was yet to come was extremely urgent.

Magnus Johannsen, the only known employee of Fontaine still living, was allegedly responsible for yesterday's decimation of Thunder. He was tied to the floor with a sack on his head, as the four of them waited for EVAC to arrive. Johannsen would then be taken somewhere unknown, and The Skull and her guys would get in their Ryder truck and disappear, waiting for their direct deposit somewhere.

But for now, The Skull had questions. "What about the other locker? The first one, with the whiskey bottle?" she demanded.

"Different M. Valoso!" said Yuri. "It was some guy taking photographs for a publicity thing. I think he was with the eight-year-olds. Eight-year-olds and whiskey, hey?"

Anders chimed in, as if defending himself. "There are over half a million M. Valosos in Italy. I looked it up. Like, one in twenty men are named Marco or Mario or Massimo Valoso. And I'm sure they all travel with whiskey."

The Skull shook her head. The shed was beginning to lighten with the morning sun.

Suddenly, the man on the floor let out a long, anguished sigh. He flexed his arms and legs against his ropes. Perhaps he thought he could writhe free with some muscle. Veins bulged in his elbows and forearms. The three soldiers looked at him but without much interest. It wasn't yet time.

Yuri continued: "Anders stood there with this claw in his hand, and these bags on his shoulders. And he was feeling a little sick because this claw was... well, Anders?"

"Oh my God, it was so gross. I could feel the weight of it, and it was like I had an extra hand! It was literally as big as both my hands put together. Marco had said it was rooster claw, but it didn't look like that. It was disgusting." Anders leaned back and looked from

Yuri to The Skull. His Swedish blue eyes were wide and dead serious.

Yuri went on: "Anders wished in that moment, yes, that Marco would be all better. And then he went back inside the coach's office."

<h1 style="text-align:center">53</h1>

ANDERS PUSHED THROUGH the blue doors and stopped in his tracks.

Marco was squirming on the floor. But he didn't seem to be in pain. Instead, he looked euphoric, as if he were cuddling with the floor. He smiled and writhed and stretched out on the linoleum, as others watched him with growing interest. Marco started to lift his head and then quickly reached for the orthopedic brace that had been fashioned to his neck. He snapped it off and tossed it aside. Slowly he stood up and rolled his wrists and neck. He couldn't believe it. He felt perfect.

Anders stood agape, positively dripping at him. Just five minutes ago, he had dropped all his weight onto Marco's face, from two meters up, and heard the crack. He had smothered him! And here Marco stood, not a mark on him. He was fresh and without bruises. Without scars or lines as well, not even the ancient cigarette burn on his right forearm, the one his "amici" had tagged on him when he was seven years old.

Marco had healed.

He looked at Anders, not confused but rather with a knowing smirk on his face. He looked like someone who had naught to say because all words were a thousand words beyond their time. He was somehow advanced. Advanced a thousand words.

Marco looked around the coach's office. The people stared at him like an audience. If the crowd upstairs could see this, they would scream so loudly the cheers could be heard in Berlin. But down here, no one spoke.

He nodded his head with a kind of kingly, all-knowing approval, then turned and walked calmly out of the office. Eight-year-olds, parents, and producers were left to marvel at nothing.

Anders followed, but once he was outside the arena, he couldn't find Marco. Anders was not particularly relieved by Marco's recovery. In fact, he realized, standing out in the dark night, he was trembling.

Anders waited out by the trucks with his cellphone in his hand. Yuri never called. Nor did Marco.

After a while, he got in a cab and went home.

54

THE SKULL WAS still listening, although she did not enjoy being the second party on the block. Not while she was on the job and especially not while there was a man tied to the floor.

She picked up her walkie-talkie again, but instead of scanning the channels, she resigned it to her lap. She looked at Anders and Yuri, who were now smiling at each other.

The Skull wanted the rest of the story. Fast and full, so they could go on with the procedure, which seemed to be commencing early somehow. She wanted everything, right now. But then she noticed that Anders and Yuri seemed to be sharing a different kind of enjoyment altogether. They looked as if they were getting to something. *Were they really just telling a story?* The Skull didn't think so. As the shed gathered light, so did her mind. Things were becoming clear.

So why all this fancy footwork? she wondered. *Were they stalling? Diverting?*

The man on the floor started hissing, toothy breaths that were anything but regular.

"Come on, you two fucks, keep talkin'," The Skull said. "Tell me about the fucking dresser!"

55

L IGHT SPILLED THROUGH the forest in blue glittering tendrils. Trees were both plenty and sparse. Pine needles covered the ground, softening the world.

Hell Finn put his right hand on the side of his Wagoneer, spun himself to face the woods, and bowed.

A thin mist approached his feet.

He straightened up and proceeded through the forest, heading straight for the shed, the thing driving his lust. Whatever was in there was magnetic, and it made his guts want to ball up. It wasn't a great feeling, but it was important to Hell. It came with a sense of duty as well as a kind of craving.

He moved swiftly, like a black ghost. A vapid, yet stimulated horror, into the woods.

56

Y URI WAITED FOR everyone (except the man on the floor) to get quiet. Then he continued.

"So Ufe's freaked out, and she has no idea that I was just at the arena, just before. And *I* don't know what's happening either. She's looking at me crazy, but a different kind of crazy, like she knows what's up, somehow. I don't know why! She was furious. *Wiley eyed*, I think is the expression.

"So, she creeps away, and I go into the parlor to sit down and ask myself what's going on..."

57

Yuri sat down in the same armchair that Ufe had sat in a moment before. It was still warm.

He tried to gather his bearings, staring hard at the cat-skin rug, which had been badly mutilated. Its head was gone—*ripped off* was more like it. A disgusted cry scampered up his throat, but before it could be released, it broke apart and bled slickly back down to nowhere.

Reality was in question. The wall had fallen away like bloody ribbons, and behind it was his house. He couldn't understand how.

He gripped the brass-studded arms of the chair. He had to squeeze his hands to keep from trembling. His knuckles were white and bloodless, like his face. After a moment that felt strangely long and quiet, Yuri began to rise, to find Ufe and see what was going on. But as Yuri leaned his weight forward to rise, he turned his head and saw Ufe. She was moving fast towards him, with a large cedar wood chest on top of her head. Her skinny arms were balancing it, and her head was cocked to one side as it perched on her neck, head, and one shoulder.

58

SHE CLOSED IN on Yuri, grinning a desperate grin that rushed at him from the other side of madness, wide eyes like headlights on a fast approaching Mack truck.

The chest was bigger than Ufe, more than twice her size. The veins in her hands and elbows bulged from her skin. They looked like fat earthworms struggling to breach the surface of her tiny frame.

Rather than throw the dresser at Yuri, which would have exuded her strength, she tipped her whole body forward and fell, directing her momentum so the dresser would land squarely on top of Yuri. But she was too slow; the weight of the chest had put pressure on her legs and halved her power, and Yuri was able to roll backwards out of the chair and land on the floor just in time.

The dresser crashed into the chair with a loud bang. The floor thrummed as the chair and the dresser exploded apart. Yuri fell onto his back, shielding his face with his forearms, as pieces of his chair and cedar chest scampered over him. He scuttled backwards on his heels and hands and came to a stop underneath the grandfather cuckoo clock.

Ufe jumped up to see what she had done. That suspicious *bastard* never expected his pippy-dippy blue-eyes to do something like this!

She hoisted her hair out of their pigtails. She did not shake her hair to plum nor comb her fingers through it. The lumpy nest of blonde made her look twice as crazy. She walked around the mess, over the cat-skin rug, towards Yuri. Her hair veiled her face, which was flushed and smoldering underneath. The grin was gone.

She stood over Yuri, her long arms hanging by her side. With her feet together and her hair in tatters, she looked like a day-lit ghost, an ambulatory doll.

"I read your letters," she said.

"What...."

"Åsa from Sweden?"

"Who—"

"Giuseppina? From Ostia?" She was breathing hard, working herself up, accelerating past exhaustion and into a panic.

"Ufe," Yuri started. "Baby those women don't—I mean, I never! There's nothing there!" He was dumbstruck. And innocent. Her display was intense and ridiculous. "Those women are just women! I had nothing doing with them—with anyone!"

"Silence!" she spat. One of the drawers from the dresser had fallen out of the frame, and it lay on the floor by Yuri's feet. Ufe floated over to it and stepped up onto it. She hooked her neck downward and stared at Yuri. She resembled a woman who had hanged herself to avoid heat exhaustion. "They both said they love you. That doesn't read like nothing! It doesn't *smell* like nothing!"

"Baby, people say that sometimes. The word *love* can be mis-used! Or interpreted in lots of different ways. Shit, baby, did you just try to kill me?"

"Ha!" she barked. "Don't be so dramatic. And don't turn this on me. I just tried to bruise you. I would have punched you in the face, but it wouldn't've hurt you nearly enough. You ruined my life, Yuri! You trashed it like garbage! Everything we had! And I *knew* it! I did the research!"

"What research, baby? That's impossible. You're being fucking crazy!"

The taught, quartz-like frame of Ufe's body softened a little, and she shifted her weight from one bare foot to the other. The cedar wood plate that had once been the bottom of the drawer (and was now the top) sagged under her feet. She still appeared to be hanging by a rope, but she was merely suspended by a feeble plane of cedar wood. She brought up a hand to rub the right side of her neck where the dresser had been perched, then dropped it back to her side.

"What research?" She scoffed, as if all her long months of work had gone *impossibly* unnoticed, as if she had sculpted a twenty-foot sand mermaid, and Yuri had stood in front of it and said, "*What sand mermaid?*"

"You've been skipping work! You've been hard to reach! Trips to Munich? Trips to Rome? Gee, isn't Rome just minutes away from... *Ostia*?"

"Babe—"

"You told me you had a gig at the stadium tonight, and then you come *shouldering* in here like the police or something? You're being suspicious of me now! A classically mental thing to do! You're scared because you have a guilty conscience. Look at your hair, for Christ's sake!" She rubbed her neck again, absently. "And what, you forgot about this gig? This so-called big event? You can't keep your lies straight! That's the thing about lies, Yuri—"

But as she opened her mouth to say "Yuri" the cuckoo bird exploded into her face. Her head flipped back in a bramble of blonde hair. "Yuri" sounded more like "yup!"

"That's the thing about lies, *yup!*"

Ufe fell backwards, and with a worrisome snapping sound, she landed on her back. Her head hit the chair, and she fell unconscious. She looked like as if she had failed to hang herself and died instead from heat exhaustion.

KA-HOOOOO!

Ufe was not permanently injured. She was just taking a little break.

She needed one.

59

"T HAT'S *IT*?" THE Skull hollered. "Well, what the fuck happened?" She had put down her walkie-talkie and was digging through a duffel bag for something to eat, all while furtively— *doubtfully*—watching the man on the floor.

"Yuri's wife tried to murder him," Anders said. "Which makes him a badass. And she did it with like the dumbest weapon."

The Skull ignored this. She looked at Yuri with millimeter-thin patience.

"There are lots of stories, boss, but that one was the one about the dresser."

"Yuri, what about the FUCKING CLAW?"

A moment of silence hung thick between them. The Skull didn't move. She was gripping the duffel bag and looking at Yuri. She seemed to be holding her breath.

"The claw is here, boss," Yuri said finally. "Anders has it."

The Skull's eyes pounced. Anders flinched, then reluctantly smiled.

The man on the floor pulled at his restraints with unbelievable strength. His muscles stretched and bulged. The bones in his elbows levered into the floor, and he started to scream. Anders leapt over to him, gratefully breaking eye contact with The Skull.

"Where is it, Anders?" she said, then added, "And what's the real deal with it anyway?"

217

60

As Hell approached the shed, his grin widened.

He looked like a bipedal mole. He walked on his toes with bent knees. He heard yelling in his head, and he wanted to mask the sounds by screaming louder into the wilderness. But he wouldn't, *no*. It would blow up his spot. He could see a man-eating tiger pacing the floor of his mind, working furiously to find a way out—to find a way outside and roar like the wind. But he wouldn't make a sound, not yet.

His ego, the Apocalyptic Gunslinger, was ready with all his imaginary combo guns in hand, flexed like a spring in a switchblade. His stomach rolled with anticipation. This old shed—whatever it was—had become anonymous now. But soon this shed would have a name and a place in history—he was certain about that.

The milky blue light of dawn changed to orange, with an imperceptible sleight of hand.

He spotted an owl thirty feet ahead, and a bit to the right, guarding an oak tree. A light brown cat owl. Hell smiled at the sight, imagining with childlike wonder what his new powers could do to it. He would *not* have smiled, not at nature, not at anything.

The forest had a lush diversity of ponderosas, firs, junipers, and oaks, all mingling in a great mountainous soirée. None of it held any esteem for Hell Finn. But now, seeing the animals made him smile. Not with admiration but with destruction. That made Hell feel just fucking great. He felt connected to them all. The wildlife was his lure, his disposable muse. And Hell was their death, their reaper, their God. Hell thought to himself that he had better hold on to his last four teeth; he had a lot more smiling to do.

He took three slow steps toward the bird and whispered, "Boo!"

The owl ticked its wise head, remaining smug on the oak.

Hell began to mumble under his breath. Something like, *I'll poof you, motherfucker. I said BOO, you fucking bird!*

But the bird was unphased. It didn't flip upside-down and die, nor pop out of existence like Meatface had. It didn't get eaten by a sudden lion as Hell had hoped it would. It just sat there, alive.

It looked at Finn, lifted one foot, and roosted one-legged on the branch.

"Son of a fucker,' Hell breathed, marching silently upwards, toward the beckoning shed.

61

ALL EYES WERE on The Skull.

She agreed that the man on the floor was beginning to turn in a bad way. It was up to her to decide what to do. Bewildered, she began mumbling in German, mulling over what might have gone wrong in self-discussion. There was no way that bamboo could grow this fast, and they did not have a plan to parallel this improbable course of nature. If this man were to die, that would mean the bamboo–their "organic torture stalks"—had grown roughly seven inches in only eight hours.

Bamboo can grow at incredible rates, sometimes as fast as a foot in a day. But from a sprout to a dagger in an old sandy patch of dirt overnight was impossible.

Yuri, still sitting in his chair, began to stretch. He cracked his neck twice. He always cracked his neck; it never reminded him of his mother.

He ran a giant hand over the smooth boulder of his head. "It's time," he said.

The Skull put down her walkie and walked over to the man on the floor. "Mr. Johannsen," she said. "Mr. Johannsen, talk to us. Where is Jameson? Where is your son? This is important, Mr. Johannsen! *Speak!*"

Yuri unzipped his parka, revealing his tactical gear underneath, and flung it away. But instead of joining The Skull and the man on the floor, he picked up his M4 carbine rifle off the floor and stood up.

He held the gun across his chest and watched the two on the floor, silently. His head shone a milky orange in the morning haze, a cue ball of fire. (His "long black Russian hair" had always been just a feature he added into his stories, included in his poetic license. He was an artist, after all.)

Yuri's outfit—a bulletproof vest, thermals, extra handguns, grenades—made him a video game character that you could smell. Here was a circus acrobat covered with guns, with a bald head and a focus like a mutant shark. You see these types of guys in the subways in Europe and Africa. New York, too, sometimes. They'll search your bag, and you'll be nervous that their machine gun will go off in your face by accident.

The Skull moved quickly. She dropped to her knees next to the man on the floor. She yanked a small wool blanket off his torso, pulled off his hood, then grabbed the lapels of his shirt with both hands and started pulling him off the bamboo plants, forgetting momentarily that his arms and ankles were still tied down.

"Fuck!" she screamed. "Knives, guys! Mr. Johannsen! *Mr. Johannsen*!" She pulled on Magnus, trying to get him off the bamboo while the guys got knives to free him. But she couldn't move him; they had grown in already. He was rooted to the floor. The Skull planted one foot on the ground and tried to yank. "Come on!" she wheezed. She now had both feet planted by the man's armpits and was pulling with all her strength. God help him if he should suddenly tear free. There would be no grace in that scenario. But The Skull wasn't thinking that far ahead. She was flexing against the idea of this whole thing—not quite panicking but somehow lost in the moment. "Shit!" she yelled, throwing her weight backwards, as if pulling up a rotted yet stubborn floorboard. Magnus didn't move, but he screamed. He screamed as if he were being ripped in half.

Anders cut his bonds, but it was too late. Magnus was stuck.

He exhaled his last breath. It was only a few bubbles. Blood flowed freely out of his mouth and nose. It spilled over his face and ears like a volcano and into the dirt floor behind his head.

It was not supposed to happen this fast. Nobody could have expected this; it was by all rights impossible.

Their operation had failed.

Anders stood at the back of the shed, opposite Yuri, with his carbine crossed against his chest. If he was disgusted, he didn't show it. He was very well trained.

A silence shrouded the room. It was the first actual quiet since the man on the floor had started blubbering, halfway back in Yuri's story.

But within this silence, the three soldiers sensed something new. A set of footsteps shuffling on pine needles from the woods outside. And low, lunatic utterances.

They all froze. All that moved in he shed were their eyeballs, which scampered over every surface.

62

THE MAN ON the floor had been Jimmy Johannsen's father, the last living cofounder of the Fontaine Project.

When Fontaine was raided and shut down, Magnus Johannsen was restrained from returning to Thunder and his family. It was early 2001, only three weeks after Alice became pregnant with the twins.

Magnus was tried in a military court. The building, Fontaine, did not belong to any state county and was many dark roads from any town.

Magnus's estate was impounded, his money cleaned and recirculated, mostly into the government. Alice was left in Thunder, with nowhere else to go. The government gave her a trailer and plot of land roughly the size of a postage stamp. She did odd jobs and handled the kids on her own, until she got that house. The worst house in town. It didn't even want to stand up. Now Magnus was dead, having outlived Alice by only six hours. Alice had only lived long enough to see her daughter die, her twins pulled apart in New York City, of all places, her life torn to shreds once more.

63

THERE WAS A bang on the door, like a boxer's jab into sheet metal.

Then silence.

"ARE THERE ANY FUCKFACES IN THERE?"

More silence.

Definitely not EVAC.

Outside the shed, Finn was rubbing his crotch with his Magnum in his right hand, his left hand swinging his shotgun in wide circles, aiming all over the woods and the shed.

There was only one door to the shed. But Hell Finn didn't know it, so he circled around to investigate the sides and back.

A lone Ryder truck stood leaning at an angle near the south wall, with no one inside.

The Skull stood up fast and stepped away from the body on the floor. She gestured to Yuri and Anders. She flicked her right hand towards the right side of the doorway. *He's circling. One man. You two go out the front and split sides. I stay here with Magnus. Defend us.*

They nodded.

The shed door clanged open. Yuri and Anders stepped out and mirrored each other back to back with their guns up, ready to lock on anything that would move.

They began bisecting the perimeter of the building. But before they could take two steps, a sudden scratching sound made them both turn their attention to the roof.

Something was coming towards them, crawling fast.

A grenade fell off the south side of the roof and landed prankishly on Anders's shoulder.

Anders leapt backwards and threw his rifle on the pine needles. His hands flew up like birds. He whirled his arms around and dove away from the grenade. But before his feet could leave the ground, it exploded.

Anders Lund made his final leap in a million pieces.

"*HOOOO!* That's some good aim you got!" Finn cheered. "Yeah, it's getting better!"

Yuri was already on the side of the shed, the north side. He rushed towards the back, gun leveled.

When he got to the corner where the north side switched to the back, he crouched, introduced himself with three shots, then peeked around. A wave of white smoke ran past him. It smelled of burnt sap and entrails. *Anders,* he thought, grimly.

Yuri knew that this man (whoever he was) wasn't behind him, because The Skull would have spotted and tagged him from inside, if he had crossed the front door.

He hoped that The Skull hadn't suffered from the grenade blast. He thought the wall of the shed had held, but Yuri didn't see any of the details. He had been in pursuit along the north side of the shed since he saw the bomb, small and black, drop onto his friend like a snake.

He rounded the back corner and saw there was no one behind the shed. For a moment he thought he was in the clear. Then he remembered something that made him freeze in place.

Shit, he thought. *Wasn't there a ladder to the roof? On the south wall by the Ryder truck—*

"Hey, fuckface."

Yuri looked up.

64

H ELL FINN WAS standing on the edge of the roof, directly above Yuri's head. His shotgun dangled lengthily between his legs.

They looked at each other. Yuri's machine gun still paralleled the ground.

"Boom," Hell said under his breath. He halfway expected shotgun pellets to fly out of his mouth and splatter this small man like a wild turkey in a doghouse. But that didn't happen. "Worth a try," he muttered. Yuri didn't move.

During the blast that had killed Anders, the loaded rifle that Anders had thrown on the ground was incinerated. The full cartridge of bullets went off all at once, blasting through the wall into the shed. The grenade did not blow in the wall of the shed, but the assault rifle blew thirty bullets straight through it, near the base. Tiny shuttles of death. They mutilated The Skull, leaving her in two halves. The flight case she had returned to collapsed, and her body lay in an impossible shape inside of it. Her lower half was kneeling, hips propped on the edge, as if she were retrieving something out of the bottom of the case. Her upper half lay backwards on the cloven lid like a sunbather, staring up at the roof.

Hell stood over Yuri. He had holstered his Magnum, and now he dangled the Remington between his legs with pleasure, hanging its weight over the first-person shooter circus clown dude trapped below.

65

Y URI SPOKE FIRST. "What the... hell are you doing here?" he asked, squinting up at the roof. He mustered surprisingly little conviction in his voice.

Yuri realized that he didn't care *what* this man was doing here. He felt precious in this moment, eggshell thin. Like a thousand lives resided in him, and all were about to die. He felt his training, his loved ones, his stories....that last one had been a bit cynical, the one about the dresser. He wished he could tell one last story. Maybe a good one about Ufe. One to show her better side.

"Is that a question? Or are you *privy?*" Hell smiled with crooked gums. His black trench coat flipped around him in a wind, like wings. To Hell it felt like purple energy waves and icy flames. "Now," he continued. "I *was* coming up here on the roof to smother you with bullets. But now I'm seeing something really fun, like a friend. A buddy." Finn sat down on the edge of the roof, dangling his Remington even lower, but still out of the soldier's reach. His black boots stood on an invisible pane of glass. "So," he said. "Tell me a story."

"Who do you—" Yuri began but retracted the question. He was getting a crick in his neck from staring up at the roof. The gun was heavy, and his arms hurt. He hadn't slept, and his vest smelled terrible (he hadn't washed it before this operation had begun), but he wanted to live through it all. And this guy wanted to hear a...a *what?*

"Yeah, I want to take a little break. Tell me a little story, and then we'll both go see what's in that shed."

"What in the *hell?* For real?" But Yuri knew it was futile to argue with him.

Finn smiled again, harder this time. He was getting used to feeling this action in his face. "Yes, you have something amazing in there," he said. "I want it."

"How do you know?" asked Yuri. "You're the first guy to ever find the claw, or even come close. Or even *try,* so far as I know."

"Don't know what you're talking about!" Hell barked. "Sounds like a good story, though." Hell's rictus smile quivered a little, then regained itself. "I got a story for you, ready? I'm fuck-assing up north on 89, minding my own, and I see this light in the mountain, and your *shed* hits me like a bunch of laser pointers! Then, I come all the way up here to investigate, and I can see an invisible beehive of *evil* buzzing inside the shed through the wall! And then, and *THEN,* I find *FUCKFACES* here, too! And then I got one squared under my *DICK* right *now! AND* I blew one up with a *BOMB! AND* that's not the *first* fuckface of the day, neither!"

Hell Finn might have laughed, but it sounded more like the honk of a seal. His four teeth flashed in the sun above Yuri, and his body contracted as if he were laughing, but only a bovine *HAAAAWW* came out.

"So what's your story, buddy? I need a break. Gimme a quick one 'fore my legs go numb."

66

A STORY, YURI thought.

A quick one.

He thought the convenient time-out might provide The Skull or Yuri the chance at some kind of advantage. But Yuri had a feeling it would not. He'd found that when he wished for something in the presence of the hand, he'd receive something terrible, some sardonic misfortune that he would never wish for whether in his right mind or even drunk and enraged. Something paradoxically destructive. Sometimes, something that's not even possible.

When Marco Valoso unwrapped the claw in the package, he forgot momentarily the warnings he had received from the old Navajo man. *Wish well or wish null,* he had said. Marco had been tired. Marco wanted the show to be over with. He wished that his Munich Arts performance would pass like a dream.

He didn't know his own foolery. He didn't even know that he was making a wish, really. It was more like an unbuilt thought beneath his conscience, a fluttering idea of his nerves before the big game.

He didn't hold the claw in both hands, and he didn't click his heels together three times. The catastrophe he'd caused that day on the field was so utterly terrifying it could only have been a dream. It was a nightmare: one of fishhooks, clouds that Anders pulled down around his face, and multiplying zombies. Of course Marco would not have wished this if he knew what he was doing. But he wished it nevertheless, and he'd paid the price for it with a bad neck injury. He had been ushered off the field before the zombies could get him. If the zombies *had* gotten him, Marco may have woken up somehow. But maybe not until after he'd felt their dead hands all over him, like cold lizards trying to pull him apart.

Fate must have been taken aback when Anders came in with the claw and the whiskey nippers and wished him all better, healing him on the spot, and mystifying everyone in the sports arena basement.

Marco was leveled up. He might even be a superhero, his *real life* dream.

And what now? Yuri was doomed. Last time he'd wished near the claw—nothing more than a thought—he had been teleported into his wife's madness and almost killed because of it. Now, in his own shame, he absently wished he could say something nice about Ufe. And now the sense of dread was downright nauseating, a hundred times worse than the regret he'd felt moments before.

A story, he thought. *A quick one.*
A nice one about Ufe.

The man on the roof was silhouetted in sunshine. His coat flapped about, and rays of light slipped through onto Yuri.

Yuri's neck was cramping. Blood was choosing to course in directions other than the one that led to his brain. He saw flickering, bright constellations. His gun was a useless ten-pound prop.

A nice story about Ufe.

Yuri squinted crazily up at Hell. "Can I get your name, sir?" he asked.

"Hell Finn," said the black flapping demon.

Street name, Yuri thought. *Whatever.*

"Well, Mr. Finn, you want a story? Okay. Here it goes. I had a wife once, sweet as can be! She was truly amazing. Her name was Ufe—"

"OOF?" Hell shouted. "What kind of a stupid fucking name is *that?* What, was her mom named *POW,* and her dad named *THWACK? Ha!* This is a great story, by the way."

Yuri could smell the pine trees in waves with his foul flak jacket. In one breath it would be foul flak jacket, cool morning breeze, foul flak jacket. He continued. "Yes, her name was Ufe. She's German, and it's not that weird."

"My name's German, too," Hell said. "Now go on. Don't leave me hanging like this."

Yuri was thinking about The Skull. Somehow, he didn't think she would come to his rescue anymore. Something must have happened to her.

"Yeah," he said, coming back to Finn. "So Ufe and I were leaving our favorite biergarten one beautiful day in Munich, and we were holding hands and not looking where we were going. Her blonde hair in the sun looked like silk made of honey. My black Russian hair was long and princely. We were great for each other."

"Hurry up."

"Yes, sorry. So we're walking, and we saw a dog with only *two* legs! Its two back ones! It was on a leash, walking around, and its head and torso just hovered over the ground! *Hovered* there, like a metal detector!"

"Okay, good story!" Finn said, apparently satisfied somehow. "Now tell me what's in the shed." Finn stood up again, and not too slowly, Yuri noticed. It would've taken Yuri twice that time to stand up on that roof. "Is there anything I should know about in there? Bombs? Booby traps? What about you, buddy? Who are you, and what the fuck are you doing here in this... this fucking *Kaibab* Forest? Are you shooting a *Predator* movie, or what? Tell me everything. Fuck the story. It was a good one though, good stuff."

Yuri's upper back spasmed, and his arms were detaching from his shoulders.

"May I lower my gun, Mr. Finn?"

"Yes," Finn replied. "That would be great."

Yuri's carbine touched the ground. His eyes never left Hell's silhouette, which looked like amorphous fabric surrounding a large twenty-gauge shotgun barrel, dangling a foot over Yuri's bloodless face like a black sun.

"My name is Yuri Pitzkov—"

"*PISSED OFF?*"

"Jesus, no! Pitzkov... Yuri!" Yuri began to think this man might actually be an amateur, an easy fix. His flippancy, his "breaks," were not a display of employed arrogance but rather a warble in a badly improvised plan. He, Yuri, might be able to think his way out of this one. As he started to form an idea in his head, he continued to give Hell the information that he'd demanded. "I'm here with my friend and partner, Anders Lund, who you killed a minute ago. And a rogue superior who goes by the name of—get *this*—"

"You're WHAT?" Hell went completely rigid. His coat stopped whirling. He inched his left hand to the butt of his shotgun. Then, speaking lower this time, he asked, "Is there someone else in the shed, Mr. Pissed Off?"

Silence.

The shotgun exploded. Yuri was flattened with a *BOOM!* and a skitter of dead leaves.

67

ELL FINN THREW his shotgun onto the ground next to the bloody pile that, moments ago, would have responded to a name that sounded like "Pissed Off". He swiveled easily off the edge of the roof, hanging by his hands first, then dropping five feet back into the dirt and pine needles. He picked up the shotgun and scanned the woods feverishly.

He listened, panting lightly, his breath puffing like a downshifting locomotive.

He could not detect anyone.

Then, he heard a soft, female moan from inside the shed.

He spun on his heel and charged across the north side of the shed, back towards the door.

The door was open. Branches of sunlight slanted down through windows set high in the walls. A dead man was strapped to the floor, his upturned face marinating in blood. A woman lay in two halves, still breathing ebulliently, her body steaming like hot tar, half inside of a flight case.

Hell sensed evil inside the shed as palpable as mustard gas.

His gums were drying out. He licked them and moved his lips around in circles. "Hello," he said politely, as he entered the shed. "May I come in?" Then he thought of a good joke because it was so early in the morning. "Rise and shine, m'lady? What? No?"

He moved inside with slow deliberation. He didn't need to check the corners; the shed was obviously empty, except for them.

He noticed some duffel bags, a ruined flight case on wheels

with the woman in it, an unpowered generator, and a folding table with instruments, note pads, walkies, and old soda cans. One dead man lay on the ground, once bound by ropes but now affixed to the ground by living bamboo. *Normal,* Finn thought, with indulgent sarcasm. The woman appeared to be in two pieces. Most of her blood had spilled outside of her body, running out of the flight case in one corner like a wine spigot. There, the dirt floor of the shed was a brackish red clay.

Finn walked over to The Skull. Her butt was in the air, on the edge of the lid. It looked like she was reaching for something behind a couch. The lid had caved in at the center, where her torso lay, reclined, as if in a beach chair.

With a little help from Finn, her legs could go in the case and she could take an *actual* blood bath. He stood over her, exalted but calm as a man inspecting his own toolbox. He patted her ass. She stared down at it in horror.

Opposite the room, on the south wall, a hole the size of a human head shone near the floor, leaking an arrow of red sunlight across the mud. It was the hole that had been rammed open by the bullets of Anders Lund's automatic rifle.

Hell found the claw in The Skull's blood-soaked right hand. It was old and hoary, and he could smell it over everything else. A twisted leather insect with cobbled skin. The Skull clutched it in her death grip. It was big, and its size was exaggerated by The Skull's smaller feminine hand. In his mind, Hell saw the beehive, a sub-visible electron shell, orbiting the claw.

Evil, meet evil.

Hell lunged over The Skull and snatched it up.

He held it up to his face and pored over it for a full minute. What planet was this claw from? Why did Finn love it so much, despite its horrible musk? Finn felt as if it were his *own* claw, broken off him long ago and rightfully returned at long last. His guns felt like mere toys to him, but *this* felt like a weapon. A smelly, ugly, awesome weapon.

He removed his stare from the claw and looked around the shed again. The Skull was breathing, but each intake was becoming shorter, more clipped. She stared at Finn.

Her expression betrayed pity mixed with revenge. She looked scared but more like she was watching someone else die rather than herself. Her eyes were clear. It was the stare of a suicide bomber.

Finn flinched at that thought. He thought about running, as if the woman actually *was* a suicide bomber, but he sensed no real danger from her. And the claw was far too unusual to be a bomb. Finn felt safe. Alone again, just as he liked it.

The morning was abundant with death. It smelled of pine, juniper, smoke, and blood. And the sight of The Skull running out of lung space was hypnotic. It gave Hell Finn a feeling of calmness and quiet reflection. He was resetting the population of the world. Wasn't he? Cleaning up the clutter. Yes, it was his job. It had been far too crowded in the Kaibab Forest. Now it was better.

The Skull died, her breaths wisping out like a candle. Finn heard a faint wax-like hiss at the very end.

There was a notebook on the worktable and a folder with a tag on it that read, "Thunder, AZ." Finn grabbed them both.

He left the shed, certain that he had everything he needed. He had grabbed the rifle lying forgotten by The Skull's body, beyond the reach of the man who was spread-eagle on the floor with sprouts coming out of his stomach.

He stuffed the bloody claw into the ankle of his right boot.

He turned the Remington over to his left hand—the hand with worse aim. His father had once said to him while as drunk as a monster, "You should get a shotgun, Hell 'cause ye don't never need to aim it! Ye just need to point it forward, and BOOM!" His father found a lot of humor in this. He barked out laughter as he stood up and vomited on the floor.

Hell never forgot that lesson. His father had a way of making things stick. The only problem was that Hell's father was never the best judge of what kind of advice to give in such a successful way of delivery.

Hell clutched the assault rifle in his right hand, the shotgun in his left. The guns were very heavy, and Hell doubted if he had the best setup for himself here. But his self-esteem was somewhere in the clouds, and he believed—he was *sure*—that he was powerful and probably magical, especially with these two huge guns that were definitely not going to throw his back out. He also had his magnum on him, another four pounds. He felt like a warrior, clad in heavy steel.

Battle at first light. A red sun rises, he mused, pausing to acknowledge the faint but distinct smell of grenade smoke. *His* grenade smoke. His destruction.

He needed to destroy something now, something more.

He wished he could blow that first fucker up with a grenade again. And he wished he could use the shotgun on the other guy, "Pissed Off," again.

He wished those things very much.

68

FINN STARTED ON, back out the open door of the shed, past the leaning Ryder truck and into the forest where Douglas firs were having early brunch with Engelmann spruces.

But at the mouth of the woods, a disturbing noise behind him made him stop, toe to toe with his old footprints.

It was a slithering sound, like a heavy reptile but much more wet, more like a bag full of organs rolling slowly towards him, surging through the leaves.

He turned to see what was going on.

Just then he felt as if he were being watched. A moment before, he had felt like the only man on Earth, but now there was something here.

Ok, he thought. *I think this madness is just beginning.*

Then he saw it.

It looked just as it had sounded, a small mound of fleshy chunks. A bloody blob of guts mixed with leaves and pine needles. He spotted bones sticking out of it. It was on the ground, sliding with slow intelligent shifts in Finn's direction, making sounds like *sshhhlll, ssshhhlll.* It almost sounded like words, like speech.

The trail of red mud led clearly toward the black spot where the grenade damage still smoked. Between the Ryder truck and the shed, near the door.

Hell Finn's eyes widened. His mouth fell open, and for the

moment, he forgot that he was carrying thirty pounds of weapons. He dropped both of his guns on the ground. Then he started to say something, but before he could, he did something he hadn't done in almost three weeks.

He dropped to his knees and vomited.

PART

SIX

69

A RED SUN rose guiltily over Thunder. It crawled up and pussy-footed low in the sky.

Despite himself, Jimmy thought that it was the most beautiful sunrise he had ever seen. He wondered how he could be capable of such appreciation in the wake of so much horror.

He needed a car. He had to get someplace, anyplace more populated than here.

Well, the moon *would be more populated than here,* he thought.

It had taken Jimmy a long time to walk to town through the icy bog, and when he got there, cars weren't easy to find.

The whole town had been ambushed by ice, and the earthquake, too. What was left of Thunder was a junkyard at best.

The auto shop near the school was still standing. It was easy for Jimmy to find. The world still had that focused, magnified look to it, and Jimmy could see the garage from across the whole shattered wasteland.

In the auto shop, he found a garaged Nissan Pathfinder with the keys in the ignition. It was parked haphazardly with the hood open, probably having bounced around the garage in the earthquake. It was dented up and cock-angled, but otherwise it seemed to be in good condition.

He didn't cry about his mother.

He didn't mourn the death of Chester's family.

He had seen a lot of people die. He had imagined his own twin sister screwing death on Eighth Avenue, for Christ's sake. It was a shock at first, but what did he feel now? Nothing?

He had seen Jackie Wells and Christian burst into flames. Did he need to remind himself of that?

What's wrong with me? Jimmy wondered. But he put the thought out of his mind for the time being. He had to get out of Thunder. It was already just a blank space on a map, and he didn't want to end up the same way.

There were drinks and sandwiches on the floor of the garage, huddled near an open refrigerator. Jimmy picked up some items, lots of water bottles, and loaded them into the truck. He dropped the hood with a loud slam, swung into the Pathfinder, and closed the door.

Oh, he hated cold cars. He sat there smelling the annoying cold-car smell and pouted internally for a moment. He hated cold cars more than he hated his family dying. What in the world was wrong with him? His twin! His mom!

He felt as if he had grown his family *out* of himself miraculously, like splinters out of skin. Like molted skin that just fell off and then you were all new again, no regret!

If he had, in the night, suffered a broken heart or endured the injury of sadness, then by now he felt recovered, healed up and signed off on. Good to go.

But then Jimmy felt something. It was not sadness.

A spooky feeling.

A chill crawled up his back like a spider. He was facing the back wall of the garage, with tools hanging vertically in front of him. Silence surrounded him in the car.

This is a place of ghosts, he realized. *This is a place of death!*

His heart went up in his throat. He flipped the key over, and the ignition snarled to life. He backed out of the shop in a knot of forward and backward lunges. He imagined smacking into zombies as he lurched in all directions.

Then he spun out of the garage, painting an arc of blue tire smoke behind him. He didn't care if the oil had been changed or if it was about to get changed.

At least the check engine light wasn't on.

70

T HE PATHFINDER WAS full of gas.

The auto shop was conveniently close to Copperhead Canyon.

He sped west across Copperhead Canyon, away from what used to be Thunder. But his eyes stayed locked, like dogs on the rearview mirror.

71

M*EGA MAN*. H*E* thought of Mega Man, though he didn't know why. It had been Jimmy's favorite video game as a kid. He used to play it at Chester's house. The protagonist was a little boy in blue armor who ran around between realms, shooting big pellets out of his hand, which was also a gun. Mega Man had been Jimmy's idol when he was seven. He'd had only one facial expression—happy and determined—and he looked like he was ten years old, Jimmy's senior by a whole three years.

Now, at nineteen, a part of Jimmy still wished he was that little blue warrior boy in the TV. Why? Jimmy had no idea. Some dreams die, and some dreams don't. Some dreams are like tattoos, so old that they become inscrutable, unnoticed, yet remain in the same place they were born long ago. Funny. He was a student, not a warrior. And even though he still had a lot of growing up to do, he was a man of nineteen, no longer a boy.

He had been driving for over an hour, but he was still a long way from any motel.

He could use a Motel 8, not *Mega Man*...

Maybe Fredonia. Maybe Colorado City. If he found coffee, he could make it all the way to Hurricane.

He hadn't slept since long before the fire at The Dockside, about fifty hours ago. (His math was slower than it had ever been). Maybe that was why his heart was so dry. Maybe he shouldn't be driving. He swerved a lot, and he knew that. He wouldn't tell any-one this, but he also blacked out in moments while he drove. Every guard post was an animal running into the road. The road lengthened out in front of him.

As he journeyed up route 89, it never got fully warm inside the SUV. But although he was cold, and it pained him to stay awake, the drive was somehow refreshing, almost pleasant.

72

ELL FINN STARED at the pile of guts in front of him. It smelled like feces and bananas and blood.

The woods were silent all around him.

The gore-pile stopped moving when it got right up close to Finn, just two yards to his bow. Hell thought it was sniffing his vomit. That almost made him throw up again.

Can it see me? Hell wondered. *Does it know I'm standing here?*

Finn imagined eyes looking up at him. Puppy dog eyes. This image made him feel cold, confused. There were definitely no puppy dog eyes in there—and if there were, they would definitely not be cute. They would be sightless and empty and bloody.

Still, this sickening aberration seemed to be staring directly at him.

The dark trail of blood curved back to the scorched clearing, where the blonde man had blown up. There was still smoke there, pale blue in the morning sun. There was only a little, but it was enough to give Hell a very clear idea of what had happened. The man he had killed was invincible. A vampire or something, and after he blew up, he'd magnetized back together, somewhat, like nothing of this world.

Hell couldn't confirm this idea, but he looked around to verify the silence that enabled this theory. It felt like a certainty.

He bent down slowly into a squatting position. He picked up

the shotgun and carefully steadied himself, putting one knee down.

He blew a fiery scattershot into the center of the pile of guts. He imagined the sound it made, like a cannonball dropped into a bucket of pudding, but he didn't hear anything under the concussive blast of the shotgun.

Aside from an appetite-bursting jump of blood, the mound remained the same, with those imagined puppy dog eyes, staring up at him, as creepy as ever.

Finn hesitated, then picked the rifle back up, his eyes welded to the blob.

He hoped that this filthy mound of death would stay here in the dirt, eventually going to sleep in his memories. Then perhaps, one day, it would leave his memories altogether, the way a guest checks out of a hotel, never to return, the way that all scary half-believable things always leave our memories eventually.

Where Finn was headed, he was sure to have no memories of any kind. And that was fine with Finn; so long as he had a few little white stones he could smoke, he would be right where he wanted to be, sure enough.

Finn turned to leave, even though the resin smell of the shotgun tantalized him again. He was warming up, and he wanted to stay here and kill more things.

He was a hunter now. He would have to find his fortunes using his nose, and his instinct and his woodsmanship. *Start your hunt,* he told himself.

Yes, but he shouldn't get lonely. He never had before, but then, he had never been a hunter before. He had hated everybody, but hadn't he also changed over the last two nights? He was starting to like having people around.

He had asked Meatface to come along with him. Meatface had

been so willing to be his buddy that he'd disintegrated with enthusiasm. He wanted to take Yuri "Pissed Off" with him, too. *He* was a badass; he looked like a goddamned video game character, but Hell had killed him as a precaution that there might be another fuckface in the shed, which there had been. But *she* died, too. She wouldn't have made a good buddy though, judging by the look of her. *Too stiff,* he thought. *No fun.* Pissed Off would've, though. Damn, this was tough!

These thoughts rushed through his mind like speeding cars on an abbreviated highway.

He swiveled away from the blob of guts, facing the forest and his path, a skeleton in a long black coat. His guns were larger than the arms that bore them. He looked like a human crab, with heavy metal claws. He began to walk.

Hell descended into the forest. It seemed happy to greet him.

But as he passed the first tree, the sound of slithering crackled into his ears once again, bewildering him from behind.

He spun around. The mound had moved.

Again, it had come towards Finn. It seemed to maintain a two-yard distance from him, just like a stray dog, wherever he went.

After shooting it many times, investigating it up close, smelling it and all, Finn decided he could either spend the day with it (with a big lump in his boot, don't forget), without lunch, or he could move on. Mound of guts or no mound of guts?

He went for the latter.

73

H E WALKED FAST, as if pushed through the forest, back the mile to his Wagoneer.

The bloody cow pie pursued him at a two-yard distance.

When he got to the car, he faced-off with the filthy lump. It stayed by the passenger side door, on a cushion of pine needles, and continued to puppy-dog him from across the cab.

Hell shook his head, hawked up a huge loogie and spat in the dirt. Then he got in the car, tossing his guns and his notebooks and his claw in the passenger foot well. He threw the keys into the ignition.

The blob jumped at the car and stuck to the passenger door with a slam. It was bigger than half of the door. The car rocked on its suspension, and Hell cried out in surprise. But the aggressive thing just stayed there, unmoving, looking like a tumor with leaves in it, dripping blood. What looked like a wrist bone stuck out of it like a hitchhiker's thumb.

Hell closed his eyes and waited. He could hear the blob tighten on the door. It would only be a matter of seconds before the blob pulled off the door and ripped the Jeep into pieces, like The Incredible Hulk.

After a moment, when nothing happened, Hell opened his eyes. The Wagoneer was fine.

"Get out," said a ghastly voice next to the driver's door. A huge shadow tackled Finn. He spun on his ass to see what it was. Within the shadow stood a grotesque figure. It was Yuri Pitzkov, the video game character, only his head was half gone. His collar bone was shot up, and two thirds of a glistening skull was resting on his shoulders, in the basin of his scarf, like a broken egg in a bloody nest. He still had his bulletproof vest on, and he still had all his gear. There was a long ribbon of flesh that looked like it had once started at the top of his head, but now it hung out of his neck almost down to his stomach.

"I'm coming with you," he said.

Terrified, Finn crawled out of the car and complied.

Yuri Pitzkov got in and slid over to the passenger seat. He was huge, barely fitting in the large cab of the station wagon. Finn got back in. The guns, cold and heavy, piled on their laps, created a web around them.

In a wood-paneled Wagoneer, with a bloody scrotum tightening on one side, Hell Finn and Yuri Pitzkov ventured on.

74

U. S. Route 89 runs north, then topples south before whipping west. It staggers in every direction except east (unless you turn the car around). It eventually stumbles into Route 389 at Fredonia, Arizona.

There is a place along the drive where the Kaibab Forest ends, its brunchy mingling of flora continuing out of sight, and the desert returns, burnt red and breathtaking.

Technically, the highway is used by more snakes than cars.

Jimmy was able to score some coffee and breakfast at a gas station-diner combo just before Fredonia and hitting Route 389. It was noon. He was breasting a big beige dome when a sign rose up declaring, "FOOD GAS LIQUOR FIREWORKS NATIVE AMERICAN CRAFTS." His stomach rumbled in harmony with this rising apparition. His blistered hand singed, *blazed,* in agreement.

He parked the Pathfinder on the side of the building in the sun, hoping to warm up the cab while he ate.

The gas pumps were mere yards away. Two Mack trucks lingered on the other side of the building, along with three ATVs and a small gaggle of Harley-Davidsons and Vintage Indians.

The horrors of the night before were already disappearing like an old dream. He felt as if he hadn't seen his family in months. He no longer felt emotionally tied to his twin, Charlotte.

He wondered if, after a hot meal, his mind would absorb everything terrible and grind him into a mortar and pestle of sadness.

But until then, there was food.

And gas and maybe some liquor.

He walked to the front doors. He saw the ashtrays in the trash stones and, fleetingly, wondered why the smoking area was so close to the pumps. But he brushed it off. The sure feeling that Murphy's Law was cashing in all its chips and coupons had left him. He didn't disregard that notion, but rather that notion seemed to have disregarded him, somehow. All that remained of the idea was the pain in his right hand, which throbbed worse than ever.

So it was on to the next necessity: bacon and eggs, but most importantly, coffee. He wouldn't sleep here; he wouldn't even snooze in the car. He was too close to Thunder. Eighty-six miles. And much less, as the crow flies.

Keep going.

The thing that stood out to Jimmy the most, as he moved into the north wing of the building toward the restaurant, was not the old hot dogs rolling in place in an incubator, nor the chilled Starbucks double-shot cans or Red Bulls in the fridge. It wasn't the muffins or popcorn, not the Arizona centennial T-shirts, nor the beautiful Route 66 sweatshirts. No.

It was a girl.

She was sitting alone in a booth, looking out the window. The sunlight shone in her hair so bright, she was impossible *not* to see. So much red. Lit up like that, it looked like smokeless, magical fire.

Suddenly, Jimmy had a crazy thing for redheads. He floated over to her, half asleep, half in shock, and asked to sit down.

"Sure!" the girl said, smiling, with camper's companionship.

Jimmy sat down and smiled back at her. He was charming, always, even after his whole world had been smashed to a brackish pulp. "My name's Jimmy," he said. He held out his hand. She took it.

"Kaye," she said. "Nice to meet you."

"Nice to meet you too, Kaye." He looked out the window, then back at Kaye, still smiling. "Are you from around here?" he asked.

Her eyebrows shot up, implying adventure. "Here?" She laughed. "No. Nothing's from around here."

"Of course," Jimmy chuckled. "Can I ask where you're from?"

"Denver," she replied. "Well, near Denver. What about you?"

"Arizona," he said, and although he felt a shadow creep across his face, a momentary forfeit for good old Ay-Zee, the girl with the autumn fire hair did not seem to notice. Then a thought occurred to him, and he quickly added, "Where you headed, Kaye?"

Kaye looked him up and down. Surely after the night he'd had, Jimmy looked more like a refugee than a young traveler. He didn't look like he had gotten lost for days on a hike—he looked like he had been to war, and he hadn't slept yet.

But Kaye didn't seem to mind his appearance. She only blinked her eyes and said, "Vegas. I'm just taking a break here."

She had a cup half full of black coffee before her, and nothing else. "You?"

"Um," Jimmy wasn't sure yet. "Los Angeles, I guess?"

"Ah, what are you doing out there?"

She gave off a vibe that was neither flirtatious nor overly interested. She seemed to him relaxed, wide open, free, like a good college student, enthralled with people in general. She was welcoming for conversation, at the very least.

What am I doing there? Why am I going to LA?

Jimmy felt as if he were giving birth to his first thought, slowly. "Call my school, I suppose... Tell them I'm not there. Maybe ask them for advice, if they're still good for it..."

He trailed off.

It seemed he might now have no idea how to continue living.

He was exhausted, and his thoughts were mere millimeters deep. He thought he should go to California, to the beach. He didn't know why. It seemed like a destination that was far enough away, but finite enough for him to make it there.

"Why aren't you at school?" said Kaye, breaking through his thoughts. "Did you book a movie?" She was getting talkative now, and her glee was gaining.

"Yeah, movie *rights*, more like. No, I... Let me get some coffee first. I'm feeling a little... sugar dip. Then I'll tell you everything."

Jimmy got his coffee and a big, steaming lumberjack breakfast. After the coffee came, he sipped up half the cup and said to Kaye, "Did you feel an earthquake last night?"

Kaye said that she hadn't felt one. So Jimmy continued carefully, searching for the right words, fumbling his ideas, like a man trying to connect the events of a previous night's dream.

"Everyone from my hometown died last night..." he began.

And vaguely, he told the story, the way he barely remembered it.

75

H ELL FINN DROVE the Wagoneer fast. The scrotum on the passenger side door never moved or slid back.

Zombie Yuri found the notes that Finn had picked up from the workstation. Magnus Johannsen's notes.

He had been on his way back to Thunder.

Yuri glanced at the notes with one eyeball, from a head that looked like a dinosaur egg that had fallen off a cliff and landed in his scarf. He had read these notes before. In fact, Yuri had memorized them, and although his brain had been destroyed by his chauffeur, his memories had stayed connected somehow, perhaps in his large, fibrous body.

Magnus Johannsen had been the founder of the Fontaine project, and he'd kept all its secrets hidden. Many of the Fontaine notes were in these folders, along with profiles of Jimmy Johannsen—Magnus's son.

Magnus had been riding toward Thunder three days ago, before all hell had broken loose in the Fontaine mines. On his way there, presumably to try to stop whatever was going to happen, he was intercepted by The Skull and her crew. They interrogated him and planted bamboo under his back, causing him to grow a few extra tracheas while the questions came in. He had carried files of Jimmy with him, data that he had slowly garnered over the years, while Jimmy himself believed him to be dead from cancer.

"Have you ever been on three meter stilts?" Zombie Yuri asked.

"What?" Hell said, still lost in his own thoughts. He looked at

Yuri and wondered grimly how a man with almost no bones in his head could speak with such clarity and diction.

"Stilts, stilt walking. Like three meters high. You have to climb on top of a boxcar to get on them. It's awesome. It feels like you're flying. And the people, they're so small from up there."

"No."

"It's really nice," Yuri said. "That's Anders Lund, I'm guessing, on the side of the car?"

Finn swerved, as if away from the blob glued to his truck. "What?" he said, again.

"Your friend there," Yuri continued, gesturing his thumb to the door next to him. "He used to be *my* friend." He paused. "Do you know anything about that claw?"

Finn hesitated. "Yes. I suppose I might," he said, unsure of what he was saying. "I might have it."

Yuri laughed. What remained of his head swelled up like a lake raft and then sucked down into his shoulders, as if his body had tried to inhale it. When it was somewhat normal again, Yuri touched it, worriedly. "You're completely fucked," he said at last. "You're running off to somewhere in Las Vegas?"

Finn didn't reply.

"Wherever you think you're headed... you're not going there," Yuri said, and returned his one-eyed gaze to the windshield and the oncoming day.

76

A FTER SHE PAID her check, Kaye stuck around with Jimmy. She liked him, and despite his woeful and frenzied appearance, she didn't pity him. She'd seen worse looking guys while hiking.

They checked the newspaper bins for recent news about Thunder, but the papers were all gone. It was nearing mid-afternoon already.

They pumped their cars up with gas.

For a moment they stood together in the sun, leaning on the Pathfinder, looking out at the mountains. Jimmy told Kaye that he planned on sleeping in Hurricane tonight. She asked him if he wanted company. He told her he wanted that more than anything.

77

THUNDER HAD BEEN a four hour drive to Hurricane. Jimmy naturally enjoyed turning four hour drives into six hour drives. He explored the worlds between worlds, which felt spacious and free to him.

He thought about Chester during the drive, revering his presence, trying to feel him, trying to miss him. That skinny, hilarious bastard. Jimmy realized that *Chester's* hand wasn't burning anymore. Jimmy was the only person still suffering. How many jokes had Chester told in his lifetime? How many hundreds of people had he cracked up before he finally cracked up himself? Chester had enriched Jimmy's life. He had meant a lot to him.

The Pathfinder cab finally started to warm up.

78

HELL FINN RODE hard for Hurricane, with the coppery smell of blood in his sinuses. And Jimmy followed, like a tiny roadrunner chasing a vicious coyote through cliffs and canyons, into the heart of Utah.

Jimmy met Kaye in Hurricane, at a Mexican restaurant called Molcajete. It was directly across the street from the Days Inn, which had the cheapest rates.

It didn't take more than two hours to get to Hurricane from the gas station near Fredonia, but Jimmy was hungry again already. Ravenous, in fact. Kaye was close on his heels the whole way. Now she was at the motel, washing up. She would be here any moment.

Jimmy felt the same as he had before. He didn't sorely miss anybody. The people in his heart were absent, yes, but he didn't long for them. He started to wonder if he was becoming an asshole, if he was *cursed* or something. Even his feelings for Kaye were, so far, perfectly flat. His crotch didn't swell up at the sight of her, except that first time. Jimmy and Kaye were jamming, but they weren't *really jamming*.

Jimmy thought, *maybe later we'll be really jamming!* Then he wondered if that was an insensitive thought, what with his mom dying on top of him earlier this morning. But in turn, it didn't matter. Jimmy wasn't interested in anything except companionship. He decided he would buy her a drink, then knock out across the street for a while. Catch up with her later in the night.

That is, of course, if Kaye ever showed up.

Wasn't she like five minutes behind me? Jimmy thought.

He tried not to panic. It was too early for that. *She had to use the bathroom, that's all. Freshen up. You could've done a little better yourself, Mega Man.*

The restaurant had a full bar. Jimmy got a ten percent discount with presentation of his plastic motel room key card.

The walls were bold, important colors: green on one wall, orange on another, yellow, red, purple. No two walls were the same. Admiring the confident flamboyance of the decor, the desert flowers and aloes, and smiling waitresses, Jimmy began to feel alone in the world once more. Even with Kaye supposedly approaching, only minutes behind.

He sat in a red pleather booth for five minutes. It was enough time to begin to stick to it, but not long enough to order a glass of water. Kaye walked in. Her hair was red hibiscus, her body still soft, white, and audacious. She sat down just as the waitress arrived and ordered a whiskey.

"Jameson, please."

Jimmy smiled. "That's my *name*, girl."

She erupted in a good belly laugh. "Well that's what I want," she said.

She wasn't being flirtatious. She was still a campfire companion.

Jimmy smiled at the waitress. She was plump, wearing red, and she looked like the kindest person he had ever seen.

"El mismo," he said to her, then lowered his head shyly.

"Do you feel any different now, after the drive?" Kaye asked. She had taken out a small journal and was writing something in it. Then she folded it and put it away.

"Eeh, not really. The ride was nice though! Pathfinders are amazing."

"Jimmy, you've been blowing my mind since I first met you, you know that?" She looked him up and down again. It was just as she'd looked at him at the gas station restaurant, but better this time. "Don't you have some clothes to change into? You don't have any clothes?"

Jimmy groaned. "Eugh, no," he said, accepting the compliment. "I'm fucked up right now, and I don't know what it is, and even though I seem okay, I'm really not. Something's wrong with me, and it's serious. I bought some clothes at the gas stop. I'll don them fabulously later, after a drink or two..." Storm clouds were beginning to form just behind Jimmy's eyes. But they broke apart just as quickly as they'd formed.

"I'm glad you're here, Kaye. If you want to bail—I mean, I know you couldn't possibly because my story is so implosively captivating, I know—but if you wanted to bail, go ahead and do it. I don't even know myself anymore, anyways. But I do like you, though, a lot. And, I'd like it if you stuck around with me more." Jimmy adjusted his position in the booth. He put up his fists near Kaye's head and squinted his eyes, making a magician-like star-bungler poof.

"Blowing your mind," he said, smiling. "We'll sort this all out over some drinks, okay? And let's get some fucking nachos, too."

Kaye and Jimmy ate and drank there for an hour, munching while talking, as the end of their stories arrived, grinning, cloaked in black.

79

ONE SPICY SALSA chip away, in this dry, Utah tarantula motel Mexican restaurant, and it all went out the window one last time.

Finn remembered that he'd wished he could shoot Yuri with the shotgun again. It hadn't taken long to find this epiphany because he made the same wish a second time, while enduring the zombie's ever percolating smell. *So this is what it's like when zombies* don't *attack,* he thought. *When they just hang out and ride shotgun and read notebooks to you and show you photos.*

Acknowledging Yuri riding shotgun made Finn think about his *own* shotgun. After that, Finn wanted only one thing: to be stepping out of the Wagoneer and hosing Yuri and the blob away with shotgun spray, never to see them again. He thought about blasting Yuri inside the car, feeling a wave of desire, and that's when the wishes sifted up.

But he drove on instead, zombie and barnacle blob in tow. He wanted to get to a town before dark.

The Jeep Wagoneer blew into Hurricane and stopped dead at the driveway entrance to an old house. The bluish paint had long since began to chip away, and it had an extension converted into a general store of sorts.

The driver's side door popped open. Finn crept out and turned around, whirling his trench coat and his shotgun around, and before Yuri could draw down in his own cramped space, Finn webbed him with the shotgun. It felt like premature ejaculation, times a billion.

Finn wiped his nose with the back of his wrist and spat. Then he stepped away from the car towards the driveway, turned, and looked at the house storefront in the distance.

It was a military surplus store. Finn had known it somehow.

Finn took one last glance at the stalled Jeep and the dead monster inside. The shotgun trick seemed to have worked. The car was useless now, of course. How he had made it this far with over a hundred pounds of roadkill on the side without getting stopped by police was a mystery. Chalk it up to Hell's new superpower—whatever *that* was. Part of him believed that he had destroyed the not-quite town of Thunder all by himself. He *had* willed it to happen, hadn't he? Maybe he'd sent out ghosts of himself while he slept, vague messengers in the night. Maybe these shapeless creepers had stolen all the life in Thunder, then brought it all to him like vampires.

As if hearing Finn's thoughts, the blob of guts started to move. It rolled off the door and landed in the dirt with a *flump!* Then it crawled like an octopus, slowly, in Finn's direction.

80

Hell Finn walked casually down the driveway to the front of the blue house. There was some snow on the ground, scattered in small pockets throughout the mountains, but Hell remained bathed in a warm late afternoon glow.

As he came to a loft in the driveway, he spotted gas stations below him, a Days Inn farther down the hill, and a Mexican restaurant, too. He realized with sudden certainty that he needed a hot meal.

But as the sun began to descend, like a tail between a dog's legs, Finn was struck by a different idea. One that took priority over food.

81

Finn slipped into the house's extension, noting the crooked sign that read, "THE SERGEANT'S LEGITAMATE SUR-PLUS" and the sign underneath it that read, "FUCK THE DOG, BEWARE OF OWNER!"

The blob of guts had practically led the way.

He spotted movement in the back of the shop. "I need some grenades, buddy. You got any?"

There was a pause. Finn heard some shuffling, and then the shopkeeper spoke up. "Sure do, buddy! In the secret back room, right there!" His voice was loud and jerky. Finn suspected that the man was now too old to use meth but had enjoyed his fair share in his younger days. He had long grey eyebrows, like sprawling storm clouds over pale blue eyes. They glimmered at Finn over his spectacles. He was sweating, despite the air conditioner, which rattled loudly in the corner. He smiled when he saw Finn, either recognizing him as one of his kind, or just glad to get one customer in the books before he closed up.

"Follow me sir," he said. "And flip that there window sign over!"

Finn did as told, then followed the man through the dank military surplus store, which was overstuffed with surplus, fatigues, gas masks, and duffel bags. The aisles were heaped with fabrics, and the ceiling was thick with low hanging flight suits and long underwear. Finn ducked under a XXXL hazmat suit, following the owner into a "secret" back room. Apparently, Finn didn't need a password—just white skin, no badge, and a charming set of gums.

The selling man was very eager to help. When Finn arrived in the back room, the old sweat hound leaned against a high counter, grinning like a carnival merchant, selling grenades as if they were candied apples.

The back room was also sloped with clothes, giving it a sinking ship feeling. It also had an air of illegitimate, controversial material. Stolen things. Nazi swag, unapproved weapons.

The carney began his lecture. "Alright, bro, check it—I got M61s, M67s, and I got the V40 Minis. They're all fragmentation grenades, and they're all badass and *really* good at making decisions! I also got some baseballs and some pineapples, but they're old and they probably ain't working. World War II shit. I got guns, and knives… The only *registered* weapons in this room are my two hands and my Glock, but they're not for sale—heck no!"

The man tipped his head forward, set his blue eyes over his glasses again and gave Hell Finn a rehearsed wink. "Watch'oo like, son?"

Finn looked at the grenade-pawning creep with openmouthed astonishment.

The blob waited silently at the store's front door.

82

Hell walked out of the shop house with a sack of bombs in his hand, the other hand shielding his eyes from the glaring sunset. Everything seemed big, bright, and airy after being in that dank store.

He looked down the driveway at the flesh-bespattered cab of the Wagoneer.

Who's pissed off now, motherfucker? He thought, smiling.

He turned the other way and faced down the hill, in the direction of the town.

Hurricane waited for him. Enchiladas waited for him.

Must be Main Street, right there.

I see some fuckfaces, too. He approved.

Hell descended the hill, toward the restaurant.

The slithering flesh mound followed.

When he got halfway down the embankment, Hell turned and plunged a mini frag grenade into the blob, right between the puppy dog eyes, which were quite surprised, and then cartwheeled away to safety behind a rock. The blob burst into a red mist, and a cloud of smoke the color of old manila drifted away.

Finn waited for his ears to normalize. Three minutes of silence should be enough to pass the neighborhood curiosity.

He thought for a moment about the tiny pin he'd pulled on the mini frag, how death, fate, and evil all rely on a long and delicate chain reaction. One wire pin, *minutia*, releasing one small handle, one drop spring, releasing one chemical charge delay, detonating 3.5 ounces of explosive composite, killing, releasing an entire destiny, perhaps removing a jinx, opening worlds of changes.

Then he wondered how he was going to manage to kill people and eat food, both in the same evening. In what order would he accomplish it all?

While catching his breath behind the rock, Finn decided to leave his weapons there, while he went into town looking like a normal lunatic to eat some food. He'd come back later, when it grew darker.

As he laid the guns out, safe from any view, lightening his load considerably, he came across the sticky claw in his right boot.

He pulled it out and slowly held it up to his face.

Hell closed his eyes ritualistically, as if the old claw might magically give him eyebrows. His black cowboy hat touched it. Then his forehead caressed it, then his nose and mouth. He began to kiss the claw, cold sticky blood and all. He licked it, and French kissed it. Just a little. Just a little to show it a "thank you," from his heart.

Hell wished that a *real* hurricane would come to drench everybody around, to simply erase the town of Hurricane, and maybe Colorado City, and *VEGAS, TOO! YES! A HURRICANE OF PROPORTIONS! BLOW! WIND! BLOW! DOUSE! WASH AWAY THE WHOLE SOUTHWEST!*

Hell didn't notice that he was making wishes, he only felt like he was generating pleasant thoughts.

BLOW, YOU FUCKING HURRICANE! FOR REAL!

Then suddenly, Hell shuddered. As he opened his eyes, still in make-out face with the claw, he saw that it had begun to move in his hand.

Hell froze, holding his breath.

He felt it soften. It was as if it was...

Kissing him back.

Then all at once, it snapped shut into a bird's fist, slashing Finn's face from hairline to chin, missing his neck by mere inches. The pain sent Finn into a panicky whirl.

He dropped the claw. It hit the dirt like a stone, dead.

Hell's face exploded with pain. He wished that the searing intensity would go away, but it did not.

Finn staggered. What at first had looked like a huge beehive in his mind's eye now looked like a dull piece of litter in the dirt. No more special than an old, dead bird's foot.

He wished it would come back to life. He wished he could rub it, stroke it like Aladdin's lamp. *Rub it, stroke it, and it will come back to life!* Hell thought. Then, he had a clearer thought: *What does Aladdin have to do with anything? And what's this fuck-talk of* wishes?

Hell didn't know or care what wishes had to do with anything. But he noticed quite clearly that he seemed to be feeling good luck and bad luck in *huge,* icy and hot waves.

It was serendipity and malice, slow dancing with one another as the world swayed between their breasts. He was charmed, and he was cursed. He was powerful but powerless over his powers. He was being played, and he was being rewarded.

His face, meanwhile, fizzled like a live wire, bleeding badly. He needed to get it to stop.

This would weigh heavily into his plans.

He crouched over his guns, behind the rock, with the claw rolled over in the dirt, to the side. He tried to clench his face and stonewall the pain. Doubled over, he cried hot tears into the wounds. He sat there for a long minute, unable to move.

❖

When his tears finally stopped and his pain had settled somewhat, Hell caught his breath and looked slowly up at the sky.

Through his bleary eyes, he could see darkening arcs in the clouds.

It looked like a change in weather.

Hell felt a cold wind scoot across him, and oh, how it cooled his face, cleared his conscience.

Nothing loved a cold wind like big, smiley gums.

83

THE HOUSE WITH the military surplus store was at Finn's disposal. Since he had initially paid for the grenades with warm lead, he could go back in there easily, clean his face, maybe shower and dry off before the storm.

Then he thought better of it. *No,* he decided. *Just clean your face and go get food. And wash your damned hands; they're disgusting.*

So Hell ran back up the embankment and into the house, wiped himself off with the store's components, dumped alcohol on his face, dried off, and came back out, somewhat composed. A casual psychopath, as usual. His normal self.

With sunglasses, a scarf, and myriad surprises under cloak and hat, Hell lowered himself into the town of Hurricane.

He flowed straight into the trench that was Main Street, hooked right, and walked toward the Mexican restaurant. His hands were inside his black trench coat, four teeth waiting hungrily in the wings.

84

THE WINDOWS SHUTTERED, as if from a large, distant explosion.

Jimmy put both of his hands on the table.

His heart leapt up into his throat. Pain flashed up through his blistered right hand. His eyes widened.

Kaye put her hands soothingly over his left hand.

"Jimmy, it's just a storm. It's nothing," she said, her eyes never shifting from his.

But Jimmy's heart was racing now. He looked around at all the innocent diners going about their business, all their worries happily sunbathing on the beaches of another continent.

He looked out the window to see wind, but it really wasn't bad outside. He spotted some people by the motel outside, wagging their chins at each other. They didn't seem bothered at all.

Kaye was looking at him, her hands resting over his. Jimmy's nerves were smoking like live wires. Maybe she was right. Maybe it was just a—

"WHOA, did you feel *that?*" she asked.

"Feel what?" Jimmy said.

"Like a *wind*, like a *whoosh!*"

"No. Not at all," he said. Jimmy now remembered that he barely knew this girl. For all he knew, she could be a total loony. From Nevada or something. Disguising her identity, psyche ward escapee. "Um," he added. "That's weird though."

"No, seriously. I looked at the window, and it's closed. And the curtains are like... not moving. But I felt it!"

"You know what?" he said. "I believe you. The whole world is going crazy today. I can see it, too. Almost as clear as day."

No one else saw it as clear as day, though. Not like he did. Only Jimmy saw the glaring cartoon clarity of everything. Shiny and somehow magnified. "So," he began. "If you're scheduling a time to get your head checked out, maybe I could come with you. It wouldn't hurt to get my own engine tuned."

"WHOA!" she shouted. "There it is again! Holy crap, Jimmy! I'm freaking out!" Kaye was looking around herself, searching for a vent under the red pleather booth, or a hole in the wall. She touched the window shades. She looked at the front door. It was closed.

Then she leaned forward, until her small but prominent breasts were on the table. She squinted hard at Jimmy. "I'm still feeling it, dude! And not a single hair on your head is moving right now, even though it feels like they should."

Jimmy understood what Kaye meant, and his throat tightened. She was feeling it. The monster was here, in this restaurant in Hurricane. It was happening.

"Not one on yours, either," he said lamely, taking the opportunity to admire her blazing, smokeless red hair. The sun was beginning to set. Out the windows, the mountains shone bright gold against a darkening sky. It lit up the restaurant, like a scene from a movie, and Kaye's natural hair was lava flow on white, unscorchable skin. Mariachi music trickled out from the corners.

But then, from the edge of his view, it appeared, wearing all black. The door chimed, and he heard a series of "Hola" greetings by the front door.

A draft tumbled in, and Kaye's beautiful hair finally moved a little.

❖

Jimmy recognized the man. He had seen him in Thunder just before he'd left for Columbia.

The man was scary as hell. Kind of a movie-matinee-scary, though in his mind, he might have been even scarier than that. He looked like he was possessed with hunt, overbearing, with the weight of a wild boar. He looked much older now than when Jimmy had first seen him. It was probably an illusion of some kind. *Oh shit,* Jimmy thought. Were those lacerations across his face?

Yes, this was definitely the man from Thunder.

Jimmy felt cornered, and he felt cold. He wanted to take a huge breath and hold it and shut his eyes until this man was gone.

On second thought, he could drop a couple of twenties and bee line for the hotel across the street. *And change your stupid clothes.*

But the man walked up and sat in the booth next to Jimmy and Kaye's, the back of Jimmy's head floating mere inches from his. Kaye could barely see him, as he faced away from her, also blocked by Jimmy's pale and desperate face.

"You're Jimmy Johannsen," he said. His voice was like a stone rolling down a hill.

Jimmy didn't reply.

"I'm Hell Finn," he went on. "I'm from Thunder, but you probably know that from my name, don't you? That's right—you do. Because I'm famous. Everyone knows my name. I'm a fucking super-villain. I learned your name from a very unlikely person, just today on the drive over here. I think he was pissed off. He showed me your picture. But you know *my* name. Yes. I am the hand of fate. *I killed your people.*" Hell turned squeakily around in his seat. "And you're a *fuckface,*" he said. "I'm going to kill you... and then marry your girlfriend. We're going to be buddies, me and her."

Jimmy stared at the fleshy slashes in Finn's face. Like gills in the wrong place. "How did you get here?" he asked stupidly. "Who are you, and why—why are you so fucking angry?" Jimmy immediately flipped the student card. His only defense was inquiry. Meanwhile—perhaps it was the whiskey talking—he had picked up his fork and put it halfway in his sleeve.

Jimmy got up slowly, then turned so he stood upright over Finn, who was crouched and black, spider-like, in the booth.

Finn smiled calmly up at him.

After almost an hour sitting in the booth, Jimmy's legs were weak. But by the time the blood got down in his feet, all he had was instinct. Jimmy sprang on Finn, the blunt fork welded to his left hand.

Finn punched him in the nose with his right arm, stood up, whirled around, and pinned Jimmy's face to the table, putting pressure on his nose, which had broken and was bleeding freely. He slipped handcuffs onto his wrists, then yanked Jimmy up out of the booth, holding a huge handgun to the side of his head. Jimmy was still holding the fork.

Finn spoke: "Hey, girl, see those enchiladas on the table right there?" He nodded towards the table next to theirs, where sat a fresh plate of enchiladas, yellow rice. "Grab that shit. We're getting out of here."

Kaye sat in the booth, stricken.

Finn looked over to an old, bald man who sat a few booths down, drinking a beer with his back to them. The man must have been deaf. He stretched out his arm and blew the man's head off, sending a wave of shock and panic into the corner of the restaurant.

"Let's go, bitch! I'm not fucking around! Grab it!" He turned and fired the revolver again, this time in the direction of the sweet waitress, backing himself and Jimmy towards the front door. "Grab that shit! Grab that fucking shit! And don't worry about the fork! We got one!"

Kaye spun out of the booth, grabbing the enchiladas on the way up, and hurried towards the front door.

85

WHILE THEY RAN, Finn forced Kaye to feed him the enchiladas so he could hold his gun on both of them. He picked off other people who got in their way, thinking *they* were superheroes—and that they could fight him, and that they could defeat him. But Finn was Poof The Motherfucking Gunslinger, and these people were nothing but pissant Mormons with puppy dog syndrome. It's like shooting puppy dogs. In a barrel! *Marvelous!*

They ran for the Pathfinder, which was across the street, parked by the Days Inn reception desk.

Four teeth, Kaye counted, as she gave him a big bite, cringing.

She could smell the gun, even before they got in the car. It smelled like pot resin to her.

"You're driving, girl," Finn said, with a mouth full of food.

"Me?"

"Of course you—I ain't driving. And I don't have the keys to those handcuffs. I took 'em off a cop and forgot the keys! It's a bad habit of mine, hard to break."

He shoved her into the driver's seat, plate of enchiladas crashing to the ground and tossed Jimmy into the back. The door slammed on his toes, shooting electricity up to his knee, where his leg seemed to explode. His foot was stuck in the door. He wailed and curled up around his blister-marbled hand.

Kaye started the car.

The wind was incredible, ripping through the town in broad, cold strokes.

It blew the black cowboy hat off Finn's head, up into the air, and away.

"Where are we going?" Kaye said, trembling as she backed them out of the driveway.

Finn was reloading his Magnum. He looked her up and down. "Mexico, I guess. Through Las Vegas. Take the 15 all the way, that's easiest. Drive as fast as you fucking can. I feel like a bad storm is coming." He buckled his seatbelt, as if to reiterate his command.

Jimmy was curled up in the back seat, with his nose dripping blood all over his face. Toes in his slammed foot were broken. Probably a few metatarsals, too. He groaned like a wounded animal being carted to the vet.

86

THE WIND INTENSIFIED as they drove. In moments, the Pathfinder seemed to be shoved from behind.

The clouds then swallowed the horizon. Grey stripes crossed the sky in front of them. Then within minutes, it became night.

No one followed, except for the storm, which snowballed fast. It thundered and screamed until it seemed like they were all speeding through darkness into nothing. A world where no human had ever been created. A black world, full of protozoa and sounds. A land before time.

Jimmy slipped into a semiconscious daze. He curled up on the backseat, with his crushed left toes still in the doorframe, only conscious of bouncing up and down on his side, and some distant pain.

He never marveled, in all his scholarly wonder, *why* Finn was keeping the two of them alive. Finn was an insatiable killer, and he seemed to have somehow gotten nature to go along with his dirty work. The sky had a murderous look to it—maybe Finn had caused the ice storm that had killed Sarah and his mother (and tried to bury him alive). So why was he still here now, helpless and in handcuffs? And Kaye. Kaye was a sweetheart. What use would Finn have for a sweet girl like her? Then Jimmy had a thought that almost made him laugh: *He's starting a family.*

No, Jimmy was delirious, obviously not seeing the whole picture.

Finn didn't do families. He was born without the family gene.

Also, he couldn't control nature. *We are not the storm*, Jimmy thought.

He was sure he would die in the storm, though, just like Charlotte and his mother and everyone else had died in the storm.

Maybe it had been an hour. Jimmy lay semiconscious, dreaming up possibilities and forgetting them right away. Each time, before his thoughts could snap together into a circle, he forgot where the thought had started, losing the connecting end.

He was just about to sit up when the car blew off the side of the road.

They were in a violent mountain stretch of Interstate 15, red rocks jutting jaggedly in all directions, two lanes of blacktop twisting through a fissure, with a two foot guard rail smirking along one side.

Kaye could feel the hurricane blowing at her back, shoving the car with powerful hands. She imagined God himself drunk off his ass, in a fiery cyclone of rage, stamping out his creations like a lovesick Francis Bacon, destroying his own artwork in a frenzy.

The back wheels spun up off the road, and the car crashed through the guard rail. It drove on a steep angle along the drop for a moment, then righted itself up onto the lane again, smashing through the guard rail a second time.

Jimmy was wide awake and in pain again, but it was impossibly dark outside There was no light along this part of the interstate. The only light was their headlamps, which lit a few yards of television static in front of them.

Kaye peddled scenarios in her mind.

She couldn't crash the car intentionally. Jimmy might not survive. He had no seatbelt on. Finn hadn't strapped one on him, and Jimmy was incapable of crossing his own lap.

And Finn actually *was* wearing a seatbelt.

It was a pitiful image: a thirty-something year-old demon with cobwebs for hair, sniffing his gun, grinning like Gollum—and wearing a seatbelt. He looked like a large, ghoulish child.

So Kaye drove hard and fought for purchase on the road with all her will. They had about fifty minutes to Vegas.

The great shrieking storm rampaged through the blackness. Another minute of this, and they would be bushwhacked off the road, for good this time. Kaye couldn't form a plan in her mind. Her head whirled right along with the wind. Directionless.

The Pathfinder blew off the road.

For good, this time.

87

WHILE THE CAR flew in mid-air, emotions slammed into Jimmy like a storm.

Tears flew from his eyes like cannonballs.

He felt his duck feather face burst out of a cocoon. He saw Kaye and Hell Finn's arms go up, and he heard them scream, all three on a rollercoaster gone right off the track.

Charlotte. Mom. The Galls. Jackie. Everybody. *Me.*

You're really going to miss you, he thought. *How sad.*

Jimmy shut his eyes. He might have screamed. He might have moaned.

The Pathfinder tipped forward in the air, starting to nosedive. The hurricane gave them a lilt. Jimmy felt weightless for a moment.

They hit something big, and Jimmy's door banged open. He flew out of the cab, hands cuffed behind his back, somersaulted twice, and came to lay on his stomach, heaving, head turned to one side as he sobbed in the mud, arms pinned behind him.

The Pathfinder bounced off its nose, flipped over, and landed somewhere below him in a grassy fissure. It splashed into an orange ball of flames and disappeared in the darkness.

Hell Finn was dead.

Poor Kaye from Denver was also dead.

88

From: *THE NEW YORK POST,* page one

GROVER THE LINE! Midtown: A man in Times Square dressed as Sesame Street's "Grover" was brutally killed by police yesterday evening, after a shouting match he started with an angry mob—cont'd page 2

[] Roberto Vasquez, 33, was smothered to death by police in Times Square last night around eight.

Vasquez was dressed like Grover from Sesame Street. He worked as a sidewalk tourist attraction, collecting tips in exchange for photo opportunities.

Vasquez, American, was chased off his usual beat between 42nd St. and 43rd St. by police, after a long-winded anti-Semitic tirade got a huge mob frenzying with outrage. Vasquez had screamed obscenity-laced diatribes at the public, scaring mothers and children alike.

One spectator from Florida said, "He was the scariest Grover I've ever seen! He said things like, 'start a business in New York and the Jews will come for you!'"

The crowd in Times Square reacted harshly. They provoked him, yelled back at him, and eventually formed a mob in front of him, making the big blue-costumed Vasquez look like a furry dictator from another planet.

When the cops realized they couldn't talk him down, they decided to book him, but Vasquez turned and ran, still wearing his mask, through the streets of midtown. Two police officers, who won't be named because they are not yet under arrest, tackled Vasquez and pinned him to the ground. But unfortunately, as they were putting him in handcuffs, they smothered him with the costume mask.

Vasquez died on the scene from asphyxia.

Luis, 26, an immigrant from Peru and fellow Grover, says the Grover community is not affiliated with Vasquez, and hopes that he does not have to buy a different costume.

Vasquez's family so far has not been available for comment.

The two police officers will not be tried for wrongdoings. The police commissioner assured that since these officers could not actually see the man in the costume, they could not be presumed guilty in any way for his sudden death.

The public asks this question: Do the police have the right to kill skiers? Astronauts? Anyone you can't actually see?

FEBRUARY 25, 2021

From: *THE NEW YORK POST*, page five

BUS-TED! A woman in Hell's Kitchen was struck and killed by a bus yesterday afternoon. Charlotte Johannsen, a 19-year-old Barnard student, was tying her shoelace in the street when an MTA Bus ran her over, spraying blood "absolutely everywhere."

John Walter, the bus driver, has been charged with manslaughter.

Walter refused to comment, but according to one bystander, "He looked pretty [buzzed] up."

MTA-NYC apologizes to any and all witnesses who might be suffering psychological damage but also denies liability.

As of now, Johannsen's family is not available for comment.

FEBRUARY 25, 2021

From: *Palm Beach Daily News,* page 2

EEL-ECTRIC CAR! El Cid: An elderly man drove his electric car into a swimming pool full of children yesterday afternoon, killing thirteen people, ten of whom were small kids. He also died on the scene.

Melvin Kirchner, 79, who lived in Flamingo Park, was out buying groceries for his *own* pool party, when his brakes suddenly failed.

Authorities first assumed that Kirchner was simply too

old to drive and fell asleep at the wheel, but officials later discovered that there had been a loose wire under the car that triggered the brake, and it was this same loose wire that had shocked the pool at such a horrific level.

Kirchner drove a Nissan WIND, Nissan's newest electric powered...

FEBRUARY 25TH, 2021

From: *The Las Vegas Evening Sun*, page 6

SHA-NANNY-GANS! Henderson: Trustworthy, reliable, and mentally stable woman murders two children last night in south Henderson.

Leslie and Scott Johannsen, three and five years-old, respectively, were being cared for by Jennifer Brownstone, a local babysitter of Las Vegas, while their father, Magnus Johannsen, was on holiday.

Brownstone allegedly tied the two kids' feet to a ceiling fan in their living room and left them overnight to centrifuge. When she returned to the house the following morning, the two kids were on the floor, along with the ceiling fan and bits of the Johannsen ceiling. The kids were still tied to the fan blades like meat carcasses, and in turn, *also* like meat carcasses, they had been partially eaten, probably by coyotes.

The children were both dead.

The time and cause of death are both undetermined so far. The bodies are currently in autopsy at UNLV.

Brownstone called the police early this morning and

explained to them that she had "found them like that." When asked what the small children had been doing alone at night, Brownstone said she had been visiting her boyfriend.

The boyfriend has not been identified.

Later, Brownstone confessed to the manipulation of the Johannsen kids and was consequently arrested and charged with criminal negligence.

Magnus Johannsen, the childrens' father, has not been informed nor contacted by authorities or anyone known to him. He is, as of now, unreached.

Jennifer Brownstone is currently being held in the Cameron St. Police Station where she awaits a competency hearing...

FEBRUARY 25, 2021

From: The London Herald, page 16

FLOWER POWER! A monumental discovery was made yesterday evening, when a man near London was about the woods hunting.

Frank Barmen was locked on a shot when he noticed a rare, prehistoric-looking flower devouring a fox carcass. Barmen called the police, and when they arrived, their forensic assistant discovered something he had studied at university: paranormal activity.

Zachary Bethel, forensic scientist with a PhD from Oxford, claims that this type of large carnivorous flower has never been seen before on Earth. While examining the surrounding habitat, he documented several rare trees and yet-undiscovered flora.

Theories on where these plants came from are in circulation among the British government, the British Museum, the Norwegian seed repository at Svalbard, as well as the Global Crop Diversity Trust and the Nordic Genetic Resource Center in Sweden.

The Vatican declares that these plants are genetically engineered experiments, although proof of their origin is as of now undiscovered...

FEBRUARY 25, 2021

From: *Le Figaro*, page one

[translated from French] WHERE DID THE LOUVRE GO? The nation was mortified yesterday, when an explosion ripped through the Louvre Museum, killing 87 people and destroying over 200 works of art.

Damon Gaspard, 29, from a small town near Calais, set off the enormous bomb in the security-check lane. The security checkpoint is set apart from the monumental three-wing museum, but, apparently, not far enough.

Half of the Louvre plaza was blown to cinders, exposing the sub-terrain and sinking the entire North Richelieu Wing of the museum.

Gaspard worked at passport control at the Calais/Dover Ferry for six months, but he has no work history prior to...

FEBRUARY 25, 2021

From: *Rossiyskaya Gazeta*, page 2

[translated from Russian] SNACK-PACK SERIAL KILLERS! Dmitri Atoll, Russia's most feared psychopath, is still roaming the country, killing young women and taking heads. Unfortunately, resources for his pursuit are thinning out, making his apprehension nearly impossible.

Here's the hang up: St. Petersburg Police disclosed this morning that there may be more serial killers in western Russia, perhaps as many as *nineteen* total, all responsible for at least three murders, some for as many as thirty-two.

S.P. Chief of Police informs us that of these psychopaths (which there are far too many of), half of them might be female, which is highly unusual.

There is speculation among Russian authorities that the recent natural disasters and accidents that seem to be happening in abundance across western Russia are somehow connected to the sudden rise of serial killers, and some go so far as to associate it to the abrupt crash in world stock markets.

The Moscow Exchange, as well as the London Stock Exchange, has exhibited unexpected...

FEBRUARY 26, 2021

From: *U-T San Diego*, page one

[This publication contains only one page, due to lack of staff and closed print facilities]

HURRICANE FROM HELL!

13,000,000 DEAD!

An act of God? The worst hurricane the world has ever seen came and went last night in a total of six hours.

Stymied, NASA has not confirmed that the storm was naturally occurring, as it could be the result of some kind of weapon of mass destruction. The possibility remains that this devastating weather may have been a terrorist attack of sorts.

Homeland Security and the National Meteorology Union are working furiously for clues as to what, if anything, may have caused this horrifying abomination.

The hurricane started in Southern Utah and moved southwest towards Las Vegas. Its behavioral pattern was erratic, with supernatural overtones. When it reached Las Vegas, it remained there, unmoving for two hours, then began a devastating path southwest to Los Angeles, where it stayed for almost three hours. Eventually it continued southwest, diffusing into a rain shower, and then an otherwise peaceful night.

Las Vegas lost seventy percent of its population. Los Angeles, ninety-one percent. San Diego maintains seventy-six per cent of its population.

At least twelve million people were killed in the storm, and the search for survivors continues. However, there are no roads nor hospitals to facilitate most of the wounded.

Not much information has come to me, for obvious reasons. I am the only U-T journalist who came to work today...

89

THE WORLD CLENCHED. The US swore that they would "dig to the very bottom of this terror." The Department of Homeland Security went into double overtime. The United Nations became a whirlpool of conversations, putting feelers out all over the world.

But the evil stopped—like a thunderclap and a lightning bolt all at once—and there was nothing afterwards. Only peace. Weeks went by, and although the world's population decreased by almost two percent in one week, everything else seemed to remain calm and undisturbed.

None of the hellish events that had swept across the globe were tied to radiation or underground fallout in any way. Fontaine never existed. Neither did Semipalatinsk, or any other nuclear test sites of the sort. No Amchitka, no Novaya Island, no Pokharan in the Indian Desert.

Sandia National Laboratories had the official undisclosed list of underground nuclear explosions.

Fallout would remain in the atmosphere for decades. Underground fallout would stay for much longer.

Nobody thought about evil itself. Nobody compared evil to

a little squirrel running down the Realms Tree and scampering across the universe, four front teeth chiseling its way into Earth's realm and killing lots of people, wiping a town off the map and then dying like a flock of birds in the mud.

90

BACK ON INTERSTATE 15, the storm passed away. Two days later, Jimmy was discovered and brought to a hospital way out in Phoenix.

A week later, he was released, and he went back to New York. Without his mother in Thunder, or his sister across the street at Barnard, he only had his classes. He decided to return, if only to have a place to mourn and fail the semester away.

But he didn't fail the semester, and his grief was more manageable than he had expected. It seemed that Chester had left his optimism to Jimmy before he died. He felt okay as long as he didn't listen to music—music made him heartsick, and it didn't even matter what style.

On his first day back at school, Jimmy was struck by an epiphany. It came from nowhere, wafting through the open iron gates of Columbia, right there on Amsterdam Ave. The idea stopped him on the sidewalk and echoed in his mind like truth, amusing and strangely visual: *Life is like a five-hundred-piece jigsaw puzzle,* he thought. *With ten-thousand pieces in the box.*

He had looked up to Chester. Without Jimmy's father around, Chester had been his masculine influence. He had been better than Jimmy in most ways. Funnier and smarter, better looking. He had made love to his chemistry professor, while Jimmy was still a virgin.

How could the people you looked up to die so young? What were you left with then? Jimmy had envied Chester's life. It didn't make sense.

Jimmy decided to major in nuclear physics, to piss off Chester's memory.

He also pursued answers to what had been baffling the world since his tragedy. After all, he was the only one alive who actually knew Thunder.

He had heard stories about those mines. Stories about his father and Chester's dad too. He knew it was not a hurricane or a "desert typhoon" that had torn his world apart. He put the pieces of his memories together, reflected on Chester's drive for nuclear physics, and decided he would start there. Come May, Jimmy would go back to Thunder to find his answers and see what remained of his mother's house, a strong foundation with a missing heart. A missing town on a map.

His blistered hand healed fine, except for one time when it squirted pus in his face while he was writing in class. He didn't get a new dorm mate. The board department at Columbia cut him a sympathetic deal.

From there, Jimmy went on.

THE END

THE RESULT OF MARCO VALOSO

W E NEVER FINISHED the story of Marco Valoso—the dancer from Naples who found the enchanted bird claw...

PREMIERE

OUTSIDE OF LAS Vegas, in the middle of the desert, it was scorching—130 panic-inducing degrees.

There were four of them inside the tank: Marco Valoso, our Neapolitan circus dancer, the protagonist, or *"Superuomo,"* as he was called. There was a guy named "Kill-Swipe" and another named "Fuckslinger," and a blonde, smirky girl named "Ass," who rode shotgun.

There were two other tanks, each one yielding similar cargo. *Gladiators. Teammates.* Enemies, really. Each of them were made up to be terrifying, armed with nothing but adrenaline and ambition.

The tanks started out in a single file, Marco's in the lead.

They had an hour-long ride from Vegas. Inside the tank, the teammates had time to talk. They all knew they would eventually kill each other, so they kept the conversations short. Ass smelled terrible. Her blonde crusty pigtails fumed like old vodka and cigarettes. She stank, but her eyes and her complexion were clear, so sharp and odorless, as if they could cut Marco clean in half. It was uncanny. She blazed with bloodlust. With a simmering rage just below boiling, she was always smirking or half-smirking.

I'd like to see you try, little girl, thought Marco.

He began to size up the other guys. His enemies.

Fuckslinger, sitting to Marco's left, was one hundred and thirty kilos, a hulking, sad-faced mother. He was probably Marco's age, late thirties, but he looked much older, maybe late forties, with a big old grey mug that sagged like a forgotten Michelangelo sculpture. He looked like a feral half-giant with a rock in his shoe. Fuckslinger looked out the half-opaque window, grunting to himself, his thoughts dark, his eyes like predatory rocks.

Maybe he's killed lots of guys, Marco thought.

Shit, maybe Ass has killed lots of guys, too... But she looks to be happier about it. He couldn't see her face; she sat in the front passenger seat of the vehicle, but her energy was murderous. Yes—having only just met her, Marco knew that Ass was more than a good deal partial to destroying people. Especially men. She was aggressive. She had a short fuse. She performed magic tricks with men's hearts. She sawed them in half, perhaps enveloped them in smoke, or just plain made them disappear. She was a sex bully, a *mean girl*, and rumor had it, she knew Kung Fu extensively.

Which brought him to Kill-Swipe. Kill-Swipe was lean and positively *ripped*, comic book style, and all clad in leather. He had things arranged on his waistband, and big, Belle Époch, H.G. Wells-looking goggles on his eyes. Kill-Swipe didn't talk. Maybe he didn't speak English. Marco spoke English fairly well. Kill-Swipe drove the tank.

There were cameras in the tanks. The Boss had said that The Initiation had already begun. The Boss had said to feel free to look directly into the cameras whenever they wanted. The Boss had said use as much profanity as they could dig out of their vocabulary. Didn't matter which language—they had subtitles for that.

And fuck my little cat! Marco squinted at the distance through the windshield. *Other tanks were approaching!*

West of the highway—northeast of Las Vegas about fifty miles— in the middle of nowhere, military tanks approached them head on. They were beige, not black like their own. Five abreast. They must have been the vanguards of the Initiation.

Marco's tank was a Hollywood set piece, labeled, "MODEL 2.1: FUTURE / MARVEL." No VIN number, no serial number—the DMV certainly had never heard of it—and it was air conditioned, designed for actors, not soldiers.

Marco knew that the moment he debarked this tank, he would appear in a hundred-and-thirty-degrees of desert. It was a crematorium out there, a trembling flare of death.

But making it out of the frying pan is always the first step, right? The tanks moved into view. They appeared to float on the Siamese cat-colored desert. They grew, warbling in the heat refraction. Then they disappeared in a frightening cloud of smoke. There was an explosive sound, *BAKKA-KAA!* Before Marco could guess what was happening, the earth pistoned up beneath him.

"Whaaa—" he thought he yelled, but it was noiseless under the explosions.

The tank landed broadside to the approaching tanks. Kill-Swipe, the driver, at first calm and commandeering in his big goggles, leapt out the driver's side door, which faced the vanguard. Ass, there in the shotgun seat, now revealed by the open driver's side door, started fumbling for her door handle. The heat rushed in. Marco and Fuckslinger lay sprawled out and dazed in the back seat. The first sensible thing that Marco thought was that he was glad he hadn't been sitting where Fuckslinger was sitting, with his head framed in the window of five perfectly clear tanks.

Ass got outside. Now both front doors were open.

The burning air on his face brought him around. But it wasn't the desert generating the heat—there was *fire* in the desert, the flames appearing all around him.

Marco took one last look at Fuckslinger, who wasn't moving but for his mouth. He saw all the other tanks through the window. Fuckslinger saw them, too, turning his head with regretful slowness. But he was too shocked to move his body.

Marco shoved his door open and danced backwards through the flames, away from the burning tank. Again, before he heard the *BAKKA-KAs,* he saw the smoke and blast come off the cannons. Marco dove away from the tank, rolled, leapt up, and ran. Fuckslinger and the tank went up in flames, as an orange parachute of fire fanned open underneath it. Marco looked back and tried to cover his face when the second black tank blew up, knocking him onto his ass. A moment later, the third one started smoking, then flipped onto its back with a finalizing crash.

Eleven gladiators, all large and heavily costumed, arranged themselves behind the flaming wreckage of their vehicles. Orange and black flumes spread out and danced between them. Opposite the wreckage, the five beige tanks resumed their approach, now only one hundred yards away.

The gladiators looked at each other, stunned, their hands clenched into fists. They were scared, like earthquake survivors; but they also looked determined, and admittedly, badass.

Helicopters went up in a roar around them, in a thousand-foot closed parentheses. They were each lumbering aerial cameras and cranes. Camera men clung to the cranes like monkeys.

Marco couldn't hear the helicopters at first. He thought it was some illusion. But when his hearing came back, it was all real again. *Yup, helicopters.*

Marco saw tufts of sand popping up off the ground. It reminded him of rain on the beach. But there was no way it would rain here today. Then, he registered a low crackling sound in the distance, and then the smoking tank remains before them were making loud banging sounds.

He hit the ground and covered his head. The rest followed suit. A second after the gunfire stopped the bombings began.

They were Master Bombers, also known as Pathfinders, though Marco hadn't been educated of that at the time. There were six of them. They dropped smoke bombs and flare bombs all around them, not wielding too much lethal strength, but it looked totally awesome, and the warriors, too, looked totally awesome when the fire cleared and they were seen in HD standing like the Avengers, covered in smudges and burns, sweating, arriving from all corners of the world to blow audiences' minds with entertainment.

When the smoke cleared, their ruined tanks were gone. The helicopters were still there, but instead of the open desert beneath them, there was what looked like a titanic television stage, sprawling in the blown-out sunlight. It was on a grade, four large stairs with two hundred-foot plateaus connecting them, and at the top, the five beige military tanks stood abreast, facing the warriors below.

It must have grown up out of the ground, Marco thought with total amazement. *This is getting good.*

The doors of the five tanks opened. Ten men got out and closed the doors.

The warriors, totally confused at the bottom end of the stage, saw the men buttoning their suit jackets and facing them, lining up in front of the tanks. The warriors looked at each other, then looked around themselves for a director or some kind of leader.

No leader. It was just them. Eleven gladiators. Gladiators of the year.

Aside from Fuckslinger, everyone had made it to standing. And everyone looked equally confused in the background, confused as to what exactly had just happened and what would happen next.

"I should have had my agent read the contract for me," Marco muttered to himself.

Then, above the surrounding noise of the helicopters, a single man's voice, loud and wet boomed: "WELCOME TO THE WARRIORS!"

His voice echoed and then met silence but for the steady, droning chopper sounds.

Was this a *welcoming* or was this an *initiation?* Because in Naples, where Marco was from, those two things could have a very different feel.

"SUNSET!" blared the voice, and its echoes sprawled across the vista. Among the huddled gladiators, an Asian man, tall and lean and dressed in a tattered black suit that looked like it may have been top fashion before he dove out of his exploding tank, began to walk forward. He had a sharp, tanned Asian face that the sun glared at. There should have been music blasting, top forty or something, exploding confetti, and pyrotechnics.

But instead it was quiet and stark. The emptiness spooked Marco. Even the stage itself seemed to have an anticlimactic, communist look to it. It was dull and industrial, as if they were standing on a kitchen appliance the size of a racetrack. A 1950s-style colossal stainless steel meat grinder.

A few long, photographic moments later, Sunset was at the top of the stage.

One of the men in suits gave him a letter, or a permit or something, and another man gave him a necklace. He shook three people's hands, and then he began to walk back toward the clan of gladiators who wavered like mirages in the heat, far below him.

"KILL-SWIPE!" the voice boomed again. The sound seemed to visibly strike Sunset's back as he descended.

The ripped man in leather and goggles started walking forward.

RECAP:

TWO MONTHS BEFORE, in Munich, Marco Valoso had been given a wish: to be all better.

In turn, he received a curse.

They came in tandem. He himself hadn't wished to be all better. His friend Anders Lund had wished it for him, because Marco had been indisposed at the time, suffering a badly sprained joint in his neck. Marco had been semiconscious on the floor, And Anders wished for Marco's wellness. The workings of the magical claw was somehow thrown askew.

So the curse was adhered to a third party. Not Anders and not Marco.

It was Marco's sister, Paola, back in Naples.

Paola fell ill exactly one week after Marco had gotten all better. She came down hard with pneumonia, checkmate style, and she went to live, barely, in a hospital. Marco knew he had to get money to bail her out of the hospital and put her where she belonged, at home, with Mama and Papa. He knew that Paola might die anyways, but he believed that money could save her in some way, if only just to make her better temporarily.

So he came out to the press with evidence about his powers. He showed them the smooth arc of deltoid where his vaccine scar had always been. He talked to the public, set up a few interviews, and before long his fame had taken off like a brand new bicycle. He got himself sponsored by CANAL Studios in Rome, Rai Studios, CNN, ESPN, Fox, and a dozen other networks worldwide.

He auditioned for the biggest game show in the world. And he booked it.

The cash prize was too big to put in writing.

When the day came, he wasn't very nervous. The power he felt overcame his nervousness—or rather passed right through it. He believed, whole-heartedly, that he was going to win, even though he was half of each gladiator's size.

COLOSSEO DELLA MORTE!
Presenta di Giulio Mercola

MEGA 2 e STUDIO CANAL 1 • 24 Aprile PALASPORT
FLAMINIO!
ROMA!

Marco looked at the poster on the bus shelter. He smiled at his face. It was perfect.

All his teeth, unbelievable. No burns on his arms, impossible. No scar on his neck, staggering. And hold on—what's that you say? No Photoshop? *Truthfully?*

There had been no touchups applied to Marco *"Superuomo,"* but many, all due, to the others—their characters all centrifuged, like an explosion of faces.

Marco totally had these guys. Kill-Swipe, Ass, Fist Machine, Blacko, and even big Kroksen. They would be dead in the water. All of them.

The bus sat idling on the Roman hillside of Monte Mario. It was a modern bus, nosey and silver, an aberration in such an old city.

Most of the others were already inside the bus. By Rome, there were only six gladiators left.

Also in the bus were Giulio, the producer (there were many producers on this show, but Giulio was known as "the producer" because he was always around and had the most artistic input), three actors that Marco never met, and Bicho, the liaison, who was not Italian but Argentinian. Somehow Bicho was Giulio's cousin. Marco had no idea how, and he didn't much care.

The networks all traded footage and worked together. Their respective directors had their own version of *Colosseo* which they angled diversely in presentation, making it palatable to their country's unique television style, but they shared clips, dramatic angles, and sometimes entire episodes, pooling footage. It was aired in fifty-nine countries. It toured to ten.

Italy, Romania, the United States, and Germany all had their own networks that showed coverage of *Colosseo* twenty-four hours a day.

Sometimes Giulio rode in his jet plane. Once he arrived, he'd hop in his rented black Hummer. Sometimes he rode in the creatives' bus, and often in production's. But today, for reasons of his own, he rode on the artists' bus, with the gladiators.

Rome was a good place for producers, but it was also a good place for artists. And what artist was better suited for Rome than a gladiator in a colosseum to perform and be observed in his ancestors' hometown? *Roma*, good old Roma.

Bicho sat in the front of the bus with the driver. Giulio sat behind him in repose, typing on his cell phone while his cast of characters loaded the bus behind him. Like all producers, he was extremely proud of this year's season.

The trucks had already set up the tents in the west of Rome, past Flaminio. Rai Studios was far away, in the center of Rome, and the CANAL Studios were farther still, to the south. Cine Citta was there, and they would have provided studio rentals, should *Colosseo* need any extra gear, but no one wanted to go that far south in Rome. There was nothing there but roundabouts, laundry, and quiet shockwaves over empty nights. Past Flaminio, to the west, sat a park, surrounded by residential apartments.

The trucks slept in a line, while the arena was built up behind them. Big tops, parking lots, tents, and boxcars with cafes in them. One hundred and twenty-three thousand seats. Seven billion dollars in advertising space. Over one thousand networks in fifty-nine countries. Four billion viewers worldwide.

And that was just on *Earth*—who knows how many more tuned in out there?

Chain link fences were rolled out and set to divide sectionals, for parking, and for video trailers. They removed the sides of production semis and fixed two of them together, creating larger vessels for offices. This type of double rig also accommodated a catering department, bathrooms with showers, a red carpet room, and most essentially, the medical truck.

The circus big tops gave *Colosseo* a gala-type feel and a freaky, fun theme. The tents also acted as canopies; shrouding the convention from above added a wash of mystery, intensity, and an "anything's possible" intrigue—because this show was a primetime tryst, and everyone knew it.

Marco savored a last glance at himself in the bus shelter poster.

He had been a performer his entire life. He had struggled for work most of it. He had studied circus arts, ballet, and various contemporary dance styles, but he'd missed out on stardom and the fancy gigs there attached, as most dancers did (all contemporary dancers, in fact). The TV studios didn't want him, not even for music videos, even though they were plentiful in Los Angeles. They were simple and crappy, but the City of LA practically ran on their economic yield, just as his tour bus ran on diesel fuel.

Marco smelled the fumes eddying on the side of the bus. He smiled one last time at his image in the poster. He had worked hard all his life. Not for fame but for money. Now he was the star of a show so big it had its own franchised restaurant in northern Germany. "Morte," it was called, which obviously meant "Death." One of their signatures was a kind of elk sushi with dragon fruit eel sauce. Fine dining to the max.

I'm the biggest superstar on Earth right now, he thought, as he scratched his thinning brown hair. *And the cash prize is so big it gives me vertigo!*

But then his mood slid into a darker place. He asked himself how he could murder eleven people for money and maintain his good conscience, or any conscience at all. He had never thought about killing anyone before, not realistically, not anywhere near the *neighborhood* of realistically. Morally, how could he live with that? Or fuck living with that—how could he even do it in the first place?

Well, first he would have to change his mindset.

What kind of person would murder people with his bare hands for cash?

It's not just cash, he thought. *It's power. It's everything. Cash is the power to save people. Starting with Paola. Her quality of life is only possible with enough cash.*

And furthermore, who would be so evil as to *deserve* to be killed by him? Well, maybe the kind of lowlife who would kill people for cash, that's who. Assholes, that's who.

Marco thought about himself in the realm of all this. He believed that he was a nice guy, a goodhearted Neapolitan *pisano,* and he always had been. He was, in all truth, an upstanding citizen with no criminal record.

Maybe they all were. Maybe everyone in the tournament was a regular Joe in a wild costume, just doing this for no reason except for what the TV commercials alleged: a release of ordinary life, money, and fame to the wicked. People loved it because it felt a little wrong, a little evil, just to boost the economy.

And why not? Plenty of people out there in the world had secret fetishes—dominatrixes, occult religious gatherings, squatted drug zones for on-again-off-again meth heads. The basements, the dredges. Everyone had a dark side. Every*thing* had a dark side. The earth, its cities, the weather, love. *Colosseo* made it all okay.

Every warrior in the show had a squeaky clean record. Everyone except for Macavinta. He was a wife-killer, but that was just a little twist in the overall story line. And he was added later, anyways. It wasn't the Hunger Games or some military experiment. It wasn't some Lionsgate film or a Philip K. Dick story. It was real. It was on TV. Pit fighting, plain and simple. It was scumbag versus dirtbag, in HD, 3D, live—you could see their DNA puffing off them with each bone-crushing punch. Blood and sweat and mist on the camera lens—that's what this show was about. Pit fighting and nothing more.

The moral complexities within *Colosseo* were saved for other television shows that reported on it (cutting the producers of *Colosseo* a little slice of the bacon, of course). Even ESPN produced a show on this show, one in which a black meathead and a white beefcake, both in suits, discussed things like strategies and the chemistry between fighting styles. About strength versus intellect versus speed. It was basically two grown-ups passionately discussing who would win in a fight: Batman vs Superman, Leatherface vs Freddy Kruger, or Mega Man vs Post-apocalyptic Gunslinger.

And the grand prize for the last man alive was not going to prison.

Genius.

The euros fell in by the billions.

Killing the girl was going to be hard though, really hard. Here's why: Marco pitied women. He didn't see the evil in them that he saw in men. They always seemed to have a good half, at the very least. He could thwart a woman's evil half, or beat it right down to a paste, but he didn't believe that he could kill the rest of her. A woman was too precious, too beautiful. Even if she had a name like Ass. Marco was an artist after all, and that kind of beauty, the good light of a woman, had too much value to destroy. Throughout his life he always searched out the good half of women, always had one eye open for it. He would try to uncover it or to chisel it out like a sculpture from a stone. But now he was putting himself in the path of killing one.

To kill a woman, to make *no one* love her ever again, he would need to navigate his conscience around it somehow. He was just not *that* kind of man. He had always tended to women. He'd protected them as if they were his half-finished sculptures—a compulsion.

He would enjoy beating her though. She smelled so badly, like old vase water, heavy and offensive. And she would fight back too, no doubt. It would be exciting! But how would he move past the pillow fight and into ending her life—removing her karma forever?

Sex, he presumed. And not in a good way.

She was sexy. Marco could pretend that he was a rapist murderer of some kind, only temporarily, to get into character. He would have to get sick in the head, subscribe to their fetishes, try to get turned on by it, pretend to enjoy it as he felt the rush of millions of people watching them—*would he do it? Would he murder this cute little girl in cold blood?*

It would be role-play, but it would be horrible, and he would feel disgusting, possibly deserving of his own death, but he would do it. For Paola. Because he believed he would win.

But what then? This is why killing the girl was going to be so hard. Because he would not do it for justice, and not for sport either. He would do it for pleasure, forced into character though it may be. And that would haunt him forever, he knew that. He might not ever look at women the same way again, which is a shame because of his superpowers and his ability to perform—in other ways besides television.

He looked at Ass's image on the poster.

She held her left hand by her face in a Kung Fu gesture, obscuring part of it, but the visible part revealed a beautiful and sharp face, with a Hollywood sugar glaze, even though she was snarling, and her teeth were pink, blood running out of them onto her chin.

She might actually be the hardest one.

Marco laughed uncomfortably and turned toward the bus. Kroksen (the big Ukrainian guy) and two actors, Jane and Sebastien, were smoking by the door. Everyone else was on board.

Showtime at the arena, folks. Time to go.

Jane walked up to Marco as he approached the bus. She seemed shy around him. Everyone seemed infatuated with Marco these days, and not because of his stardom, or his somewhat smoldering Italian look, but because of his superpowers. He was a demigod, and in his native country, nonetheless. The goddam trees were infatuated with him.

"Hey," Jane said, her arms folded across her chest. She met Marco apart from the others, so they wouldn't be overheard, and she spoke in room-temperature tones. "You know Steve, the British truck driver with the ponytail?"

"Uh... with the black hair?"

"Yeah, quiet guy," she said, leaning into him a little.

"Yes," Marco said. "I mean I didn't know his name, but I know who you're talking about."

Marco liked Jane. They had only been on the road for six days;

they had done one show in Hong Kong, one in London, and the long drive across Europe.

Jane had been on the road a bit longer and had been to some rehearsals. She had stayed five days in each venue already. She knew the routine. But Marco, being a fighter, only joined up on tour a week ago, after The Initiation, near Vegas. He hadn't yet found time to lather Jane with his smoldering Italian salve. And now it was, in Marco's experience touring with dance companies and circuses, the inevitable bomb time, the time when the tour upgraded, and you nail the floorboards down on the hot girl. She seemed fun, too. You would have to be to book *this* job.

Marco followed her lead, and they angled away from Seb and Kroksen.

"He's got cocaine, dude," she said. "He's got a lot of it—you just gotta ask him." Jane relaxed a bit, as if they were friends. Marco liked that.

"The truck driver?" Marco asked. "Well that is some very—wow—information. Thank you, Jane."

"Yeah, you know. I tour a lot," she said. She kept her arms folded.

"Do you have some on you right now?" Marco added.

It always happened so fast. First week, floorboards nailed. Every time.

The bus closed its doors with everyone on board and started slowly down Monte Mario into the center of Rome.

Marco and Jane did not sit next to each other (too soon!). But they did play secrets together like school kids on a field trip, looking at each other and smiling private smiles that nobody on the bus noticed or even would give a shit about. But that news would be big if it *did* get out, should someone decide to give a shit. Marco was one of the biggest celebrities in the world! If he was alive in a week, he would not be able to go into public without bodyguards. Not that he would need them anyways.

What if he got her pregnant? Would their babies have super-powers? Marco had been tested for abnormalities by scientists. They found no outstanding chromosome in his blood work, nothing augmentative, nor thyroidal, nor supernatural.

There was nothing scientifically identifiable about Marco at all, except that he had this ridiculous strength, this bewildering intelligence, and these animalistic reflexes. And no skin blemishes or scars, not even a hangnail. It was as if he were under a spell.

And Jane was sexy—it would look like perfectly normal tour behavior if they had a little humpy-pumpy on the side. That was one of the things that made touring appear so glamorous to the general public, aside from the romance of traveling itself. The humpy-pumpy! Needless to say, this was an extremely graphic, murder-encouraging, swear-fest-of-bad-messages television show, so the artists were encouraged to show their dark sides as much as possible. The more loathsome they appeared, the better the show looked. Sexual promiscuity, harassment, all of it was encouraged— even production-paid prostitutes weren't expressly excluded. And if one artist said a cruel or embarrassing thing about another artist on camera—let's say in relation to cock size or vagina smell, a little *bonus* might be direct-deposited into the little shit-talker's checking account.

They each did a load of coke in the bathroom of the bus, separately, and Marco had to fight back hysterics as he pushed out the door and saw the backs of everyone's heads in their seats. They were all different colors and styles, and all hilariously backwards and blameless. They had no trainers, no managers; they were each alone, and all of them but one were headed for a dead end. Literally. That was funny to Marco, not bitter at all.

He and Jane shared a bond now, and he was proud of it. The connection to a girl is one like no other.

When they got to the arena, there were plenty of places to galavant off to, to frisk each other and do more blow. Marco also liked being with someone he wasn't eventually going to kill.

Jane had light brown wavy hair, soft features, and cowboy boots. She was from the United States and good friends with the choreographer. She was hanging out with a murderer, and someone who might die in as soon as five hours. Marco couldn't get that off his mind.

It had only been six days of touring, so far. Two shows and one fight.

He'd killed a man named Sledgehog in London. His real name had been Victor Black, also known as "Tennessee." He had been the American.

Kill-Swipe was Brazilian. Kroksen, Ukrainian. Ass was Norwegian, and Blacko, Nigerian. Fist Machine, British. Father, Chinese. Sunset, Japanese. Alla was Pakistani, and Machete, Mexican.

Fuckslinger had been from Lebanon.

An ugly man named Jorge Macavinta was added after Fuckslinger died. He had been a UFC Champion, a superstar of the past, but he'd killed his wife. He chopped her up and put her in cement in two separate Rubbermaid bins, and for that he'd incurred life in prison. He had lived in Las Vegas and got pent-up in Ely, but they let him out to do *Colosseo*, because they needed twelve Gladiators, and they would have busted out more inmates if that's what it had come down to after the Initiation. Also, they had other applicants, the callbacks from the auditions. But they chose Jorge Macavinta, the wife-killer. How do they come up with this stuff anyways?

By Rome, Sledgehog, Father, Machete, Sunset, Alla, Fuck-slinger, and Macavinta were all dead.

And now it was showtime again already!

Better party it up! Pretend it's your last day on Earth!

RAGAZZI, LUCI! MUSICA! PRONTO, E…

Episode 4: Colosseo Della Morte, in Rome. They tried to book the actual Colosseum for the show, but they were almost denied entry into the country for asking. So it was Flaminio Palasport Arena instead. Symbolically, it was just as good.

Episode 1 was *The Initiation*, filmed in Vegas. "Welcome to the Warriors," they called it. It was also a worldwide memorial for the hurricane that had demolished the American Southwest just two months prior. The entire planet tuned in religiously, observing the higher power of The Network. Los Angeles had been scrubbed off the map, which gave birth to *Colosseo*. Death reminded the world to never forget.

They lost Fuckslinger that day, in Episode 1, and since then, the "Warriors" all had the all-too-real, sour taste of blood on their tongues.

Episode 2 was in Hong Kong.

The Hung Hom Coliseum shimmered, looking like Heaven on Earth. It was gold, glittering, and cavernous, until it flooded with mud and broken glass. The Warriors wrestled and strangled each other in thick white slime, and eventually they became monsters, toothpastey-looking swamp things.

Blood came in every fight, as the heavenly glass set exploded at the top of each of the Round Twos. The Round Ones were just for show anyways. Let 'em duke it out. Let 'em *slime* it out. Round One was fun, but Round Two was where the money was.

It ended up being a ceremony of blood, olympic in size. By the end of the first fight, the coliseum looked like an enormous bloody zit. By the end of the whole night, it was a sea of blood.

The viewers cried and screamed and banged their foreheads against their television sets at home, elated.

First, Blacko fought Machete.

This fight was memorable because it occurred in pure white mud and glass. Visually, it became an instant classic, a monument to Asian art design. It was Neo-Kabuki theater. The only plot was the lives of the gladiators. These were real men, perhaps destined to lose everything and to paint the white canvas with their finale in blood.

Blacko creamed Machete in the second round. It was the first death of the season, and Blacko made a big spectacle of it by cutting off Machete's head with a shard of glass. The world watched the light in Machete's eyes go out, as he became what they called "Dead in HD."

Central America was wounded by his loss, but their networks didn't suffer, not one bit. They never did. *Colosseo* was a six-episode obsession.

Next Alla fought Kill-Swipe.

Alla fought well, first running towards the bloody area of Machete's death to look for shards of glass that might have been overlooked during the cleaning interval.

But in the end, all the way in the opposite corner of the arena, in Round Three, Alla lost his life to Kill-Swipe. Kill-Swipe grappled Alla, who was still wearing his turban, and briskly managed him into a full-Nelson and rammed him through a glass wall that had malfunctioned when the set exploded. Alla blacked out, bleeding to death in the slime, about to be called out, when Kill-Swipe flipped him onto his back and straddled him. He grabbed a large shard of glass and sliced Alla open, pelvis to collar, unzipping him like a duffel bag full of blood and guts.

Ass was incredible.

Fist Machine, the enormous Brit, was able to postpone his death until the second round, but as soon as their beautiful set exploded, Ass grabbed two shards of glass, one in each hand, and ran fast at him, carving a wake of white and red peppermint slime in her path. Fist Machine was down in thirteen seconds, and he was dead in sixteen. Episode 2, all told, had been a great success.

Episode 3 took place in London. Marco killed Sledgehog by rolling him up into a ball with his head between his legs and squashing him with his arms, emitting a painful *crunching* sound. That sound was the number one text tone for the summer. Marco broke Sledgehog's back in eighteen places, and Sledgehog died on the spot.

Kroksen, the Ukrainian, skewered Father, the Chinese man, in the throat with a tree branch.

The O2 Arena had a "park" theme, with lots of trees in it.

Kroksen suffered a smashed AC Joint in his shoulder. It was a nasty break, but he was deemed eligible to continue onward to the next episode.

Sunset, the Japanese Ninja in the black dinner suit, killed Macavinta, the Vegas wife-chopper. He kicked Macavinta repeatedly, staggering him backwards into a tree trunk, then spun him around and slammed his face into a jut, braining him.

Marco thought about his sister as he watched.

Episode 4 took place in Rome.

Jane was sweating so much her hair was dripping. She was bent over, exposing her teeth in a sex grin. Marco was doing her from behind. He was calm, also grinning but with good humor and delight. He felt crazily sober—there, right there in the sports arena bathroom, lights glaring, body thrumming on cocaine, he had a hot American hellcat in his lap squealing. He felt like checking his phone for new text messages. *Fa niente,* he thought. *Wherever you go, there you are!*

Ironically, *she* was doing *him* like it was *her* last day on Earth. Like they would be her last beads of dancer sweat that ever spattered a floor.

She definitely was not thinking about having super-powered babies.

Done and satisfied, Jane left the bathroom. She went to go find her choreographer, Brandon. Marco had seen him around but had never met him. He seemed like an asshole.

As Marco came out a minute later, he heard his name being called on some sort of God Mic. It echoed throughout the arena. He hadn't heard it inside the bathroom, but as he walked out, he heard it clearly, and Kroksen the Ukrainian was walking towards him.

"Superwoman, you go to *steege!*" he said. And he turned and walked back from where he'd come from.

Kroksen had tentacle-looking hair that sat on top of his big shoulders, like an octopus perched on a rock. He walked with a slow, steady pace. Marco imagined that if Kroksen were to hit him, he'd hit with soulful, profound meaning. Kroksen shook his head slowly as the octopus shifted its position. "Superwoman," he mumbled under his breath, amused with himself.

Hopefully Kroksen was leading him toward the stage. Marco would have had no clue where to start looking for the stage if it wasn't for Kroksen. He didn't remember how he had followed Jane to the bathroom twenty minutes before. He would have thought the layout of an arena would be simple, but no; the signs were only every hundred meters.

Marco followed Kroksen, and it was a four-minute walk back to the stage. He wondered nervously if he would be billed to fight Kroksen for tonight's episode. He hoped not. He liked Kroksen.

The walk felt much longer than four minutes with the voice of the PSM officiously paging him: "Superuomo to the stage, please." Then, "We're looking for you, Superuomo!" Next, "No cold feet—we're going!" Eventually, as the walk began to seem endless, the voice of Giulio Mercola, the producer himself came on: "MARCO, STAI ROMPENDO IL MIO CATSO! CHE *CATSO STAI FACHENDO?*"

When Marco got to the stage, he felt boyish, and utterly non-deadly. His shapeless brown hair was sticking out, his lips held in a straight crease. He cursed the stupid Adidas jumpsuit he wore.

The pit where the matches would take place was elevated three meters off the floor.

Marco climbed a small ladder onto the stage. *It's some kind of swimming pool or Jello bowl,* he grimaced. *Or... an alligator pit or something. This is going to be a mysterious pain in the ass.*

The ring looked like a giant snare drum to Marco, and it was decorated with cross-ties and a drumhead-looking platform, to complete the style. *We're going to fight on a drum? What is that?* But he anticipated that there was more to this evening's show than the initial set up. After all, this was Rome—the birthplace of pit fighting!

"Hey, Super-homo, where you *been?*" Jane asked, smirking as she headed to the stage with Brandon the choreographer and the other performers. They were going to run the opening number. She was smiling, and Marco realized that he didn't care if he was going to fight in a deep swimming pool. He would win anyways. The time spent between "action" and "cut" would be only a minor nuisance, and then he'd be on to the next city, little Paola that much closer to health.

Marco was instructed to get a physical checkup in the medical truck. He came out fine. Better than usual, in fact. Then he went to another truck to get his legal spiel, then another for "talking points," and finally, he saw the night's lineup and show list detailing who was to fight whom and in what order. There was no talk about what to expect. Everything was improvised on the spot, as agreed upon from the outset.

The big tops began opening their doors to the Roman public. The PSM poked his head into Marco's dressing room and said, "Thirty minutes, Marco."

Showtime, folks.

Marco fought first, courtesy of his home country.

Kill-Swipe was his challenge.

The crowd went berserk, as Marco walked alone down the ramp towards the ring. The overhead speakers burst with White Zombie's "More Human Than Human" slamming heartbeat rhythms under a caterwauling guitar. But louder still was the earthquake of cheers and jeers the crowd made. A little slice of fear wedged its way into Marco's chest.

Kill-Swipe's theme song was unknown to Marco, but it was a great one for sure—loud and fearsome and fast. The cheering grew louder, but Marco could tell no real difference in overall partisanship. This season was the best one yet, by far.

Kill-Swipe and Superuomo faced each other from opposite sides of the drum. Kill-Swipe wore scaly grey leather and a techno kind of goggles new to him. But Marco was the superhero, dressed in a blue soccer uniform and high top blue soccer shoes. *What's blue and Adidas and Italian all over?* His friend Anders used to say that, wherever *that* guy was these days. Marco hadn't seen him since that shit-show happened in Munich. He figured Anders was watching *Colosseo* on TV. He never imagined that Anders would join a team of mercenaries in Germany with Yuri and eventually explode and reform into a blob monster off Route 66 somewhere in America.

Marco's hair and his makeup were the only two things making him look at all professional. He wasn't even muscular, not compared to Kill-Swipe, who had at least seven inches of height on him. Kill-Swipe looked like a villain. Superuomo looked like a thirty-something dancer from Italy.

They stood on opposite edges of the ring like goalies in a soccer match with no teams. They walked to the center, where they shook hands.

The crowd screamed, which caused the stage and overhead rigging to rattle around him. The floor thrummed like a timpani drum.

The announcers, who were nowhere to be seen, yelled over them in English and Italian simultaneously.

Then came the horn blast, and they were off.

It started with a kick to the balls (Just like a real soccer match!) and Marco went down instantly. *Fuck,* he thought. *Who kills someone by kicking them in the* balls?

Kill-Swipe was on him fast, climbing up his back. Marco could smell his breath right away, like bananas and bacteria. He reached over his shoulder and cinched together enough leather to purchase Kill-Swipe and throw him over his head onto the ground. Kill-Swipe got up fast, but he seemed to have hurt his knee, perhaps sprained it.

Kill-Swipe didn't put his weight on his left foot. Marco saw this and took a step back, as if to check him out, and Kill-Swipe stood there. *He can't run,* Marco thought. *He can't use that leg.* Marco almost smiled, but he knew it would not have been appropriate in the current situation. Marco was just relieved that he wouldn't have to fight too much. He hated fighting. He just did it to keep his sister alive. So tonight he was happy for this easy win. He was glad to be able to earn so much money for so little work. But still, Marco didn't smile.

He sprinted at Kill-Swipe, who was negotiating with his knee, trying to use time to his advantage, using it to get his bearings. *Dead in the water*, Marco thought. He was more right about that than he knew at the time.

Before Marco reached Kill-Swipe, the drumhead vanished, and they fell suddenly into a giant pool of saltwater, thrashing and sinking.

What the fuck? Marco screamed inside his head. He hated water. Until now he hadn't realized that he almost had a phobia of it. He had never liked to swim, and he wasn't very good at it. *I can't throw a punch in this,* he bellowed to himself.

They scrambled towards each other like dogs, grappling with one another.

Three blades then dropped into the pool around them. One of them struck Marco's shoulder hard, and he began to bleed into the water. Kill-Swipe noticed his injury, caught that same knife in the water, and slashed Marco across the chest in a broad gesture, armpit to armpit. Marco curled up and kicked Kill-Swipe in the stomach with both feet, pushing backwards off him, and dove to find another blade.

The crowd, from underwater, sounded like loud television static.

But Marco discovered that he could swim exceptionally well. Better than he ever had before, anyways. He turned and dove, and through the blood rising from his chest he saw his blade, although Kill-Swipe was guarding it.

Kill-Swipe held two blades in one hand, pointed in either direction out of his white-knuckled fist. His other hand was treading water desperately. He jerked and wiggled, and he looked badly hurt. But Marco could see him smirking under his goggles.

The third blade was lying underneath Kill-Swipe's flailing legs, on the floor of the tank.

The movement, underwater, caught on camera was beautiful and lyrical. The diffused lighting was "spot on," as the directors would say, and the show had gone off without a hitch.

Blood was leaking out of Marco's chest and shoulder. As he swam for Kill-Swipe, a red flume trailed out behind him.

He didn't go for the blade at first. He went to break Kill-Swipe's arms.

Looks like I'm working after all, he thought.

Marco went in fast, but Kill-Swipe, crouched and ready with a full lung of air and his goggles allowing him to see underwater, managed to tag him on the back of his head, right behind his left ear.

It was deep, and a lot more blood floated out. A red thundercloud grew in front of Marco's eyes.

Blindly scrambling with his hands, Marco found Kill-Swipe's arm– the one with the blades clutched at the end–and broke it. It sounded like a car axel breaking, and he felt it against his body. Marco yanked the two knives away from Kill-Swipe's limp arm, again using his feet against his chest as a leverage point, swirled around and sliced him across his throat.

Kill-Swipe's mouth dropped open in a gasp. He drowned instantly. A moment later, the pool was overcast with blood and darkening.

Marco submerged his head in the water to dampen the audience's screams. The blast horns blared, the announcers yelled over each other, and as if that weren't enough chaos, White Zombie's "More Human Than Human" thundered through the stadium.

The thick, turbid pool strobed darkening blood-filtered colors, and Marco floated in it, one hand clutching the back of his head. The lights and pyrotechnics around him looked like nothing he'd ever seen before. He smiled, feeling a little better about having murdered Kill-Swipe. It was all a storm of stage lights and fireworks.

Next, Ass fought Sunset, the Japanese Ninja. Thirty seconds on the drumhead sparring, then bath time.

The water hadn't been changed between matches. It got darker and more bloodbath-like as the night went on.

Ass won, slicing Sunset to pieces. Some of the pieces floated delicately to the bottom. Most of his body was removed from the tank.

In the next match, Blacko and Kroksen drew a tie, killing each other in the second round. Blacko died first, awarding Kroksen the victory, but then Kroksen died before his song could finish. He lay on the side of the large blackish-red pool and bled out his death on the rim.

His song, Tool's "Sober," rocked on for a minute after his ghost was already gone.

LATER:

MARCO AND ASS sat quietly in the medical truck. There were massage tables, blue Pilates mats for stretching on, free weights, and a smell of soggy feet. The back half of the truck was walled with medical supplies.

It was just the two of them from this point forward, and just one of them—probably Marco—would remain in three days.

Jane hadn't felt like a long time ago, until now.

They were silent for a while, Ass and Marco, reflecting on the eleven dead men and the chaos that it was probably causing out in the real world.

They reflected on these men with shame. Because backstage, everything was different.

"Are we evil?" Marco said.

Ass looked up from her hands, blinking away her own reflections. "What?"

"I said, are we—"

"Do you think we can call it off?" she asked. "The rest of the show?"

Marco was taken aback by this. He hadn't thought of it until now. "Do you want that?" he asked.

"Maybe," she replied. "If we can. Maybe we can split the money or something. Or we can give some of it to charity!" Her pigtails were wet and still offered that horrible smell. "We could make it look like a world press event! A big universal movement for peace. Like—uh, Martin Luther King! That's the only way, right? We have to make a big meaning out of it. A whole *movement*. We can't just pussy away and give up—they won't buy that, obviously. This is a TV show. But we can—oh!—we can stage a *riot!* Shit, we can make a bigger show than anyone ever expected! And if we show blood, up front, the world will believe us! And follow us!"

"Hold on—I don't know," Marco said, disbelieving. Ass was looking very small in her exhaustion, and, for the first time, helpless. "But," he added. "There's no harm in asking."

Marco could hear a group of dogs outside the medical truck,

ten to fifteen meters away. They were barking vaguely in his direction.

There are police dogs in the parking lots and near the trucks, too. Marco remembered causing problems with the dogs on his first visit to the medical truck in London. These dogs were not going to let up, Marco knew that. The only way these dogs would let up was if they somehow got excited to death.

"Anyways, *Superuomo...*" she said, changing her tone to one more aggressive. "What do you have against the obvious?"

"What?" Marco didn't relate. "What do you mean? Why?"

"They're going to kill you, you know." She stared at him. Her lopsided pigtails and sharp blonde face were frozen. "After the show. You know they will try to kill you. Put you in jars. This show is all about *you.* You are not just a celebrity; you're a phenomenon. A *freak!* You're the second season of Morte, and they're gonna nab you on the way out of the studio, the *second* this is over. All the scientists and armies. You're going to be probed and chopped up until you're just a brain in a tank. They're going to figure out how to make someone else like you for the *third* season!"

"That's not possible," Marco said, remembering the Navajo shaman in Arizona. That man was probably dead by now, possibly by his own reckless, stupid curses. Even if the feds had persuaded Marco to give the man up, they would never find him. But they would try, if they believed him at all and didn't think Marco was just shunting them with absurdities.

"You might as well die here," she continued. "By me. You know, die a hero."

"No, I will not," he said. *What is she talking about? She's desperate.* Marco gave her a soft, apologetic look. *I wasn't expecting this,* he thought. *What if she starts begging?*

"That would be to die a failure," he continued. "Let them try to catch me. Maybe I'll get even stronger. I seem to be improving a little bit every day. I can get out of this. I can fight my way through them, starting with *you,* Ass. And like you said, it's great for the press."

Ass looked at him without blinking. She didn't even move, despite her broken wrist, which she wanted to jerk around very badly. It lay motionless in her lap with her other wrist, which was not broken. "Can we try my way first?" she said.

"Yes. Of course," he said. "*Perche non?*"

There was a pause, and Marco listened to the dogs' worried woofs. They started to crescendo, and then they were barking full out and with feeling. Ass only stared, unblinking at Marco's face. "So, how super... *are* your superpowers, anyways? From what you know?"

"Well, not that super, actually," he said. He looked boyish. "Like I can think faster, and heal faster, *move* faster. I'm stronger and smarter, but I was not very smart or strong to begin with, you know, so..."

"Great. So what does that say about *us?*" she asked. "That we're not great, right? *Barely* stronger than average? That my Kung Fu is just a very small upgrade from the fat, normal public?"

"Well, I suppose I was *kind* of a strong to begin with. Stronger than most, I guess, realistically. I *was* in the circus."

"Yeah, and Kill-Swipe? He was a Brazilian strongarm! Never killed anyone, but he got a lot of people to do what he wanted. Using force, of course, not Portuguese."

"I was lucky to break his knee at the start." Then after some thought, he said, "You might actually stand a chance against me, you know. I mean I wouldn't know, but the way you killed that ninja with the suit? It's like I said—I'm just a normal Italian guy, but better! *And,* I don't have a strategy, you know! Kung Fu is all about strategy."

This seemed to give her hope, and she leavened noticeably. Marco thought she almost smiled. On any other day this would have made her pretty, but it was hot in the medical truck, and her stink was coming back, almost vengefully.

"Kung-fu is all about momentum," she said. *And you, little man, are breaking the bank in that department,* is what she wanted to add, but before she could, they were interrupted by the sound of ferocious barking.

The dogs looked like they had poison oak on their noses, scratching their faces shamelessly against the doors of the medical truck, barking and snarling in outrage.

Marco, with better-than-average hearing, caught one of the policemen—the *Carabinieri*—saying, "It's the freak-o with the powers. The dogs can smell the powers on him, and it burns their noses. Come on, let's get 'em outa here."

They knew about the dogs already! His secrets were getting out. This was bad. He was leaking—*how* long before he *sank*? Sank into the military labs for all eternity?

Marco was beginning to feel more like a specimen already. He had only come out with his powers three weeks ago, and since then everything had been about putting this show together. The big game. But what would happen after that?

He had been blinded by the prize, and now the blindfold was coming off.

Episode 5: Sao Paolo.

Ass's pigtails were washed for the first time, and they even looked kind of pretty, believe it or not. Her broken wrist was wrapped tight; it was not as bad as she'd thought it was, and she'd been able to score some pain killers before the fight from one of the truck drivers—Steve, the one with the black ponytail. She figured if she was going to hell, she might as well grab one for the road.

Her plan hadn't worked, the one about the peace riots.

The fight was brutal. At one point, Marco had a blue soccer shoe on the top of Ass's head and a pigtail in each hand and yanked. He ripped her pigtails right out of her scalp, as if they were useless shoelaces.

The stage was themed "sensory deprivation," complete with long blackouts, bright flashes, smoke, fake blood mist, all synchronized to the cameras, which switched between night vision, infrared, slow shutter, and other effects. It was a horror show, designed so that the fighters would forget who they were fighting in the darkness.

It took a long time for the match to end, (Episode 5 was only one fight) and by the end of it, in their imaginations, they were each fighting a badly decayed yet active monster. After Marco ripped Ass's pigtails out her head, he lost his grip, and she escaped, but the cameras followed her. Sometimes she would attack the cameras instead of her opponent. When the lights strobed, her face lit up in horrible grimaces, the remainder of her hair blowing out everywhere, ghastly expressions on her face. The fight went on for over an hour and a half.

Eventually she just laid down and let him mount her.

The world watched in elation. The arena vibrated and seemed to shrink into darkness like a point. Like certainty.

Marco closed his hands around Ass's throat and gripped it until it made a *crick* sound and then finally snapped. The lights flashed once, just after the final snap—perhaps at the very moment she died.

They had hired Cirque du Soleil to do a festive opening number. Now the acrobats sat in the basement loge, in a clump, watching the video monitor in silence.

The lights went up.

Marco looked at Ass's greyish, blank face, stunned. He didn't hear the crowd leap into a hellish wail around him. He didn't hear the music, nor see the confetti and indoor fireworks.

His face cracked and dissolved into tears.

Money shot! Superuomo was now "The ruthless, deadly beast with a conscience." He knelt there weeping, in a white sphere of spotlights, as transfixed viewers frothed at the mouths and networks choked on champagne.

Episode 6: Moscow. "The Memorial."

He had won. He would get the cash prize and save his sister.

He would build her a mechanical dome that would purge the deathly sewers from her lungs.

Jane did not go to Moscow. She and most of the performers had gone home. Marco was alone out there. Well, alone among thousands of people—backers, investors, celebrities, press, and of course, fans.

He had known he would win since the beginning. He had simply gone through the motions. He knew he would save his sister. He knew he would kill five people, even the girl. He'd just walked straight through the mess. The initiation. The fights. The memorial. The press. The money. Jane had given him the last of the coke, too. And that somehow seemed to be part of the overall unreal, fantastical experience.

But he loathed the feeling that lingered in his hands, the sensation of breaking his opponents' bones. The ghosting feel of their limbs cracking under his arms. It upset him, even now. Especially now. His opponents were dead, but their bodies still lived on as discomfort in his hands.

They had asked him to come to the stage wearing only a small pair of Umbro Napoli Soccer shorts. They were white with a blue icon on the right thigh. That was to be his final look. They wanted Marco to show his knees, his calves, his torso. To show the world what it was up against. That was the final message. Marco was *David*, reincarnated. Fighting the monsters of the earth. Looking great, both human and godly. Blue and Adidas and Italian all over.

The cameras did their routine. Marco addressed them, following the red light that alternated atop each one, for what felt like an hour.

It was two hours, actually.

He had won.

THE END OF MARCO:

THIS IS THE story of what happened to Marco Valoso, our man from Naples.

Nine months after *Colosseo Della Morte*, Marco was asked to do a press event at Madison Square Garden in New York. He had only been imprisoned in a military lab for three weeks, and after that he was let go; the scientists got embarrassed and tired from losing every hypothesis they made.

At MSG Marco was to make a short speech about the importance of strength in modern times. Physical strength, which most men didn't need any more when there were machines to lift things, small, totable weapons to defend themselves with, and money to suit women with. Even *money* wasn't physical anymore. It had all become digital, just like strength. And *mental* strength had been outgrown as well, now that the world had calculators, camera phones, and digital maps to soften the mind's ability to grasp concepts.

It was a celebrity bullshit spiel, in other words. Arbitrary speech rhetoric, just to book Superuomo for the ratings. The speech was uninspiring and forced, but it pumped up the audience, nonetheless. Marco realized with sorrow that he could not be in front of a pumped-up crowd ever again without a certain shadow rolling over his heart, without thinking about Ass and the feeling of her pigtails freeing from her head.

When Marco finished his speech, he left Madison Square Garden to return to the Edison Hotel on 46th Street, where he was staying. It was UFC night at MSG, and Marco had no mind for fights. Paola, healthy now, stayed to watch. She loved mixed martial arts and had free tickets.

So Marco left Paola at The Garden and meandered back to the Edison Hotel. There was supposedly a good bar there called The Rum Room, and Marco was fine with drinking for the rest of the night. The alcohol was good for washing off the memories of *Colosseo* that had clotted on him the last nine months—especially tonight, after being in front of that crowd. He was still trembling a little, soured by the feeling of being on stage again.

But someone had messed up.

Someone had booked Superuomo at MSG just two days before the annual Humane Society Dog Show. By the time Marco had returned to the Edison Hotel that night, ninety-one dogs were checked in and registered there.

Although he could hear the dogs simmering and beginning to clamor even as he turned the corner onto 46th Street, he was not prepared for what was to come.

A small woman was walking her enormous Mastiff pure-bred down 46th Street. The Mastiff—named "Bong John"—made his way to the corner of Eighth Avenue and froze there, sniffing, as if he smelled a fire somewhere. He started to shift strangely on his paws. Then he sat back on his haunches and stared patiently at the corner of the building. He wouldn't walk, he wouldn't obey the small woman, and *poopie* seemed to be the farthest thing from his mind. Instead, he sat at the corner with a strange, alien obedience, waiting for someone else's command.

Then Bong John began to shudder. He crouched low on all

fours and grew tense, trembling. His thick fur fanned out over his massive body, and a low growl churned from within him.

The woman had seen Bong John do this once before, nine months ago, when she was watching her favorite TV show, *Colosseo Della Morte*, but she'd had no idea why. Since then she had forgotten all about that. Until now.

Bong John scratched his nose on the concrete corner of the building, then went back to his crouched-ready pose. His small woman was worried; she knew without trying that she wouldn't be able to budge him, if she couldn't talk him down. Physical strength was a thing of ancient times.

A young Italian-looking man strolled around the corner. Before she could recognize him from TV, Bong John was on him.

With a crazy yowl, Bong John clasped Marco's head in his jaws and pulled him down to the pavement, trampling him, bucking wildly and snarling. Ninety-two of Marco's extra-strength bones snapped like sticks. His ribs were broken into daggers, and they sliced up his insides. His super-heart was chopped up like a salad. Fortified blood leaked all over the dog and the sidewalk.

The tourists all cried and screamed, running in circles.

The locals were disturbed, but only mildly; however, most of them canceled their appointments and went directly home.

THE END